After reading *Winds of Change*, I was encouraged about the way Jeff Kelly described the problems that our youth and parents are facing and the solutions that make life a real blessing. The small-town atmosphere and sports and the horses bring back the memories of many of us growing up. The Christian experience is explained so plainly, and the book is a pleasant read.

E. Wales Lankford, pastor and
evangelist, Church of the Nazarene

This book is an easy read, and it will bless your heart. The story is testimonial and experiential. You will check your own salvation experience to be sure radical change has come to your life after trusting Jesus. I encourage you to read this book and pass it on to your friends.

Ralph Chapman, director of missions,
Beckham-Mills Baptist Association

Addison,
Hope you like it!
Jeff Kelly

WWW. THELEKITURNEYSERIES.COM

winds of
CHANGE

email — JEFF KELLY @
CHURCHESAID.com

THE LEXI TURNEY series

winds of
CHANGE

JEFF KELLY

TATE PUBLISHING & *Enterprises*

Published by Tate Publishing & Enterprises, LLC
127 E. Trade Center Terrace | Mustang, Oklahoma 73064 USA
1.888.361.9473 | www.tatepublishing.com

Tate Publishing is committed to excellence in the publishing industry. The company
reflects the philosophy established by the founders, based on Psalm 68:11,
"The Lord gave the word and great was the company of those who published it."

Book design copyright © 2010 by Tate Publishing, LLC. All rights reserved.
Cover design by Kellie Southerland
Cover photo courtesy of Tracy Smith
Cover model Tristan Smith
Interior design by Stefanie Rooney

Published in the United States of America

ISBN: 978-1-61663-680-7
1. Fiction, Christian, General
2. Fiction, Sports
10.06.14

Dedication

To Makenzie, Cassidy, Stockton, and to all teenagers who are struggling, you are not alone!

Prologue

The story I am about to share with you begins on the night my best friend was kidnapped right before my eyes. It was a dark and horrible time in my life, and it was about to get even worse. People often share about hitting rock bottom in their lives. If I wasn't at the bottom, I knew I had to be near it.

I was fifteen and rebellious. I felt like I had a reason. My dad had died two years earlier. Because of the horrible accident, it was a closed casket ceremony. I wasn't allowed to see him. I never got to say good-bye.

My mom and I had never been close. My dad was my cheerleader, my safe place. When he died, I felt lost. Soon, I became angry. I was mad at God for letting him die. I was furious with my mom for acting like it didn't bother her and everything was still okay. I was even angry with my dad for leaving me.

Deep down, I knew I shouldn't be drinking and hanging out with the wild crowd. In my heart, I was more of a middle-of-the-road type of person. I used the party scene to help me forget about the feelings of loss and hopelessness that I had carried around inside since my dad's death. Also, it was the only way that I could get my mom's attention. Every time I would get in trouble at school or come home late from partying, she would actually sit down and talk to me. Most of the time she just yelled, but I would take what I could get.

As I look back on it, I realize I was punishing myself as well. I was mad at myself. If I had been a better daughter, maybe my mom would be more interested in me. Maybe my dad would have ... Why couldn't he have been more careful? Didn't he know how much I needed him?

My name is Lexi Turney, and this is my story.

Cruise Control

S trange how you don't know your life is about to change in an instant. You would think that you could sense it somehow. I couldn't understand how I could be so blind about the fact that my bad choices were about to shatter my life into a thousand little pieces.

That fateful night, Amanda picked me up early. That was bizarre, because she was always late. She buzzed into the driveway in her red Volkswagen bug and ramped the curb with her stereo thumping so loudly that I was afraid the old man next door would come over and gripe us out again. Her cheeks were bright, and her lipstick was even brighter with gloss smeared on heavily.

I had been grounded for two weeks and had missed several end-of-school parties, so I was pumped about going out that night. I felt like I had missed out on so much fun. I was going to catch up on all of it.

We went to pick up Sarah, but she wasn't ready. The starting center on the basketball team, and my basketball buddy since fourth grade, was obviously perturbed that we were early. She walked gracefully back upstairs, her blond curls floating and weaving with each step. I would be annoyed with her perfection, but we were best friends, and our bond easily erased my mild jealousy.

When we pulled up early, I already knew she was going to freak. She wouldn't have fixed her hair or makeup this early. When we went out, she usually waited until the last minute to get ready so she could look as fresh as possible. *She didn't need that stuff,* I thought jealously. It was tough to shrug off my feelings of inferiority around Sarah.

"You guys go on without me," Sarah said, sitting on the edge of her perfectly made bed and grabbing a pillow with an elegantly curved *S* on it.

"No," I pleaded with her, "you have to come. We'll wait until you're ready." I started begging her and cut my eyes sideways at Amanda. I silently communicated to Sarah, *Don't leave me alone with her,* by raising one of my eyebrows and making a pleading face. By her quick grin, I could see that Sarah understood me, as always. She raised one eyebrow back at me and made a funny face that only I could see. It was all I could do not to laugh out loud.

"Oh, all right, but it will take me a few minutes to get ready. She rose from the bed, spinning on her toes like a ballet dancer as she made her way toward her bathroom that was attached to her room. I marveled at how coordinated she was for someone over six feet tall. It must have come from taking dance and ballet lessons since she was four years old.

I sighed in relief and stretched my jean-clad legs out on the bed. I glanced at Amanda to make sure she didn't realize what had just happened. She was clueless, as usual.

I picked up a *Seventeen* magazine and idly thumbed through the pictures, pausing to focus on the cute guys and looking at the newest hairstyles. Amanda plopped down beside me, almost bouncing me off the bed and overwhelming me with her perfume. It did smell good, but why did she have to use half of the bottle?

"Scooch over, Lexi, and let me sit. Ooh, I love those earrings. Let me see that for a sec." Amanda grabbed the magazine out of my hands, and I just let it fall. She could be so pushy.

Don't get me wrong. I liked Amanda, but Sarah was my best friend. I needed her to talk to when I couldn't handle Amanda's attitude anymore. Amanda annoyed me about half the time. Sarah and I had considered ditching her several times. The problem we faced was that neither of us was old enough to drive, and being hauled around by your parents was just lame.

Amanda absolutely loved to go driving around in the town next to us. She had gone to school there a couple of years before and knew all the kids. Also,

Amanda and I could usually find some older guys who would buy us some alcohol.

Sarah wasn't much for drinking though. Once she had told me, "Lexi, you know what people say about girls who drink a lot. I don't want people to say that stuff about me." I saw her point. As the class vice president and likely valedictorian, she had an image to uphold. Also, she was afraid we would get stopped by the cops, and her parents would find out. Even though I knew they would kill her, I needed her there with me.

I knew Sarah was probably right, and part of me wanted to be more like her. Compared to Amanda and most of my other friends, she was careful and concerned about being good and doing right. She would go along with some of the things I wanted to do, but she never really looked like she was comfortable with it.

As hard as I tried to be more like Sarah, I felt myself drawn to Amanda's motto of "Get loose and have fun." There were several mornings after a night of running around with Amanda that I swore I would never party again, but I always seemed to go back for more.

Other than the times when I lost myself in a movie or playing basketball, the only relief I found from my unhappy life was partying. For a little while, I could forget about my dad being gone, my mom's indifference, and all of the daily stress in my life. In my heart, I knew it was wrong, but I felt that I had lost the one reason to do things right.

Sarah finally finished primping, and we thundered out of the house, giggling and singing. We had driven around for a while, honking and playing our favorite songs, when Amanda started pointing and waving like crazy. "Those guys are really hot!" she said.

The guys she had spotted were pretty cute, and the car they were in was awesome. It was a solid black Dodge Charger with chrome everywhere. The driver careened around the corner, barely sliding through a yellow light, and pulled into a nearby parking lot. They blatantly disregarded the no loitering sign and turned up the volume on their sound system another couple of notches.

I was surprised that I had never seen them before. They definitely weren't a part of Amanda's old crowd; they were too slick and dressed up. "Who is that?" I asked Amanda, glancing at her from the cramped passenger seat. "I don't recognize that car."

Amanda rolled her mascara-caked eyes at me and said arrogantly, "Who cares! They are hot, and they were checking us out when they passed us a minute ago. You and Sarah worry too much."

Sarah made one of her crazy faces, puckering her lips and fluffing her hair. I shook my head, rolled my eyes at her, and giggled softly. She was such an actress, and she knew how to make me laugh.

Amanda saw the Charger on our next pass and pulled over beside them. They asked us if we wanted to ride around with them, and Amanda simply hopped out of her little Volkswagen Bug and slammed the car door. That was typical Amanda, always chasing the guys.

I pulled at my halter top and smoothed my bangs out of my eyes, trying not to bite my lower lip. Meeting new people always made me nervous. I opened my side of the car door and got out.

As Sarah slid out of the back seat, she gave the guys a shy smile. She was all lean arms and tanned legs showcased in shorts and a tank top. As we climbed in with them, I whispered, "Amanda, there is this thing called playing hard to get." She just gave me her usual saucy grin and swung into the leather-covered passenger seat.

At sixteen, Amanda was a year older than Sarah and me. She was attractive, and it annoyed us when she said she thought she was fat. We both wished we were a little curvier like Amanda. I think it was because she saw herself as heavy that she always had to have a guy's attention.

She habitually flirted. She didn't seem to care if the guys were really cute or even fun to be around. Her signature move was flipping her jet-black hair, looking back over her shoulder, and flashing her smile at the guy she was interested in on that particular day. She was pretty, but it seemed like she just tried too hard.

Amanda slid over as close to the driver as she could, sitting uncomfortably on the cup holders and center console. The driver had red hair, freckles, and thickly lashed dark eyes. Amanda was hanging all over him. He was not my normal choice for a hot guy, but he was strangely good looking. He was dressed like the guys at school except that he and his friend both had bandanas tied around their right arms. Something about him told me he was a lot older than the rest of us. I didn't mind that as much as his intense stares. They gave me the creeps.

A couple of minutes earlier, when we were getting in the backseat of his car, I had glanced over and caught him staring at me. It wasn't the kind of look that I would have expected from someone I had just met. His look was more like he already knew me but not in a good way. I racked my brain to remember if I had ever seen him before, but I was sure by his unusual good looks and red hair I would remember.

The driver didn't bother to tell us his name, but the other guy introduced himself as Cruise. After an awkward pause, I looked over at Sarah. She shrugged her shoulders, and looking toward the driver, she wrinkled her nose as if something smelled. I tried not to bust out laughing, but Cruise smiled widely at the face Sarah had made. I couldn't hold it in any longer. All three of us started laughing so hard that the driver called over his shoulder, "What's so funny back there?"

"Nothing, Red," I answered with sarcastic sweetness. That started Sarah laughing again. She laughed so hard that she snorted. She did that a lot when she laughed really hard. It was the only thing I ever saw her do that wasn't perfect.

Cruise kept looking back and forth at us with a puzzled look. He could tell he had been left out and wanted to know what was happening. Calling the driver Red was another one of my inside jokes with Sarah. Red was the name of my dog in grade school. She had helped me hang up signs all over the neighborhood when the dog had gone missing, so she knew exactly what I was doing. Sarah would laugh every time I called him that, her white teeth flashing in the dark.

It was awesome to have a friendship like ours, full of private jokes and secret looks with only meaning found between us. I felt grateful that she always treated me like a regular person after my dad passed away. She never bugged me to talk about him. Sometimes I thought if I ever could talk about it, Sarah would be the only one I would even think about opening up to.

Her dad was gone too, but what took him away wasn't an accident. He worked for a big company and had been transferred to some country overseas where everybody was Muslim, and the women had to wear scarves on their heads. Sarah and her mom had decided not to go with him so she could graduate with all of her friends. She hadn't seen him since about two weeks after my dad's funeral, two long years ago.

I didn't understand why he never came home to see his family, but Sarah got so upset when I asked her about it that I had vowed not to bring it up anymore. Her dad wasn't dead, but he was gone. If anyone could understand what I felt, I knew it was Sarah.

I shook my head slightly to put away my sad thoughts and concentrated on the good-looking guy in the backseat with Sarah and me. Cruise sat in the middle, and as we talked I noticed he was looking over at me most of the time. I was enjoying his attention and having a blast. I was thankful that Sarah didn't seem to mind.

I asked him about the bandana around his arm. "It's a family thing, you wouldn't understand," he answered.

I could tell he didn't want to talk about it, but I held his gaze so he would know that I wanted a better answer. He turned his back on me and looked over at Sarah. She asked what he had in his cup. He said, "Here, just try it and see." She looked at me and smiled tilting her head to the side. I knew that meant *you go first*, so I did. After I tried it, he handed it to her and she took a couple of sips. It was some kind of tea with a lot of alcohol mixed in it. We passed it back and forth until it was gone.

Cruise turned back to me. "I like your hair," Cruise said. He ran his fingers through my shoulder-length brown hair. When he touched my hair, it sent a tingle down my spine. "Your smile is so pretty," he continued.

"What about my beautiful brown eyes? You have got to get some better lines!" I said teasingly.

"No, they are beautiful." He looked down as if he were embarrassed.

I started thinking he was being serious. What if I had embarrassed him? I was always saying the wrong thing, especially around cute guys. He looked up at me and said, "They match your shoes."

We laughed awkwardly. I was relieved that he wasn't angry about my teasing. What would it be like to have a boyfriend like Cruise? His hand lay on his leg, almost touching mine. I wished he would reach over and take my hand in his.

Dragging my eyes away from one of the best-looking guys I swear I had ever talked to, I began to look out the window. I wanted to get a sense of where we were. After a few seconds, I realized we were getting closer to the city. I asked Cruise why we were headed that way. He just looked at me with a flirty smile. He had the bluest eyes, and when he looked right at me like that I felt warm inside. I got so nervous that I couldn't remember what I had asked him!

He was extremely cute with his dark hair spiked and messy, and he seemed to like me over Sarah, which was nice for a change. He had to be at least eighteen, and Sarah usually got all the attention from the older guys. I told myself it was because her height made her look older to them. We told all the guys we were older than our true age of fifteen. Tonight, I was seventeen, and Sarah was eighteen.

Finally, I was able to concentrate long enough to remember what I had asked him. Those baby blues were lethal and very distracting. We had left the drag a while ago, and I was worried that we would get too far from home for me to make curfew. Again, I asked Cruise where we were going; he used that smile of his on me and said, "Don't worry about it. We're just going to a party."

I tried to relax, but I couldn't come in late again

this soon. Being grounded the last two weeks just about killed me. I had been invited to three different graduation parties, but my mom hadn't given in at all. I was still furious with her, but I knew she would do it again if I missed curfew.

"No, really, Cruise," I said. "I'm not supposed to go into Chicago."

"I told you. We're just going to a party. It's not that much farther. Don't you wanna go to a party with me?" he asked, his smile flashing beside an adorable dimple.

"Sure, sounds like fun. But we aren't going all the way into Chicago, are we? I can't be late tonight," I said, feeling like a worried little kid.

Cruise looked down and mumbled something to himself. I asked him what he said, and he looked up to face me. "No, not all the way," he said. His voice was a lot more serious this time, and he sounded a little frustrated. I was afraid I would blow it with him, so I didn't question him anymore about it.

Red had obviously been listening because he looked over his shoulder and said sarcastically, "Cruise, did you get stuck with a couple of little babies back there?" I looked at Cruise to see how he was going to respond, but he just stared at Red. I was ticked.

"Shut up, Red. We're having a good time back here." Sarah giggled again, but not as much as she had a few minutes ago. Red turned back to Amanda, and I sat back in the cushy leather seat. I could feel the alcohol thawing my reservations.

The car was quiet for a few minutes until Amanda

started jabbering away about nothing. Cruise asked Sarah how tall she was. Here it comes. Guys always did this. Sarah had told me a million times that she hated it when guys asked her that. We even came up with some things to say back to let them know she didn't want to talk about it.

She used my favorite one when she answered, "I'm just five feet and thirteen inches." I laughed, but Sarah didn't join me. Her face looked pale, and she was holding onto her stomach.

I knew what was coming next. I cringed when he said, "Nice legs." Sarah looked at him and then at me. I turned to look out the window and waited helplessly. I knew she could have just about any guy, but this one had acted like he liked me instead.

"Are we almost there? I'm starting to feel sick at my stomach." I turned and smiled at her to say thank you, but her panicked expression told me she was serious.

Red started slowing down. I heard him tell Amanda to read the street names out loud. When it wasn't the one he was looking for, he would speed up so fast that it tossed us around in the back seat. I started feeling a little carsick. He obviously hadn't been to this place before tonight. That should have alarmed me, but I was just going with the flow.

We finally turned and then stopped at an old, two-story, brick building about the size of a small warehouse and went in a rusty, brown door on the south side. Sarah and I were having a little trouble navigating, and I giggled and clutched onto her as

I tripped. Going into the dank, dark room, she still looked like she wasn't feeling well with a frown marring her normally smooth brow. She had her lips smashed tightly together and was breathing rapidly through her nose.

We were obviously the first ones there. I sneaked a quick peek at my watch to see how long the ride had taken. It took me a minute to focus on the small numbers. I blinked several times and tried to get my eyes to focus, but everything was starting to get a little hazy. I could barely make out the time. It was fifteen minutes until eleven! It had taken us an hour to get here. Even if we left now, I would barely make my midnight curfew.

Horror Story

Expecting a parent-free house and teenagers milling around as I had enjoyed at previous parties, I was surprised and disappointed. A musty smell pervaded the room mixed with a disagreeable stench. "No way anybody lives here," I mumbled to myself. The guys acted as if everything was fine, but we stood awkwardly. I felt overly warm and nauseated, and I could see a faint dotting of perspiration on Sarah's upper lip.

"It's hot as crud in here," Amanda stated blandly, holding the back of her hair up with one hand and fanning her face with the other. It was hot, but her pose only seemed to purposefully accentuate her figure. Once again, she was trying to draw attention to herself.

Cruise moved close to my ear and murmured, "Let's sit down." He slid his warm hand into mine and laced our fingers. Surprised, I gripped his hand

and fell into step behind him. Based on his earlier compliments to Sarah, I thought she had another admirer. Instead, he led me over to a ratty couch with an orange flower print. It reminded me of the one in my grandmother's basement.

The place was an absolute dump. I was thankful for the open window above us that provided some breathable air. We sat down and sank so low that I thought we might go through to the floor. I stifled a giggle and fell against his side. His arm had my hair trapped underneath it, and I leaned forward to free the strands.

Sarah sat on a rickety chair pulled near the couch. She was bent over with her elbows on her knees. Red and Amanda were leaning against the water-stained wall to our left. Amanda laughed loudly and whispered something in Red's ear.

Knowing I was going to miss curfew and therefore this would be my last night out for a while, I wanted to have a good time. Unfortunately, my stomach didn't feel right. I felt dizzy and weak, but I was afraid to say that I didn't feel good. I decided to fake it and smiled at Cruise to let him know it was okay to kiss me. I didn't want him to start talking to Sarah again. We were best friends, but when it came to boys, we were pretty competitive.

I shifted restlessly and gently nudged Cruise with my elbow. He glanced down, and I could see the shadows of his long eyelashes. I waited expectantly and held my breath. He seemed to lean toward me, but he didn't kiss me.

Instead, he got up and started saying something to Red. They talked back and forth for a minute. I tried to listen, but they both spoke so low that I couldn't hear a word they said. I wondered if something was bothering Cruise. He hadn't been talking to me as much over the past few minutes. I started trying to think what I had said to mess things up. When he turned back toward me, he looked totally freaked.

I had tried not to question why we had driven so far away from the neighborhood and so close to Chicago. But now, here in this sweltering hot room, I could tell that something wasn't right. Something was bothering Cruise, and I was beginning to feel like we were in a lot of trouble. I decided to get some answers.

"If this is a party," I asked, "where are all the people?" Red said we were just early, but I noticed Cruise was acting really nervous. He had begun walking back and forth near the door. I tried to get up too, but my whole body felt weak. It felt like the flu when you just want to lie there in bed for days.

The room tilted slightly, and I pressed my hand to my cramping stomach. I tried to check for clues to what was going on by scanning the small, dark room, but I couldn't keep my mind focused. Alcohol had never made me feel this way before. What was in that cup that Cruise had shared with Sarah and me? The light seemed even dimmer in the room. I couldn't see all the way across the room anymore. Was that from what I drank?

Grimacing, I looked over at my friends. Amanda

was laughing hysterically and kissing Red. He wasn't doing much kissing back, but she was sticking with it. Sarah was sitting on the other side of them. She was usually outgoing, but now she looked dazed, confused, and even a little sick at her stomach. I hoped she didn't get sick because I knew how upset that made her.

"Sarah, are you all right?" I asked. Sarah just nodded her head, but I could tell she wasn't herself. Sarah was still bent at the waist, head down, curls obscuring her pale face. I knew she just didn't want to ruin everybody's good time. Sarah was the kind of person who wanted everyone to be happy despite what it cost her.

I leaned my head back on the couch, probably getting something gross in my hair and not really caring. I was able to collect my thoughts and sat up to tell the girls that we needed to get out of there. Before I could speak, I heard people talking outside and a knock at the door. I moistened my lips and said, "Girls, this isn't right, we need to—"

"Now the party can get started!" Amanda interrupted. Red disentangled himself from her and headed toward the door. He reached down and picked something up, but in the dark room I couldn't tell what it was. The next few moments were chaotic.

Several guys stepped into the room wearing bandanas matching those Cruise and Red wore around their left arm. When one pointed at Sarah, they rushed over, quickly taped her mouth, and began to drag her out. I couldn't believe my eyes.

Sarah was kicking and screaming. I pushed myself up, screamed, and launched myself at them. Amanda jumped on the back of one of them, and I grabbed the one that had a hold of Sarah's legs. As I started pulling on him, I saw Red hit Amanda in the head with some sort of stick or maybe it was a pipe. She crumbled to the floor, and I could see blood on her face. He gave her a kick for good measure, but she didn't seem to feel it. I saw a dark blur coming toward my face, the last thing I remembered after waking up and realizing the group of guys were gone ... and so was Sarah.

I looked up from the floor and saw Red leaning against the wall looking devilishly satisfied. "Where's Sarah?" The words were a scream in my mind, but they came out so muffled I thought maybe my mouth had been taped like Sarah's. I touched my lips and found blood. They were swollen, and my jaw was killing me.

Cruise looked at me and when our eyes met, he quickly looked away. Red was laughing at me. "Don't worry. They're coming for you next, and you'll see her then!" he said with a smirk.

Half crawling and stumbling, I moved toward Amanda, still feeling weak and dizzy from what must have been some sort of drug in Cruise's cup. She was lying face down, and her body was limp and lifeless. I got down on my hands and knees and began crying when I saw blood matted in her hair. I felt as if I were going to puke. What was going to happen to us? I wondered if my dad had these same feelings at the time of his accident.

Leaning over, I shook Amanda slightly and called her name. I never thought I would use anything from our health and safety class, but it all came back to me. I checked to see that she was breathing and found her pulse. She was alive, but I still couldn't get her to respond.

My head had been pounding since I had come to, and leaning over Amanda was making it worse. I sat up and noticed that Red was watching me. He looked agitated. "Is she dead?" he yelled at me. I just ignored him. "Whatever!" he exclaimed. "She doesn't matter anyway." He ran his hands through his coarse hair and fidgeted with the bandana on his arm.

I started to panic as I remembered our counselor warning us in a morning assembly about a new gang initiation. Boys traded girls to the members of the gang in exchange for letting them join. The counselor told us this usually happened at the gang's safe house. The girls were killed so they couldn't lead police back there.

We just laughed about his little speech. We thought he was just trying to scare us to keep us from going out and having fun. Besides, we all agreed the gangs were in the city. My friends and I knew to stay out of Chicago. We thought we were safe out in the suburbs. I felt so stupid that we had walked blindly into this situation.

I began looking for a way out of this horror story. I could see the door, but Cruise and Red were between me and the only exit. Why had we gotten into the car? The guys looked normal enough, and we had been going to that neighborhood all summer. We liked to go riding around with the older boys on the drag. They were cool and mature. We all agreed that the buzz we got from the alcohol they gave us was awesome.

I began to think that if we could just get out of this, I knew we would be more careful from then on. Out! How would I get out of this? And even if I did, how would I get Amanda out? Where did they take Sarah? This can't be happening! I kept trying to convince myself that everything was going to be okay. But every time I looked at Amanda lying there in a pool of blood, I could barely keep myself from freaking out.

I looked up in anguish, wishing for anyone to come to our aid. That gave me an idea. The window above me was open because of the summer heat. It was higher up than the normal windowsill, but I had done pull-ups all year in basketball practice so I knew I could make it.

My plan was to distract the boys by going crazy, like I thought Amanda actually was dead. Even though Red had said he didn't care, if they thought she was already dead, surely it would mess up their plans.

While they checked on Amanda, I would get to the window and pull myself up and ... but what about Amanda? I couldn't leave her. What if the counselor was right? Maybe I could bring help, but she could be gone by the time I got back. Still, without help, none of us was getting out of this alive.

Rescue

"O ver here!" I had never been so glad to see a cop. "Help!" I yelled as loud as I could. He turned around and sped up to me. I went up to the open window on the passenger side. "My friends are in trouble!" I exclaimed. I began frantically telling him the story—how the boys picked us up and drove toward the city, the room, the guys who took Sarah.

"Okay, slow down," he said. "Where are they?"

I suddenly realized that I had run so hard crying and shaking that I didn't know where they were. I began to tremble with fear for my friends, wiping my nose with the back of my hand and taking deep breaths.

How far had I run since pulling myself up and through that window? Several times I had turned the corner when it looked dark down the street on which I was running.

"Miss, you have to answer me." I looked at him and began to cry even more.

"I don't know!" I cried. "I just ran and ran."

He looked at me disgustedly. "Have you been drinking?" he asked. His tone told me that he already knew the answer.

"Yes, I drank something from a cup one of the guys had. I think it had some kind of drug in it," I confessed.

"Try to remember anything. What did you see?"

I closed my eyes tightly and exhaled slowly, forcing myself to unclench my fists and avoid hyperventilating. "I remember a big building with a picture of a loaf of bread on it." I sobbed.

He nodded his head briskly, and I could tell that had helped. "Okay, get in and we'll head that way." As he talked on his radio, I began to weep uncontrollably. He spoke to me in calm tones trying to get me to stop, but I couldn't.

"What if we can't find Sarah and Amanda?" I said between sobs. "I could never forgive myself. I don't want to be the only one to make it out of this alive! I could never live with knowing I had left them alone."

The cop looked at me with pity in his eyes and said, "We'll find them; just calm down."

When we got to the bread factory, I was still crying. The realization that I could have been killed was really sinking in, but I had to help my friends. I got

32

excited as I started to recognize more of the buildings. "There. Go straight here; I think we're close." I
hoped I was right.

We went three blocks, and I could remember I
had been there earlier tonight. But was it when I was
running or in the car with the guys? When I saw the
place where the party was supposed to be, I started
yelling. "There! It's that old two-story brick building!" I was half shocked that we found it. The cop
called it in on the radio.

"How old are your friends? Where there more
than the two you mentioned?" he asked. "What
clothes were they wearing?" He asked all of this
really fast but in a matter of fact tone. I knew he was
trying to keep me calm, but the questions upset me
even more.

As I saw their faces in my mind, I started really
losing it. "You've got to get in there!" I yelled. "Why
are you just sitting here?" As I pushed on the cop's
shoulder, two more cop cars pulled up.

"How many guys are inside?" he asked, more than
a little agitated at me by then. I didn't know what to
say. There were two when I got out the window, but
what if the others had come back?

"Two, maybe more," was all I could get out before
he slammed the door. *Please, God! Please!* I prayed,
not knowing why. I had sworn I would never talk to
a God that would let my dad die.

I sat stiffly in the squad car, staring out the window and gripping the front door handle with stiff,
bloodless fingers. Guilt washed over me in waves,

swamping me with pain and nausea. My mother's warnings swirling around in my mind didn't sound nearly as ridiculous as they had when I had first heard them.

Having a good time had been our only focus. Our judgment had been dulled by the foolish choice of drinking alcohol. We had ignored all the warning signs in search of fun. None of us was having much fun now.

It seemed like a million years before the cops went through the door. They had their guns drawn, and bulletproof vests held them in a stiff posture. The scene was chaotic with flashing lights, voices yelling, and sirens blaring as more cops arrived.

A few minutes later, my cop came around the corner with a guy in cuffs. It was Cruise. The flashing red and blue lights from the squad car reflected off his spiky black hair. His mouth was set in a firm line as he jerked angrily away from the officer. *What a lying jerk!* I bet he tried to go out the same window I had used to escape.

Suddenly, I was out the door and running toward Amanda. She was walking, barely. A cop ran up to her and held onto her so she wouldn't fall. "You were told to stay still and wait for us to help you, young lady," he said. He made her sit down right there on the pavement. I wrapped my arms tightly around her shoulders, ignoring the fact that her makeup was running so badly that it was smearing all over both of our faces as we hugged and cried.

Another cop was leading Red toward a police car.

As they passed by Amanda, she swore at him and tried to kick him. The cop that had scolded her for getting up held her down and told her to be still.

I hugged her until the ambulance arrived and the EMT pulled us apart. Words were not necessary or possible. We just squeezed each other and cried. More cop cars had pulled up and lots of cops were going into the building next to the one Amanda had come out of. Amanda and I were taken to the ambulance, and for a few minutes we cried tears of joy. We were so lucky to be alive. "Sarah will be joining us soon," I said in Amanda's ear.

○

At the hospital my mom came up and hugged me. "I am so glad you are all right," she said.

"Are Sarah and Amanda okay?"

My mom had a strange look on her face. "Amanda is shaken up, but she will be fine. Honey, they haven't found Sarah yet."

My heart sank. I didn't know what to say. I felt so guilty for talking her into going with us. I started getting up out of the hospital bed. "I have to go find her," I told my mom.

She pushed me back down on the bed and said, "That is what the police are doing right now. They are the professionals. You can't do anything to help except rest and answer their questions with a clear head."

"Is Sarah's mom here?" I asked.

"Yes, she came to see you two and to wait in case they bring Sarah here," Mom answered.

I felt like I was going to panic. "I am afraid to see her. She probably hates me. I told you before that she always blamed me when Sarah would get in trouble."

"You have been through so much tonight. We can see her mom another time," she said. We hugged and cried together. This was as close as we had been in longer than I could remember.

Next Stop: Freedom

"Honey, are you all right?" I woke up, startled by the old lady sitting next to me on the bus. "You were having some dream!" she said with a smile.

"I wish it were a dream," I mumbled. My tone and frown were intended to tell her that I didn't want to talk about it.

"Where are you from?" she asked, still smiling even after I had responded so rudely. I decided to shut her up once and for all, so without a word I put my headphones on and turned to face the window. I felt a little guilty, but I didn't want to talk to anyone and especially not some old lady.

As I stared out the window, I began to think about my mom. I missed her and hated her all at the same time. I couldn't believe she had made me get on this bus and shipped me off to her sister.

During our argument about this trip, I reminded my mom that there was absolutely nothing to do out there. She said, "Good, then I don't expect to hear about you getting into any trouble." I told her she was just being selfish and wanting me out of her hair. She tried to convince me that I needed new friends and new surroundings.

I didn't want or need new surroundings! I wanted and needed my friends. Also, my friends needed me. I should be home helping the cops find Sarah and hanging out with Amanda so she didn't go off and do something stupid.

I knew I would hate Oklahoma even more than I did last time we visited. I was only in first grade then, but I know I didn't like it at all. That family trip was the worst. I definitely expected this time to top it though. At least last time I wasn't stuck on a stupid bus.

I remember that I had cried until Dad had agreed to take my new bike on the trip. He told me there would be nowhere to ride it. I didn't believe him until he unloaded it at Uncle Patrick's house, and I started trying to ride. All of the roads were dirt or gravel. I couldn't even pedal my bike. I went into the house and told my dad to load my bike. I was ready to go home right then.

Of course, they all laughed and said we had just gotten there. Even though I cried and had a fit all evening, we had to stay for the rest of the week. I don't remember the trip home, but Mom always tells everyone that I made Dad unload my bike every time we stopped so I could ride it around on the concrete.

I don't remember much about Uncle Patrick from that trip, but when he and Aunt Joanne came for a visit last year, I decided that he was a jerk. I didn't even know him, and he jumped all over my case like he was my dad or something. "Young lady," he said, "you need to use respect when you talk to your mother."

He had no right! He didn't know what was going on in my life. My mother had stopped treating me with respect as soon as Dad had died. From the way she acted, I don't think she ever cared about him at all. It had been almost two years, and she still had not cried. I couldn't stand the way she seemed to ignore his death. She just kept working like nothing ever happened.

Now she was using her job as an excuse again. She said she couldn't take off work to drive me out to Oklahoma. She didn't even drive me to catch the bus. She asked our neighbor to take me. I was so embarrassed! As I was leaving, she said she loved me. Unbelievable!

I knew she just didn't want to deal with it. After all, I had been through that night one month ago, and she was sending me on this bus, alone, no friends, no cell phone, nothing. She even made this stupid rule that I couldn't talk to anyone from home except for her. I didn't plan to talk to her at all.

I should get off this bus somewhere and just disap-

pear. I don't even think she would care. I wonder where the next stop is. It doesn't matter. I am so off this bus!

There is no way I can put up with Uncle Patrick. I know it will disappoint Aunt Joanne and that does bother me some. She is nice and always seems to care how you are feeling about things. She is probably the only one who will really care when I don't show.

Just the thought of disappearing feels good. No more problems! I won't have to answer to anybody. I know that I can take care of myself. My mind is made up, and I will claim my freedom at the next stop. With that decided, I felt myself relax, and I fell asleep.

Bessie

When I woke up, the bus was just pulling away from the bus stop. I had missed my chance to escape! The old lady was beside me again, smiling as usual.

"Why didn't you wake me up?" I half-yelled at her.

"You looked so peaceful," she answered cheerfully. "Here, I got you a few things. Are you hungry?" she asked.

"No!" I snapped, but it was a lie. I was starving! "Oh, all right," I managed. "What did you get? How much do I owe you?"

She smiled again. "No, no, you keep your money. My name is Bessie." She paused for me to answer with my name. When I just looked away, she continued. "I got you a nice ham and cheese sandwich, some chips, and a bottle of water. I noticed that you were drinking water earlier, and I didn't know what kind of soda you liked."

"Thanks," I said meekly.

Bessie looked like the typical grandma. She had the blue-gray hair, bifocal glasses with that beaded chain thing to keep them around her neck, and wrinkles everywhere. I hoped I never got wrinkled up like that, but her smile was so kind and sweet.

"My name is Lexi, and to answer your earlier question, I am headed to Oklahoma to stay with my aunt and uncle."

"Oklahoma!" she exclaimed. "I'm going to see my relatives in Tahlequah, Oklahoma. What is your stop?" she asked as she nodded her head encouraging me to respond.

"Elk City," I answered, frowning at the thought. *Great! How am I going to get off early and run away now with Granny Bessie hovering over me?* "Is Tahlequah in the east or west part of Oklahoma?" I asked, hoping for east. I knew Elk City was the stop farthest west.

"East," she said, smiling. This lady was too happy, but her answer made me almost as happy as her.

"Oh, good!" I said with too much enthusiasm.

I figured that would give me time to escape if I had to wait until she got off the bus. She looked puzzled and then thoughtful and then she just started eating her sandwich. I joined her, happy for the conversation to be over, and my stomach was glad for the food.

While we had been talking, the bus had driven into a rainstorm. I could barely make out the road signs as I stared out the window. I pulled out my iPod and some magazines my mom had picked up for me. This was going to be a long, boring trip. The only thing more boring would be if I had to stay there with my aunt and uncle. I smiled to myself because I knew I wouldn't be staying there after all.

I stole a peak at grinning Granny. She looked like she was asleep, but if she was anything like my Grandma Mary, she would say she was just resting her eyes. I began to plan my escape at the next stop. I thought about waking up Granny and talking to her so she wouldn't be rested when we stopped again. She looked so peaceful I couldn't bring myself to do it. "You'll regret that," I told myself.

The Creep

A few hours later, we pulled up to the next stop. I was hoping to avoid the guy sitting across the aisle from me. He had been staring at me off and on for the past two hours. He looked dirty and creepy. Also, he was almost as old as my dad. As Granny and I got up, he was staring again so I kept her between us. I decided to stay close to her until I saw my chance to get out of here. We headed toward the bathrooms, but it seemed that the entire bus had the same idea.

Grinning Granny was following me all around the store, and I began to think she knew about my plan. She followed me to the deli counter where we ordered a couple of Italian subs, but she wouldn't let me pay. I figured from the way she was dressed that she had plenty of money. I guess she just rode the bus because she was too old to drive.

My mind was going a hundred miles an hour trying to figure out how to get rid of her and disappear. I knew if she saw me walking away she would call the cops. Maybe that would be okay. Even if I got caught, Uncle Patrick would have to come and get me then I wouldn't be on this stupid bus. Then again, I would have to listen to him gripe me out all the way to his house, and my shot at freedom would be lost. I decided to just get back on the bus and wait for the next stop.

After what felt like years, the driver announced the next stop. The butterflies started flying around in my stomach just like they did on the game days during basketball season. We pulled up to one of the biggest truck stops that I had ever seen. It would be easy to lose Bessie in there. "I'm going to use the pay phone and call home," I told her.

She nodded her head with approval. "I'll be at the diner getting a piece of pie and some coffee," she answered.

This would be where my journey on my own would begin! I even knew where Granny would be so I could slip out the other side of the building and be long gone before she knew it. I was a little scared, but the promise of freedom kept me from chickening out. I stopped on one of the food aisles and was trying to decide what all I would need to stock up on when the creep came up behind me.

"Sexy Lexi!" he said. "I bet you hear that a lot." His voice made me sick to my stomach, and by his smile I could tell he knew he had upset me. I hated that I had given him the satisfaction of knowing that

I was afraid of him. I looked around for help, but no one was paying attention. Where was grinning Granny when I needed her?

I couldn't decide if I should scream, run, or punch him in the face. I just froze. My face burned with rage as all of the feelings from that horrible night flooded back into my mind. I wanted to attack him with all of the pent-up anger inside of me. Instead, all I could do was stand there like a statue.

"Don't worry," the creep said. "I just wanted to tell you I was getting off at this stop. Will you miss me? I'll miss seeing you, but I'll be thinking of you out there in Oklahoma."

He reached out to touch my face, and I shoved his hand away and ran to the bus. My heart was pounding out of my chest. *Why does this have to happen to me? Why couldn't I act out my feelings and rip his face off? Stupid! I can't believe I just stood there.*

It was only after the bus was rolling away from the stop that I realized the creep had ruined my best chance of slipping away without Bessie seeing me and calling the cops. *That jerk! What if he comes out to Oklahoma? Did he hear me say what my stop was?*

Bessie found me and sat beside me with what I was beginning to think was a permanent smile. Her smile changed to a look of concern when she saw how upset I was. "What is wrong, Lexi? You look all red in the face!"

"Nothing." I looked away so she couldn't tell I was lying. I didn't know this lady, and she was so old. *How could she understand anything about me?* I turned and looked at her. She was digging for something in her purse, which looked more like a beach bag.

The creep had really scared me. I felt so alone when he was trying to talk to me. Deciding that a sweet old grandmother might not be so bad in this situation, I made eye contact and smiled just as she looked up from finding her Chapstick in her gigantic purse. I wasn't prepared to try very hard, but if she wanted to be friendly again, I was willing.

"Do you want to talk about it?" she asked.

I shrugged my shoulders but didn't look away. "Did you see that creepy guy that was sitting across from us before we stopped?" I asked. If she didn't, I was going to drop it.

She frowned and said, "Yes, I saw him. He did act strange. He asked me about you while you were asleep earlier. I wouldn't tell him anything. Did you know him?"

"No, but he must have been listening when we talked because he knew my name. He came up to me in the truck stop. He was scary. I'm so glad he got off the bus." I could feel my eyes welling up with tears as I spoke.

Bessie frowned deeply and said, "He was much too old to be interested in you." I nodded my head in agreement and she continued, "What did he say to you?"

I told what the creep had said and how he had reached out to touch my face. Just saying it out loud made my stomach churn. I did feel a little relieved that I had someone to tell what had happened.

After I had finished, she motioned for me to wait and pulled out a piece of notebook paper. She wrote out two Bible verses on one side and told me to read them. One said something about fear, and the other said God is our protector. I laughed when I read that, but Bessie just gave me a sympathetic smile.

I knew I had not told her about my dad, but it was as if she somehow knew already. I wanted to blurt out, "Where was God when my dad was killed?" Fortunately, she started talking again before I could say what I was thinking.

"Turn the paper over," she said as she handed it to me. "Now," she instructed, "write down everything you can remember about the creepy guy." I didn't know what good that would do, but I had nothing else to do so I began to write.

I wrote: old baseball cap and beady eyes. I paused and looked up at Bessie. "He really freaked me out!" I exclaimed so loudly that the guy across the aisle looked over at me.

"Write it down," she said. I could tell from her expression that she was very serious about this.

I didn't know what her plan was. I thought she would probably turn the information over to the driver. That seemed like a good idea, so I started thinking harder. I continued to write: dirty blondish hair hanging out from under his cap to his shoulders, goatee, ugly (I knew that I just wrote that out of spite, but I didn't care), skinny, wore a jean jacket.

"He talked funny," I said.

"Yes," she replied. "I've been thinking about that, and I think he was Cajun."

"What's Cajun?" I wondered aloud.

"That is someone from Louisiana," she explained. "That information will come in handy if he comes around at your aunt and uncle's house. You give that description to them and tell them what happened."

Bessie looked away. I wondered where the smile had gone. She turned back to me with tears in her eyes and began to say something. Her voice cracked, and I couldn't make out what she was saying. She stopped and was quiet again, but this time it was for several minutes.

When she finally turned back to talk to me, she said, "I sat beside you because you remind me of my daughter when she was your age. I'm guessing you are about fifteen."

I nodded, surprised she hadn't guessed older. I could usually convince people I was at least seventeen.

She continued, "I didn't want you to be alone because of what happened to her. Her name is Carolyn. Your olive complexion and beautiful brown eyes make me think of her." She paused to compose herself.

When she continued, I had to lean in to hear her. It was obvious that she was still bothered by what had happened and could barely tell me about it. "Carolyn was driving back to college after Christmas break when her car broke down. There were no cell phones back then. She knew she was supposed to stay in the car and wait for help, but she was always bold and headstrong. She thought she could walk back to the town she had passed through a few miles back. It was snowing, and after she had walked a mile or two, the snow started coming down so fast that she couldn't see to follow the road. The temperature was well below freezing."

Her words began to come more quickly, and I could tell she was nearing the end of her story. "Carolyn almost made it to town before she fell and passed out. My little girl was out there all night. The next morning a county worker driving a snowplow saw her lying there beside the road and got her to the hospital. The doctors said if she been out there in those temperatures for a couple of more hours, she would not have lived. As it was, she had severe frostbite and spent almost a month in the hospital. I thank God every day that Carolyn lived."

I hugged Bessie. It felt a little funny, but I couldn't help myself. She was so nice. I was puzzled about one thing. How could she thank God when he allowed something so awful to happen to her daughter? "Is Carolyn okay now?" I asked cautiously.

"Yes, she has a good job with a computer company in Wisconsin. She is married, but she isn't able to have children. I often wondered if it had something to do with that night," she said thoughtfully.

"My best friend, Sarah, is missing," I blurted out, and then I just started crying. We held hands and cried together. I knew I couldn't tell Bessie the rest of my story. Even after she had shared with me, I just wasn't ready to talk about it. Part of me wanted to, but it was just too hard and too real.

We squeezed each other tight, and then Bessie pulled away. She looked me right in the eyes. I was afraid she was going to ask me about Sarah. She just asked if she could pray with me. I couldn't say no, even though I didn't want to pray now or ever.

If I refused, I knew it would hurt Bessie's feelings. Besides, anything that might help Sarah was worth a try. "That would be nice," I lied. Surprisingly, I felt a lot better after listening to Bessie pray. Maybe it wasn't a lie after all.

Go for
the Gold

At the next stop, I was starting to get upset because Bessie told me she would be getting off the bus in a few hours. We had been talking nonstop since I had shared that Sarah was missing. I probably told her a hundred times that I was sorry for being so rude that first day. How could she forgive me so easily? I knew if someone treated me like I had treated her, I would be sitting as far away from him or her as possible. Instead, Bessie had been a friend to me, bought me food, and helped me settle down after the creep had upset me. I decided I would stay on the bus until we got to her stop. After hearing about her daughter, I didn't want her to be worried by my running away.

We got off the bus together and headed toward the store. It was small and packed with people, so we stood outside and waited. Bessie's usual smile faded into a serious look. "I have a favor to ask you, Lexi. I want you to promise me that you will give your Uncle Patrick a chance. I once heard a wonderful speaker named Zig Ziglar talk about how to deal with difficult people."

She told me the speaker shared a story about when miners dig for gold. They move tons of dirt to find a few ounces of gold. The miners ignore the dirt and only focus on the gold.

Bessie said, "We need to look at people the same way. The dirt is all the things they do that we don't like, and the gold is the good things that we enjoy." She made me write down the phrase "Go for the gold" on the magazine I had in my lap.

As I wrote it down, I realized that a few hours ago I wouldn't even answer her questions. Now, she had me taking notes as if I were in school. What was this power she had over me? Maybe it was that I wished my mom would care about me and talk to me as much as this stranger did. Then again, maybe I was just lonely. Whatever it was, I had let Bessie into my heart more quickly than anyone ever.

The next couple of hours flew by as she told me about her kids and grandkids. I shared with her about my dad. It felt good to tell someone how great he was, especially someone as caring and positive as Bessie. The driver interrupted our talk when he announced that we were almost to Tahlequah, Oklahoma. Bessie and I looked at each other and smiled. "I am going to miss our talks." All I could do was nod my head and try not to cry. "You never gave me that promise I asked for," she said coaxingly.

"I wrote it down; isn't that enough?" I asked teasingly. She tilted her head and gave me a fake frown. "I promise," I said in a defeated tone. Then I smiled to let her know that I was going to keep the promise.

My smile quickly faded as I felt the bus begin to slow down and turn off the interstate. I was so sick of losing people! I decided right then not to let anyone else that far into my life. I might let her be a friend, but she was not getting into my heart. Bessie would be the last one.

After we hugged, she asked me to pray with her again. I said, "I think that you're one of the nicest people I have ever met, but to be honest I am not much on praying. How about I just listen again?"

She ignored my comment about prayer and said, "I appreciate you saying such nice things, but what you see is just Jesus coming out of me." I knew she was a special person, whether she wanted to take credit for it or not.

After a prayer that seemed to go on forever, we went into the store. I bought Bessie an Oklahoma T-shirt as a souvenir. It had an Indian, a buffalo, and a bird with really long tail feathers on the front. Of course, Bessie acted as if I had given her the best present ever. She was really good at going for the gold.

Back on the bus, I looked for someone to talk to, but there were no Bessies to be found. She was definitely one of a kind. I was bored and lonely, so I started writing a letter to Amanda to tell her about my trip out here.

I knew I would have to leave out the part about the creep. Although we hadn't been allowed to talk much since that night, I had gathered that she was still extremely upset. She told me she had not gone out since then and didn't think she ever would. I figured that was just a phase, or knowing Amanda she just wanted attention.

I caught myself wondering what Bessie would say about Amanda's reaction to our trouble that night. She would probably be extra nice to Amanda. That thought was with me as I wrote the letter and helped me to see the gold in my friend.

Dear Amanda,

What's up? I hope you're doin' better. I know you're having a really hard time dealing with what those jerks did. I am so sorry! I hate those guys! Are you going to go to school this year or did you go ahead and decide to be homeschooled?

I'm really nervous about going to school out here. I'm not sure I'm gonna stay on this bus all the way to Elk City. You and I both know I can take care of myself. If I do run away, don't worry; I'll still stay in touch with you—whatever it takes.

You have been such a good friend to me. I'm sorry I had to go away when you needed me the most. I need you too. Just remember, my mom said I only had to be out here for one year. You know I would never let you down like this, but I had no choice in the whole thing. My mom is so stupid! Anyway, since I'm not allowed to call you for a while, I thought I would write you a letter. You know I'm not much on writing, but if it's as boring out here as I figure it will be, you may be getting a lot of these.

On the bus I met this old lady. She was really sweet, and we talked for hours. I know it sounds weird, but it made the time go faster. You would have liked her a lot. She just got off the bus, and I miss her already. Elk City is only a few hours away. I hope my aunt and uncle at least have cable or satellite. Think of me out here in captivity! LOL.

See ya,
Lexi

When we stopped in Oklahoma City, I had a major decision to make. I didn't want to make the wrong choice like I did when I got in the car with Cruise and Red. This stop would be my best chance so far to walk away without anyone questioning it. I was torn between the freedom I had been thinking about the entire trip and the promise I had made to Bessie.

I knew Bessie was right, but I just didn't know if I could put up with the whole deal. My mom shipping me off like this was so wrong. I expected to be miserable at my aunt and uncle's house. Even if I could put up with all the hassle and rules, I knew I would be bored to death.

The worst part of it all was that I already missed Amanda, and I just knew if I was back home I could help find Sarah. She had been missing for over four weeks now, but I still expected her to be found.

After the night Sarah was kidnapped, her mom would barely speak to me. It crushed me. She used to call me her second daughter. I felt like she blamed me for what happened to Sarah. Every time we got into trouble she would convince her parents it wasn't her fault. Still, I didn't blame Sarah. I knew it must have been hard for her to try to be the perfect student, athlete, and person that her parents pushed her to be.

If I didn't get back on the bus, I would be letting down so many people. Aunt Joanne and my mom would be worried and hurt. Worst of all, I would be putting Amanda through twice the grief. I didn't know what that would do to her.

Also, I was afraid I would miss out on any news about Sarah. Finally, I decided to get back on the bus. As I climbed the steps, the driver handed me an envelope with my name on it. It was from Bessie!

The envelope had three one-hundred-dollar bills in it. Bessie had written a long note. I tried to think of when she would have had time. I was shocked when I read the part that said, "I'm glad you decided not to get off of the bus prematurely. I know that there are great things waiting for you." So she did know my plan!

This Is It?

When I arrived in Elk City, Uncle Patrick and Aunt Joanne were waiting for me in their old blue Ford pickup outside of Hutch's convenience store. I had made up my mind to try out Bessie's gold idea. I figured that would be the best way to get on their good side. I had learned that if grown-ups liked and trusted you, it was easier to get them to do what you want. I hugged them both and said, "I am so glad to finally be here!" I may have been stretching the truth a little—okay, a lot—but I was determined to try.

Aunt Joanne, or Jo, as Uncle Patrick called her, didn't dress like an older lady. She was plump, but I didn't think of her as fat. She was a happy person with kind, brown eyes. The thing I liked most about her was her voice. Her tone was always soothing. I could listen to her talk for hours, but she rarely would speak more than a few sentences at a time.

Instead, she liked to get other people talking about themselves and their thoughts or worries. She was a great listener.

Uncle Patrick was a big, wide-shouldered man with gray hair. His glasses had huge, round rims from the old-school days. He wore boots but never jeans. Instead he always wore cowboy-looking slacks that were too tight and button-down shirts with snaps that looked like they had part of a pearl in them.

Aunt Joanne asked, "Are you hungry?" I nodded my head and smiled widely.

"What sounds good?" she asked. After all of the subs and burgers on the bus trip, I thought Red Lobster sounded good.

When I suggested it, Uncle Patrick chuckled. "We don't have one of those out here," he said with a smile.

"What do you have?" I asked.

"I am afraid the only restaurants we have that y'all have in Chicago are fast food chains."

"Like Burger King?" I asked.

"Uh, we don't have that either." Aunt Joanne winced.

"There is a good place that's known for its fish and steaks," Uncle Patrick offered.

"Sure, I'm up for anything," I exaggerated. "But do I need to change?" They both smiled widely, and Aunt Joanne assured me that *out here* it is okay to dress casual if you feel like it.

The restaurant was just outside of Elk City. It was called Simon's Catch. Outside the restaurant, there was a high fence with all kinds of animals behind it. There were zebra, ostrich, elk, and turkey. The restaurant was a rustic log cabin.

When we walked in, we were greeted face-to-face by a gigantic buffalo head. I was surprised how cool the place was. It reminded me of one of our favorite restaurants back home called The Wild. Maybe it wouldn't be as boring out here as I thought, or maybe I had gotten lucky and found some gold in the first shovel of dirt! At the very least, I had been trying hard, so I was already gaining some control of the situation.

The drive to Uncle Patrick's house felt like it took forever. Not only was I tired of riding, but they lived way out in the country. They called the area where they lived Dempsey, but it was not a town. Aunt Joanne said that in the past Dempsey had a store and a school. Now there was just a cemetery and a small building.

As we drove past the white, one-room building, Uncle Patrick said enthusiastically, "We have the Dempsey social right there on the third Saturday of each month." I tried to act interested, but I couldn't see why he seemed so excited and proud. I wondered what they did at a Dempsey social that could be so much fun.

On the way to their house, I asked them about where I would go to school. Aunt Joanne said, "It is called Reydon, and their mascot is the tiger. There will be about nine students in your sophomore class." As she started naming the kids in the class, I tuned her out. I was furious! Mom had told me it was a small school, but this was ridiculous.

I guessed it would be pointless to ask about basketball since I was sure they wouldn't even have enough girls to make a team. My mom was such a liar! Small compared to my school would have been one hundred students in a class. I couldn't even think what it would be like to be in a class of nine students.

When we pulled up to the house, I was still fuming. "What do the kids here do for fun?" I asked incredulously. I expected the answer to be ride horses, round up cattle, or something like that.

Uncle Patrick answered, "Kids are kids. I bet they do a lot of the same things you guys did back home." Before I could catch myself, I laughed out loud.

"We'll introduce you to some of the kids at church on Sunday, and you can ask them," Uncle Patrick said. His tone told me I was starting to irritate him. I was mad, and I didn't care.

I was impressed with their house when I saw it. I had been here as a little girl, but as I tried to remember what it was like on the way out here I could only see logs and a big roof. It was a nice, two-story log cabin with cedar on the eaves of the second floor. The roof was very steep and covered with green metal. There were trees all around the house. A gigantic metal barn where my uncle kept his tractors and equipment was near the house.

Aunt Joanne spoke tenderly. "You're probably tired, dear. Let's get you inside and settled in your room."

About a half hour later, Uncle Patrick knocked gently on the door to my new room. "Come in," I said, trying to speak through my spontaneous yawn.

He gave me a hug and told me he was glad I had come to stay. I accepted the hug stiffly, and he stepped back from me. "If you want, I'll take you to see the school tomorrow," he offered.

"That sounds good," I said sleepily. "How far is it?"

"It's about twenty minutes."

I immediately began to try to figure out how early I would have to get up in the mornings. "What time does school start?" I asked.

"I'm not sure," he said. "Tomorrow we'll ask Mr. Monroe, the superintendent." I was impressed that my uncle knew the superintendent. At my school we never even saw the superintendent, and most of the parents probably had never met him.

"How will I get to school when it starts?" I asked.

"Most days you will ride the bus," he answered. Then he hollered into the next room, "Jo, what time did Shirley say the bus would be by here in the mornings?" When Aunt Joanne told him that it would be about six in the morning, I must have turned as white as her kitchen tablecloth. Uncle Patrick smiled slyly and hollered back to Aunt Joanne, "We got her!"

"That's not funny," I said, faking an angry face. *Maybe this would be bearable after all,* I thought.

"Who is Shirley?" I asked Uncle Patrick.

"She takes care of the bus routes and helps keep the school up and running. She is as work brittle as they come." He added the last part with a nod and a matter-of-fact tone.

I wanted to know what work brittle was, but I was too tired to ask. I just smiled through another yawn and told him, "Good night."

Aunt Joanne came in just as Uncle Patrick left. She brought me some milk and warm chocolate chip cookies. She sat down on the bed and asked about my trip and how my mom, her sister, was doing. They were trying so hard that I was beginning to feel a little guilty about my hard feelings toward them, or at least toward my uncle.

I began to open up a little to Aunt Joanne. "Mom is fine," I answered. "She is always busy with her job." The thought of that precious job made me mad, but I tried not to show it. "The trip out here was okay," I said. I told her about Bessie, how sweet she was, and our talks. I shared with her about the creep and got the paper that Bessie and I had worked on out of my bag. I gave it to her.

"That was smart of Bessie to have you write down a description of the man. I will give it to your uncle. I am sorry such an awful thing happened to you." I didn't know why, but I decided not to tell her about the letter and the money from Bessie.

Aunt Joanne told me she had been praying for me since hearing about that awful night and Sarah's disappearance. I knew she meant it, and that made me feel good. When Aunt Joanne was around, I could feel the love in the room.

She gave me a kiss on the forehead, and we

hugged. She got up and headed to the door. "What brought you to us may not be a blessing," she said, "but you being here is a blessing to your uncle and me. I hope by the time you leave it will seem like a blessing to you as well."

I smiled sleepily and mumbled, "Me too." I had never heard anyone talk like Aunt Joanne did. I felt like we were in the movies or something.

Cheyenne-Reydon

The next day, Uncle Patrick took me to see the school at Reydon. I met the superintendent, Mr. Monroe. He was a huge man. Uncle Patrick had warned me that he liked to tease people. "So you are from Chicago?" He asked. "Do you know Michael Jordan?"

"He lives on my block," I said with a grin.

He looked surprised and then just started laughing. "She's a dandy," he said to Uncle Patrick between chuckles. We all laughed. I could see why Uncle Patrick wanted me to meet him. I liked him a lot.

We toured the entire school. It didn't take long at all. There were only three buildings besides the gym, which was separate from the rest of the school. The junior high and high school had their classes in the same building. It was connected to the elementary school, which was a brand-new tan building with a red roof.

I could tell Mr. Monroe was really proud of the school. He showed me every room. It felt more like a house than a school. Most of our school buildings were gigantic old brick buildings with huge hallways. "This is kind of homey," I commented. I was trying to be positive, but the only thing I liked about the school so far was Mr. Monroe's jokes.

Mr. Monroe smiled at my comment. "You'll find that the students here get to know each other really well. My kids have said that a lot of their classmates are like brothers and sisters." He slapped Uncle Patrick on the back and started laughing again as he said, "Sometimes they fight like family too! But the next day they get over it."

The thought of finally being in high school and still having to be around a bunch of little kids was depressing. I was having a hard time finding any gold in the situation. The school was tiny, and the gym was pitiful compared to the arenas where I was used to playing basketball. If Bessie were in my position, I was sure that she would have trouble as well.

There was one short wall of lockers shared by the junior high and high school students. *Great, more little kids!* Mr. Monroe joked that they had done a scientific study that proved that a student could leave class, go to his locker, and get to his next class in approximately twenty-seven seconds. *Why did I care how long it took me to get to class?*

I was pleasantly surprised when Mr. Monroe told

me how good the lunches were. He said that people from the community even come by to eat sometimes. The food at our cafeteria was terrible, and this school year was going to be the first time that students at my old school weren't allowed to leave our high school campus.

Last year, some guys ruined it for the rest of us when they robbed a convenience store during their lunch break and brought the money, cigarettes, and beer they stole back to the school, leaving them in their car. They were a bunch of losers. We all thought their story might end up on that stupid criminals show.

Mr. Monroe joked around with Uncle Patrick the entire time we were at Reydon. They acted like they were good friends. By the time we were ready to leave, they had planned a fishing trip to one of Uncle Patrick's ponds.

Back in the old blue pickup, Uncle Patrick said, "Do you want to see the Cheyenne gym where most of the home high school basketball games are played?"

I pointed at a gym that had a mural with a tiger painted on the side. It wasn't even half the size of the gyms I was used to playing. "I figured that was the gym," I said.

"A couple of home games are played in the gym here in Reydon. It is nice and has been renovated on the inside, but it is smaller than the one in Cheyenne." *Yeah, right.*

On the drive over to Cheyenne, Uncle Patrick

said, "The people out here love and support basketball when it is played properly. A lot of the time the entire town follows the teams during the playoffs." I smiled politely and tried to act interested. I didn't believe a word he was saying.

It didn't matter anyway, I tried to convince myself. I would not be playing basketball out here in Oklahoma. With nine students in a class, I figured they couldn't be very good, and I hated losing.

When I asked Uncle Patrick how they could even have a team, much less win any games, he said, "You are right to some degree. You have to realize that in Oklahoma, schools are put into classes according to the number of students they have enrolled. The smaller schools play each other because they don't have as many kids to choose from for their teams."

"We had four to five hundred students in each class and some years we were lucky if twenty girls came out for the team."

He raised his eyebrows and his voice as well. "You might be surprised at the level of talent in this area. Many of the small schools out here can compete just fine with larger schools like Elk City and Weatherford that have five times their enrollment. In fact, when we have a good team, they often go to Oklahoma City to find someone challenging to scrimmage."

I couldn't tell him the main reason I wasn't sure if I would be able to play basketball here. I was afraid to play without Sarah. We had never played without each other. I also worried that when she found out

I had played without her she would feel betrayed. I knew that is how I would feel if she went to another school and played.

Basketball was more than a game to us. It was what brought us together and kept us together. Even when we weren't getting along, we would go to practice, and it would be as if we had never fought.

We had played together for so long that we knew where each other was going to be every second. I could look at Sarah, and she would know I wanted her to screen for me or that I was bringing the ball down to her in the post. Even as much as I loved it, I could not see myself on the court without my best friend.

Uncle Patrick made a call as we drove into town. When we pulled up to the gym, a guy met us at the door. He introduced himself as Coach Bradshaw. He was much younger than I expected a high school basketball coach to be. From his athletic build, I could tell he had probably been a good basketball player. I was sure he was a guard because he was only about an inch or two taller than me. I played guard most of the time, but since I was five foot nine, sometimes the coach would move me down by the basket.

Coach Bradshaw took us into the gym. I was impressed. It was almost as big as our high school gym at my school. There was a giant bear head painted in the center of the court, and the seats were orange, the school color. I couldn't imagine that they would ever need all of the seats that were available.

Coach Bradshaw asked me how I liked it here so

far. "It's okay," I answered. I didn't want to talk too much the first time I met him.

"Have you met Mr. Monroe over at Reydon yet?" he asked.

"Yes, we just came from there."

"He was my coach here at Cheyenne."

"He's really funny," I commented.

"He is now, but it didn't seem like it when I was playing basketball for him," he said, smiling. "He worked our tails off every day."

Uncle Patrick pointed to the banners that were hanging on the wall behind the goal on one end of the court. "Lexi, Coach Bradshaw helped hang that state tournament banner." I nodded, not knowing what to say. He continued, "That team filled this place up every time they played."

"How many people usually come to the games?"

"That depends on how good our teams are and how hard they play," Coach Bradshaw said.

I asked because I was always disappointed at our freshman games last year. We won most of our games, but we would have been lucky to have enough fans to fill up one of the sections in the Cheyenne gym. It was so much easier to play your best when the atmosphere was loud and full of energy.

Our gym was huge, but it was so quiet that it was hard to get excited about playing. Nobody came to games except the parents and a few friends from school. The high school games I had been to didn't have many more people than we did. I started thinking how much of a rush it would be to play here when it was full.

"Are you going to help us fill this thing up this year?" I couldn't help but think that Uncle Patrick had set this whole thing up to convince me to play, but I didn't know why he cared.

"I don't know," I answered. "I am just trying to get used to everything right now."

He nodded and said, "I understand. Change can be hard. I want you to know you are welcome."

"Thanks," I said, happy that he didn't try to persuade me right then.

The three of us walked back to the pickup. The heat was terrible. I still hadn't gotten used to it. Nobody wanted to talk out in the heat, so we told Coach Bradshaw good-bye and got in the pickup as quickly as possible. I turned on the air conditioning as high as it would go.

"What do you think now?" Uncle Patrick asked. I just shrugged my shoulders, not knowing what to say. He continued with an enthusiasm I hadn't seen from him up to this point. "What Coach didn't tell you was that last year they were one game from the Big House and only lost one starter. She was a senior, about your size, that averaged 15.6 points and nine rebounds per game."

I could tell he wasn't going to drop it until I talked to him about it. "Two questions. What is the Big House, and how did you know exactly what that girl's stats were?"

"Didn't I mention that I drive the bus and keep

the books for the basketball teams?" he said with a sly smile.

I looked at him in shock.

"Your eyes are as big as saucers, Lexi. Are you surprised that your old uncle is into basketball? Since we are on the subject, you might as well know that I helped hang one of those banners in that gym and played in the Big House at the state tournament as well. By the way, your Aunt Jo thought I looked pretty spiffy in my uniform!"

I was blown away. I didn't know Uncle Patrick ever did anything but take care of cows and horses. "So the Big House has something to do with the state tournament, but what is it?" I managed to ask, still shocked by the new information.

"The state tournament is played at the state fairgrounds in an arena we call the Big House. It is the goal of every team to finish their season there and to get to hang a banner in their gym. Lexi, our team is good this year. I know that you could help them realize that goal." I stared at the floorboard of the old blue pickup. Now I know why he was willing to have me come to stay this year. I was completely confused, scared, and yet a little excited.

Breech

About a week after I first arrived, the phone woke us all up at two thirty in the morning. I got up and went to my door to see what was wrong. I could hear Aunt Joanne saying, "Well, Patrick, you know Lana would be here in a heartbeat to help you if you were in need." I laughed to myself. Even half asleep in the middle of the night Aunt Joanne was thinking of other people.

Uncle Patrick came down the hall that went by my room and led to the kitchen. I had noticed they always used the kitchen door instead of the front door, which I thought was strange. He stopped when he saw me at the door and said, "You want to go with me to help deliver a foal?" I just blinked at him and tried to figure out what he was talking about. He was in a hurry, though, so he made the decision for me. "Get dressed; you need to see this," he said and headed hurriedly down the hall.

I had been trying hard all week to get along, but this was really pushing it. I had convinced myself that if everything went well I might not have to stay here the entire year. I got ready as quickly as I could and found Uncle Patrick waiting in the pickup. As I got in he huffed so I would know that I didn't hustle as fast as he wanted me to. "Sorry," I said with a yawn.

"The foal is breech," he said as we flew down the dirt road.

"What's that?" I asked.

"It is trying to come out feet first instead of head first. We will have to try to turn it while it is still inside the mare," he explained. I figured out mare meant mom.

"Who are we going to help?" I questioned.

"Lana Merrick," he said. "She and her husband, Kent, have been our friends and neighbors for years. They have some of the best horses in the country. They have thoroughbred racehorses, quarter horses, and appendixes, which are a mixture of thorough-bred and quarter horse. Lana's father is credited with bringing the first quality quarter horses to Okla-homa, and Lana is a world champion barrel racer."

They sounded like interesting people, and as I began to wake up I was glad I had come. Some of my fondest memories were of going to the racetrack and watching the horse races with my dad. He was usually happy while we were there, but sometimes he seemed depressed when we left. I had no idea what a quarter horse or barrel racing was, so I had lots of questions. The question on my mind the most was how were they going to turn the baby around while it was still inside of its mother?

When we got to the ranch, my uncle ran to the barn so fast that I had trouble keeping up with him. Lana was comforting the mare. She was stroking its neck and talking to it sweetly. Lana looked up at us. "Thanks for coming," she said. She had a beautiful smile, slim figure, and big brown eyes. Although she was in work clothes and not wearing any makeup, I could see that she was an attractive lady.

They started working on the mare almost immediately. It was kind of gross watching them. I looked away a lot, but I was afraid to leave the barn. What if they needed something or the baby was born while I was gone?

"How do you know what to do?" I blurted out. Uncle Patrick looked annoyed by my question.

"Well, Pat, are you sure we do know?" Lana said.

They both laughed for a second, and then Uncle Patrick said, "Lexi, we've done this several times. Unfortunately, some don't make it."

I caught my breath. I had not even considered that the baby might not live. I thought horses were big and tough. What if it died right in front of me?

"Lexi," Lana said, "get that black pail right there and go fill it up at the faucet at the far end of the barn." I ran to fill the pail as fast as I could. I couldn't bear to think that anything I did or didn't do would hurt the baby's chances at life.

The baby, or foal as they called it, was coming out as I ran back. Lana and Uncle Patrick were both pulling on the foal. There was blood and white, pasty stuff all over the place. I couldn't look anymore. I turned around but yelled over my shoulder, "Is it okay?"

"He's as healthy as a horse," joked Uncle Patrick.

They both got out of the stall to let the mother clean up her baby. It was a tan color with a big white mark on its forehead. It had one white sock on its front left leg. We all enjoyed the moment. Watching the mom take care of her baby was so cool. It was amazing to see the foal trying to stand when it had just been born. It finally got so tired from all of the exercise that it lay down.

When the foal lay down, Lana went back into the stall. She sat down by the foal and began to rub it and talk to it. Every little bit the mare would stick her nose down by Lana and sniff her.

"What is Lana doing?" I whispered to Uncle Patrick.

"It's called imprinting," he explained. "Lana will touch the foal everywhere that she will need to touch it during training and riding. She will let it smell her hair and breath. All of this is to build a bond with the foal. The bond will last a lifetime and help the foal when it is time to train it."

The imprinting lasted about two hours. Although the sun was coming up and I hadn't slept but a few hours, I didn't feel tired at all. I was enjoying this new experience and wishing I could share it with my friends back home. "Sarah would have loved this," I told Uncle Patrick. He just nodded and went out to the pickup.

Uncle Patrick came back with a camera, and when he handed it to me I could see he had tears in his eyes. I looked at him with a puzzled smile. "I am always amazed at God's gift of life."

After I took a few pictures of Lana with the horses, she talked me into going into the stall. The foal was clean now, but there was still some blood on the hay. Lana took pictures of me with the foal and mare. Then she motioned for Uncle Patrick to get in the pictures with me. He did, but I could tell he wasn't excited about being in a picture.

Lana said she was going up to the house to take a shower. "Are you done imprinting?" I asked.

"No, once I take a shower I will come down and repeat the whole process."

"Why do you have to do it all again?"

"Smell is very important to a horse. I need to have the foal recognize me whether I have been working all day or just got out of the shower."

"Oh, I get it," I said.

Lana smiled and said, "Thank you both so much." I looked down at the pail of water. It was still just as full as it was when I brought it to her.

"So the water was to give me a job to do?" I asked with a smile.

"I like this girl, Patrick," she said. "She is quick!"

"Thanks for letting me see all of this."

"You're welcome, Lexi, and good night, I mean, good morning," she said. We all laughed.

Golden

I slept in the next morning until eleven. "Good morning, sleepyhead," Aunt Joanne said from her rocking chair in the living room. Her chair was different than any rocker I had ever seen. It was high backed with green cloth covering it. The arms were made of wood, and it sat on two curved pieces of wood attached to springs. It looked so comfortable that I knew I was going to have to try it.

Aunt Joanne continued, "There are bacon, biscuits, and scrambled eggs in the oven keeping warm for you."

"Thanks," I answered. "I'm starving. Everything looks so good! I could get use to this." She got up and headed toward the kitchen.

"Where is Uncle Patrick?" I asked.

"He went to check a cow that is due to calve any day. He'll be back soon, and he wants to take you to see something," she said with a wry grin.

"Aunt Jo," I paused, realizing I had used my uncle's nickname for my aunt. She smiled at me knowingly but didn't say anything about it. "Do you know how Lana's foal is doing?"

She frowned. "No, I am sorry, dear. I haven't heard. Your uncle will probably know something."

It wasn't long before Uncle Patrick came home. He greeted me with a big hug. "What have y'all been doing?" he asked. I smiled every time he said *y'all*. It was another Oklahoma saying, like fixin'. Whenever they were about to do something, they would say, "I'm fixin' to do this or that." It took a while to get use to some of their terms.

Aunt Jo told him that I had slept in a little. She said we had eaten breakfast and done a few chores. I appreciated her making me sound quite a bit better than I had actually been.

Uncle Patrick started talking loudly with a big grin. "Lexi," he said, "I want to tell you about the finest woman in the country. She makes the best food at the church dinners, keeps a spotless house and never gets tired of helping me around the ranch."

Aunt Jo's face beamed. She enjoyed his praise. It made me happy too. I had never seen this side of my uncle, but I wished he would talk like this all the time.

"So, I'm fixin' to go check cows. Do you want to go with me?" he asked. I had no idea what that meant or what I would have to do.

I looked over at Aunt Jo. She nodded her head, encouraging me to go. I knew she wouldn't send me off to do something too terrible, so I said, "What do I need to wear?"

"Work clothes," he answered as he headed out the screen door toward the pickup. I got out to the pickup much faster this time, hoping not to ruin his good mood.

We drove all over the countryside. He pointed out houses and told me who lived in each one. I got to see all of his pastures and hear the story of how he had acquired them. He was enjoying it, so I just listened and acted interested. Boredom had almost completely overcome me by the time he pulled into a big lot full of horses.

My eyes scanned the lot looking for the foal that had been born at Lana's ranch. He had told me what seemed like hours earlier that it was healthy as a horse. I had given him a frown and said, "That joke is really getting old." He just laughed. He thought he was really funny.

"Is this where Lana keeps her foal?" I asked, finally finding something interesting on this tour.

"It isn't here," he said, "but I have some foals in the stalls in the barn you might want to see." We went into the barn where there were five mares, each with a foal. One of the mares looked like Lana's. I looked at the foal, and it had the same big white mark on its forehead as Lana's foal. It even had the same white sock on its front leg.

I pointed into the stall and asked Uncle Patrick, "Isn't that Lana's foal that was going to be born breech?"

"No, ma'am," he said. "That foal doesn't belong to Lana; it belongs to Lexi."

I couldn't believe what he was saying. I turned to face him. He wasn't kidding. He just nodded his head yes. I ran up to him and gave him a big hug. "Whoa, there," he said, "you'll squeeze the stuffing out of me! Let's go see your foal."

Uncle Patrick opened the door to the stall and motioned for me to come in with him. I said, "But you said Lana's horses were really expensive." He put his finger up to his lips.

He spoke in whispers. "The mare doesn't know you yet. Don't move quickly or talk over a whisper."

I whispered this time. "I can't believe you did this." The mare didn't even like my whispering. She let me know by putting her body between me and the foal. "He is our baby now, Momma," I said.

I wanted to hug the foal and rub him down like Lana had done when he was born, but the mare wouldn't let me close to him at all. "Patience, Lexi," Uncle Patrick said. "She will get used to you in a day or two. Tomorrow you can bring her a treat and just sit with her for a while." I could hardly wait for tomorrow to come.

I stayed up until two in the morning thinking about the foal. I had never before been given a gift like the foal. I was responsible for it. I wondered what would happen when I went back home. That would be a whole year from now, I told myself.

Right now, I needed to name him. I wrote down names to see what they looked like on paper. I laughed at myself because no one would ever actually see his name on paper. It wasn't like he would go to horsey kindergarten.

I finally settled on the name Golden. He was a gold color to me, but Uncle Patrick called it buckskin. I thought about Buck for the name, but I wanted something more original. Golden would be short for Golden Boy. I loved him already.

I went to the horse barn every day. The mare let me get close to Golden after a couple of days, just as Uncle Patrick had said. Going up to work with the horses made the time until school was to start pass a lot more quickly.

Also, I was spending much of my time getting to know my aunt and uncle. Aunt Jo was just as sweet as I had remembered. I figured she had to be to get along with Uncle Patrick all these years. She thought of everything and took care of everyone else before she would sit down to eat or do anything she wanted to do for herself. She said her one vice was watching a soap opera every day at two o'clock in the afternoon.

Uncle Patrick wasn't as bad as I had expected. I liked the way he obviously loved Aunt Jo. He was always asking me questions and acted like he really listened to what I said. And of course, he had bought me the foal.

I decided that I was glad Bessie made me promise to give my uncle a chance. I did like Uncle Patrick, but he had a lot of opinions about things. That wouldn't have bothered me so much except most of our opinions were very different.

One night, we argued about my curfew. I had told him that my curfew at home was midnight. He said that in his house it had always been eleven, and it was not about to change now because nothing good goes on after eleven anyway. I tried to argue that the late movie wouldn't be over until eleven. That had worked on my mom, but he wasn't buying it. I finally dropped it. I figured I could try again if I ever made any friends and wanted to go somewhere that the curfew mattered.

The next day with Golden at the horse barn, I started worrying that Uncle Patrick had spent too much on the foal. I didn't want to feel like I owed him something. I walked over to where he was working on the hooves of one of the mares. "We could take him back if you want," I offered. "I would be happy just taking care of your other foals. I really do appreciate it, but I don't want to always feel guilty about how much he cost you."

"That is so sweet and unselfish, Lexi," he said. "The foal wasn't as much as you think. He was born in July. Lana breeds her mares to give birth as soon after January first as possible. She rarely has a foal born before that date because every foal becomes a yearling on January first."

I was confused, and Uncle Patrick could tell. "In the competitions that Lana enters her horses in, the foal we bought would have had to compete against other horses that were born just after January first. Since he was born in July, he would be about five months younger than the other horses. That is a big disadvantage in maturity and makes it even tougher to win. Lana likes you a lot, and since the horse had such a big disadvantage from the beginning, she was willing to sell him much cheaper."

I understood a little better but not completely. It was nice to hear that Lana liked me. I liked her too, but I still had one question. "Why was the foal born in July when you said Lana always breeds the mares to have their babies in January?"

He turned to look at me and said, "The Lord did it." He looked so serious that I had a hunch he was trying to tease me again.

"You mean that God is in charge of everything, like you said the other night?" I asked.

"No." He smiled. "Well, yes and no. God is in control of everything, but the name of the stud that got into the pasture with the mares was The Lord and His Ladies." He laughed so hard at his joke that I thought his false teeth might fall out.

I laughed too. "All right, Uncle Patrick, that was a good one!" I admitted. I could feel myself wanting to give in and trust my uncle, but I couldn't shake the doubts in my head.

First Day of School

The first day of school at Reydon had finally arrived. Surprisingly, my mom called the night before to wish me luck. Her call made me feel good, and we had a nice visit. She reminded me about my first day of kindergarten. Apparently, I didn't want to go at all. She said that I cried all day long for the first week. I wanted to go home and play with my toys.

She started laughing and said, "When the teacher wouldn't let you go home before lunch, you yelled, 'Teacher, listen to my brain. I want to go home!'" I was glad to hear her voice. We hadn't spoken since I left. I rejected my thoughts of ruining her good mood with my complaints about being exiled out here.

This was the first time I could remember actually being glad that school was starting. Except for spending time with Golden and the occasional trip to the gym with Uncle Patrick, I was bored to death. I was tired of trying to find something on television, and I could only take so many walks. However, from those walks, I had gained an appreciation for the beauty of the land that made up my aunt and uncle's ranch.

Aunt Jo took me into the school and helped me get started. I was so nervous. I could feel the knot in my stomach tightening. Several of the students stopped to say hello when they passed us in the hall. Mr. Blevins, the principal, walked us to my locker. Aunt Jo said she would pick me up after school and gave me a hug good-bye.

I followed the flow of students toward a fairly large room they called the lounge. Some of the girls about my age came up to me and started talking. We sat down together, and Mr. Blevins started orientation. I thought it was funny that he didn't even need a microphone to talk to the entire high school. I was not used to everyone actually paying attention when the principal addressed the students, but all of these kids did.

Mr. Blevins smiled a lot more than any principal I had ever seen. He didn't really talk like a principal either. He spoke loud enough for all of us to hear but didn't act like he was better than us. Also, he dressed more like a teacher. He wore slacks and a short-sleeved button down shirt without a tie or jacket.

Although meeting the students was going pretty well, I was still a little nervous about my teachers and classes. With only nine students in my class, I knew I wouldn't be able to hide out in the back of the room. What would the teachers ask me? I hoped they wouldn't put me on the spot.

The five girls in my class were really friendly. They were probably excited to have a new person in their school. Everyone I met asked me questions, but the question I was asked the most was if I played basketball.

I was glad to hear how many of them were *ballers*, but I didn't know what to say. When I even considered playing, I felt like I was betraying Sarah and my other teammates. For now, I decided to say that I didn't know.

When I had enrolled a few days before, Mr. Blevins convinced me to enroll in athletics to give it a try. He promised he would let me change classes if it didn't work out. He told me that his daughter, Dawn, was in my class and played basketball. Also, he said there were two other girls in my class, Addey and Kylie, who were really good players.

I met Addey in my first hour class and liked her right away. She was friendly and quiet all at the same time. She dressed cute but not too fancy. She asked me if I would like to go swimming at her aunt's pool in town sometime this weekend. "Sounds like fun," I said, glad to be making friends so quickly. However, the more I thought about it, the more nervous I became. *Who all would be there? I don't even own a swimsuit.* The teacher started talking, and I knew that I would have to ask her more about it later.

The next hour we went to science class. The teacher was new, and I liked the idea that no one else knew what to expect any more than I did. His name was Mr. Noak. He was from Canada and had only taught in college until now.

"Don't worry," he said. "I'm not going to expect the same level of work from high school students. However, we will challenge ourselves, and I expect you to ask lots of questions."

He spent the rest of the hour telling us about his life in Canada. He had hunted moose and told us all about it. He grew up working on his grandparents' farm in Canada. "Since I was good in school, I decided to be a teacher, aye," he said with a Canadian accent. Everyone laughed.

When Mr. Noak mentioned that he had taught at the University of Oklahoma, the students got into a friendly argument. Some of the students started saying that they liked him already, but the others started saying that Oklahoma State University was better. Since both of the colleges were in Oklahoma, I didn't understand the problem. I was glad nobody seemed truly angry about it.

The classes all seemed to go by quickly. All of the teachers I had met so far seemed to be nice and much more laid back than the teachers in my old school. I was feeling better about everything except all of the attention I was getting about basketball.

Mr. Monroe, the superintendent, had a senior daughter who came up to me in the hallway between classes. Her name was Leisha. She tried to talk me into playing basketball too.

Leisha introduced me to two other seniors on the basketball team. "Toren and Tina play too," she said. "We had a good team last year. We plan on going to the state tournament this year and could use another good player. My dad said you were a starter at a huge school in Chicago, so I know you must be good." She added, "This is our senior year and our last chance to play in the Big House."

"I met your dad this summer, but we didn't talk about basketball. How did he know that I played?" I asked. Leisha shrugged her shoulders, but I already knew the answer—Uncle Patrick.

I guess he really does care if I play, I thought to myself. With that, the knot in my stomach got big-ger and tighter. *How could I know the right thing to do? I wish I could talk to Sarah right now!*

The bell rang and broke up our conversation. I headed to English class, hoping I wouldn't get a tardy on the first day. I had been looking forward to meeting Mrs. Latta. Most of the kids said that she was their favorite teacher. I hoped she was as nice and funny as they said.

I quickly learned that they weren't kidding. She told us her rules, but she called them *expectations*. She had a funny way of saying things that made listen-ing to her fun. She also acted out some of the scenes from the story we started reading; it was hilarious.

Also, as part of her class procedures, Mrs. Latta had a sticky-note pool. She said that we would use sticky notes almost every day in her class. Students that wanted to be sticky-note sweet could donate sticky notes to the pool. Those students would know they had some any time they needed. But students who wanted to be sticky-note stingy and not put any in the pool would have to make sure they remembered theirs every day.

Since it was the first day, and I was new, I tried not to bust out laughing when she said sticky-note stingy. Most of the class laughed, but they didn't seem surprised at her humor. I was pretty sure Mrs. Latta was going to be my favorite teacher.

At the end of the day, it was time to go over to Cheyenne for off-season basketball. We rode over on a bus. It took about fifteen minutes. I purposely left my practice clothes at home so I could sit back and watch to see what it was going to be like.

When I told Dawn that I didn't bring my clothes, I could tell she was disappointed. Dawn said she had an extra shirt and caught Kylie before she went to softball practice to see if she had some shorts. I said I would just wait until tomorrow. I was surprised that anyone cared about the first day of off-season practice.

There were only three of us who didn't come prepared to practice, and the other two told me they didn't know if they were going to play this year at all. Coach Bradshaw came over and talked to us for a minute before he went out on the court. He didn't ask me if I was going to play. He just said, "You girls be sure to have your stuff tomorrow if you plan to be a part of the team."

He was friendly, but he was definitely serious about basketball. For the first day, his practice was super tough. He made the girls run for fifteen minutes before they even started doing drills. He told them that every one of his drills would have a winner and a loser. The losing group had to do push-ups. If neither group was doing well or trying hard enough, he would have everyone line up on the baseline to run sprints.

I knew he was going to want me to make a decision before I was ready. I hoped I would have a few weeks to figure everything out and get used to the new school. I was really bummed. This was not what I wanted to happen.

Aunt Jo picked me up after school. "How did it go today?" she asked. I just shrugged my shoulders.

When she asked me again, I said, "Fine." She jerked the steering wheel and pulled over to the side of the road. I tensed up. When my mom pulled over like that, I was about to get chewed out.

Aunt Jo didn't yell or even act mad. She just said, "I'm not just talking. I really want to know. I love you, and I care about everything that affects you."

There was something different about my aunt. I really didn't know why, but I automatically trusted her. "I'm sorry. I know you care," I said softly.

I began to tell her everything that happened during the day. I even told her about trying to decide whether or not to play basketball and how all the kids were asking me about it. She listened closely and asked lots of questions.

In my room later, I had time to think. The way Aunt Jo was with me was awesome, but I felt weird. I was so angry at my mom. Why didn't she care enough to take the time to ask me questions and really listen to what was in my heart? My talk with Aunt Jo made me miss my times with my dad.

○

I could hear Old Yellar coming from a mile away. The engine growled menacingly as Dad stomped on the gas pedal, heading toward the school zone. He braked quickly to stay just within the fifteen-mile-per-hour speed limit. I knew that restriction must be killing him.

Even though I was bummed out about my friend Traci, I couldn't help but smile as he pulled up in his '69 vintage Chevelle. My fellow seventh grad-ers all stared at the bright yellow muscle car as the afternoon sun made the black, metallic racing stripes glitter. Old Yellar purred like a tiger while I trotted over to him.

He was all smiles as he leaned over and opened the door for me on the passenger side. I hopped in, tossed my bag in the rear seat, and primly buckled the faded lap belt. Dad gunned it just a little to show off for my friends. He was so awesome.

"How was your first day of seventh grade, Lex?" He glanced sideways while shifting gears smoothly.

"Not that great. Traci Brown found out she made cheerleader. For the rest of the day, she wouldn't even speak to me and Sarah. Then she came in at our athletics hour and informed us that she was way too busy to play ball. All she cares about are her cheerleading friends."

Dad nodded. "Her loss. She can jump around and look pretty while you and Sarah play ball. You don't want a friend that is that fickle anyway."

He always had a way of making me feel better. I knew he was right, but it still hurt. At least I would always have Sarah.

"Well, that's the worst thing of the day. What was the best thing?"

I began telling him that the volleyball coach came into off-season basketball practice and asked Sarah to play volleyball. She told him that she could only play if I came too. Fortunately, he agreed, and we would start practicing with the team the next day.

Dad squeezed my shoulder, and I took a deep breath, letting the disappointment of the day exhale out of me. He suggested that we stop for an early supper since Mom wouldn't feel like cooking again, he was sure. We headed toward our favorite restaurant, and Dad turned up the radio way too loud as a classic rock station thumped the back speakers. The wind from the window swirled my hair wildly as I thought about the new lineup without Traci. She wasn't that great anyway. I loved how my dad knew that we didn't have to fill up our time with a constant flow of conversation. It was comforting just to be in his presence as we both nodded our heads to the same beat.

○

My aunt was a sweet lady, but no one could replace my dad. Remembering how Sarah would not play volleyball without me made the decision about basketball here at Reydon even more complicated.

The Party

The next day a bunch of the kids at school planned a party for that weekend. They invited me to come. I desperately wanted to go. I hadn't been to a good party in a long time. The ones talking to me about it were mostly juniors and seniors. The girls on the basketball team told me that they weren't going. I knew I was going to go, but I had made friends with those girls. I was disappointed that they wouldn't be there.

Dean was a senior boy who had talked to me in the hall on the first day of school. When he asked me if I was going to the party, I could tell he wanted to get together. He was kind of cute, but I had only seen one boy in the entire school that I would consider going out with, and it wasn't Dean.

Keith was the best-looking guy I had ever seen in real life. He was tall, and his eyes were blue, which I loved. When I first saw Keith, all I could think of was Cruise. The more I talked to him, though, the less I saw Cruise in him. He wasn't super muscular like some of the other guys in Reydon or Cheyenne, but I wasn't really into that like some of my friends.

His hair was brown, and he kept it longish but not too long. Most days I could see his hat ring where he had been wearing his baseball cap. He dressed plainly, usually in a T-shirt and jeans, but he looked good in anything.

I realized that thinking about Keith had caused me to drift off from my conversation with Dean. When I came back to reality, I said, "I don't know if I'm going or not."

I looked away, hoping to end the conversation. All I needed was some guy following me around when I wasn't interested. He didn't get the message. "Will you go if I pick you up?" he asked.

"I'm probably going with some of the girls if I do go," I said, turning to walk away. I hated to hurt his feelings, but I was going to be gone at the end of the year anyway. If Keith were to ask me, I might have to think twice about it. In fact, for him I would think about staying out here in the wilderness.

The party was going to be at one of the seniors' houses. I heard that his parents didn't care if the kids drank. Some of the girls told me that if I wanted a ride they would come by and get me. I told them that would be great. Now, all I had to do was figure out how to get Uncle Patrick to let me go with them. He knew so many people out here that I was afraid he might already know about the party.

Over dinner, I got up the nerve to ask Uncle Patrick if I could go out with some of the girls on Saturday night. "Who are you wanting to go with?" he asked. I told him their names and he frowned. "I know those kids and what they do on the weekends."

My heart started pounding. I told him that they had asked me to go to the movies. "Don't you want me to have friends and fit in?" I complained.

"Lexi, you know I want you to do all of that but not those friends," he said.

I knew I had him now. "You can't pick my friends," I declared, expecting him to agree.

"Oh, yes, I can. In fact, as I am fulfilling the role of parent while you are here, it is part of my job," he countered.

I couldn't believe what he was saying. "Mom says that parents can't pick their children's friends. She says that you like people because your person-alities click, and parents can't control that," I said triumphantly.

"How is that working out for you?" he said sar-castically. "I would say that your mom is probably rethinking that position at this time. While you are here, we will help you spend time with people that will build you up as a person. We will protect you in every way possible, and that includes what friends you choose."

I stormed away from the table and slammed the door to my room. I was so angry that I wanted to scream. How dare he think that he could control every little part of my life! I knew it would be this way. What a control freak!

Lying in bed that night, I was so angry that I seriously considered going out the window and heading back to Chicago. The entire plan went through my mind. I would get in the pickup and pull away slowly with the lights off. I saw it on a movie one time. People out here left their keys in their cars, and Uncle Patrick was no different.

Next, I would head to Elk City and get on the interstate. I had the money that Bessie had given me, and I was sure it would be enough to get me home. That was my entire plan. It wasn't complicated, but it made me feel like I was in control.

At school the next day, everyone was talking about the party. I decided I was going. I didn't care what Uncle Patrick did to me. Besides, up to this point he hadn't done anything but talk. I told the girls to pick me up at ten o'clock at the end of the long gravel driveway that led up to the house. I knew by that time my aunt and uncle would be in bed watching the news.

When they said good night and headed to their bedroom, I acted as if I were going to bed as well. I went out my bedroom window and met the girls at the end of the driveway. It was exciting when they pulled up without their headlights on, and they acted impressed with me for sneaking out of the house.

The party was a total blast. It reminded me of going out with my friends at home. I would have to write to Amanda and tell her everything about it.

The only disappointing part of the night was that Keith wasn't at the party.

When I asked one of the girls where he was, she rolled her eyes and said, "Keith is too good to hang out with us."

"What do you mean?" I asked. "He is always friendly to everybody at school."

She frowned. "He doesn't drink or smoke or anything, if you know what I mean. He thinks he is too good for us."

I didn't know how that made me feel. Part of me felt like he wasn't the perfect guy I had in my mind after all. Another part of me was even more interested in him. A guy that cute that doesn't party? I didn't know there were any out there.

I got back to the ranch at three in the morning. I was able to sneak back into the house without being seen. "Too easy!" I whispered to myself. I changed in the dark.

As I crawled into bed, I heard a rustling noise like a piece of paper. I covered the lamp beside my bed with a dirty shirt from the floor and turned on the light. The piece of paper read, "Your aunt and I are very disappointed. We will talk in the morning."

Busted! I covered my face with my hands, and for a minute I thought I might cry. I wondered what they would do to me. I finally decided it couldn't be that bad. They would probably just ground me. I would say I was sorry, but I was glad I went. I had a great time.

I was sorry that they had found out. I didn't want

to let them down, but their standards were too high. Things had changed since their kids were in school, and besides, I was acting better than I had in a long time. They should be proud of me for improving.

The next morning we all three sat silently at breakfast. When he had finished eating, Uncle Patrick turned to me. "Lexi, where did you go last night?" I rolled my eyes at him and looked away. I wasn't going to make this easy. He knew where I went. Why was he wasting time asking? He just sat there waiting for me to answer.

"You know that I went to the back-to-school party," I said.

"The point is not what I know, but that you know I said you couldn't go," he said. A flash of anger crossed his face.

"I went because I want to fit in here and have friends. I told you that is why I wanted to go," I said flatly.

Aunt Jo spoke up. "Do you think we don't want what is best for you, Lexi? Don't you see that those kids are the same kind of friends that you were sent here to get away from?"

I could believe that my aunt was siding with her husband, but I was surprised by the way she was talking to me. I knew I was going to lose this argument and get grounded anyway, so I just blew up on them.

I got up so fast that my chair tipped over and went crashing to the floor. I yelled, "You guys have no idea what it is like to come into a brand-new place and try to fit in and have friends. I have tried to make this work and put up with all of your stupid rules, but you don't cut me any slack. My mom would have let me go to a back-to-school party unless I was grounded."

Uncle Patrick stood up slowly and said, "Young lady, your tone and attitude are unacceptable. You will not yell at us in this house. As far as parties are concerned, consider yourself grounded for the rest of the year. When and if you go back to live with your mom, you can go by her rules. Until then, I expect you to obey and respect us or face the consequences. Now, go to your room."

When I slammed my door, I heard a picture fall off of the wall in the hallway. I smiled for a second, and then I threw myself on the bed and began to weep. *How had I ended up here with these people?* I told my mom it would be like this. *I hate it here!*

I stayed in my room, refusing Aunt Jo's calls for lunch. I slept most of the afternoon and woke up to a knock on my door. Aunt Jo peeked in the door. "You need to get up and come to supper."

At the table, Uncle Patrick asked me if I was ready to talk about our problem. I said flatly, "I am sorry. I will follow your rules."

"We love you," he said, "and that is why we are willing to spend the time and energy to discipline you."

I didn't quite understand how making my life miserable was a way of loving me, but I didn't want another fight right then. "Am I still grounded?" I asked.

"Yes," he answered.

"How long?" They looked at each other and I could tell they hadn't decided that part yet. I took the opportunity to try to get a shorter sentence. "Most of the time I get grounded for a few days to a week," I lied.

"As I said last night, you are grounded from any and all parties with that group of kids for as long as you are here. That is not your punishment. It is your protection. As for your grounding for directly disobeying us, you will go nowhere but school and church for the next two weeks."

I dropped my eyes to the steak on my plate. So much for a shortened sentence. They were better at this punishment stuff than I thought. I looked up and said, "Can I be finished now?"

Aunt Jo frowned, but she said, "That will be fine."

She had made one of my favorite meals, and I could tell she was not happy that I only ate a few bites. I didn't let it bother me. I was still so angry that they thought they had the right to choose my friends that I could scream.

This was worse than living with my mom. She didn't care who I hung out with as long as I came home by curfew. I figured she just didn't want to have to come looking for me or stay up and be tired for work the next day. Now I was stuck with two people watching my every move who wanted to control everything in my life.

To Ball or Not to Ball

I slid down into a desk in Mrs. Latta's room. She had told us all if we ever wanted to talk we could come in during lunch. She said she never went to the lunchroom and would always be available to visit with us during that time.

Maybe that was why she was so skinny. Mrs. Latta was probably older than she looked. She looked like she was in her twenties, but she had a daughter who was a freshman. Her daughter, Logan, was the star on the junior high basketball team. Some of the girls had told me they thought that Coach Bradshaw would pull her up on the high school team. I had seen her on the court a few times, and she was really good.

"What's wrong, Lexi?" she asked. Mrs. Latta always called us by name. When she did, it made me know she thought of me as a person. I was more important to her than just a student. No one else had come into her room yet, and I was glad. I really needed to talk.

"I have to decide today if I am going to play basketball or not," I said. I tried to choke back my tears.

She looked knowingly at me. "I read in some of your daily journals that you were having a struggle with that," she said. She waited for me to say something, but I couldn't. "What does your heart say about it?" she asked.

"I don't know. I think I … I … " I stammered and then just stopped.

Two junior high boys came to the open door and stood. Mrs. Latta went to the door, and one of them asked where Logan was. I smiled to myself. Kylie and Addey had told me that all of the junior high boys and a few of the high school boys wanted to go out with Logan. We all could see why. She could be a model if she wanted.

Mrs. Latta sent them away, shut the door, and sat down beside me. "I read in your journal that you and your friend Sarah had always had each other in basketball." I sat there with tears running down my cheeks and nodded my head yes.

"Do you really think Sarah wants you to be miserable for a year to pay for the trouble of one night?" I looked up at her quickly, surprised that she had read all of the journal entries I had turned in to her.

"I think you should be here while you are here. Do what will make you feel like you are Lexi again.

Don't let someone else decide what you should do, and don't blame your decision on Sarah when you don't know what she would tell you."

I hadn't thought of it that way, but I had been blaming Sarah for my indecision about basketball. "What if I can't play with these girls? I am afraid that is the only reason they pay any attention to me," I whined.

Mrs. Latta looked serious as she said, "If that is true, then they are not real friends. But, Lexi, I have known these girls for six years, and they are not like that at all." I sighed in relief and grinned at her. I was so glad I had decided to talk to her.

That afternoon I dressed out and practiced with Coach Bradshaw for the first time. About half of the team was on the court as the rest of the girls that would be playing this season were still playing soft-ball. Their season would end sometime around the first of October, depending on how far they went in the playoffs.

I went out on the court and started shooting around before Coach was ready to start practice. I couldn't hit anything. I was so nervous that I could actually feel my muscles tightening. Our coach last year had taught us to loosen up in our minds so that we could play loose on the court. I went over and sat down on the bench and tried to calm my mind.

I knew I would be rusty, but I wanted to do the best I could. By tomorrow morning at school, everyone would be talking about how good or bad I was. "You have got to impress them today," I whispered to myself. When I thought like that, I just got more anxious.

Dawn didn't play softball, and I was glad. I was going to need her smiling face to help me make it through this first practice. She came over to the bench and said, "Coach Bradshaw made those other two girls who hadn't been dressing out enroll in another class today because they didn't bring their practice clothes. I was all prepared to give you my clothes and take the punishment if you had forgotten yours again. I'm so glad you didn't."

"Thanks, but I didn't forget them these past two days. I was having a hard time deciding if I was going to play. I—"

"I am so glad you are going to play!" Dawn cut me off in midsentence. "We all are. The girls really like you, and we all wanted you to be a part of the team." She finished her excited statement by giving me a big hug.

Coach Bradshaw walked up while we were hugging. "Are we going to practice today or do we have too much to celebrate?" I looked up at him from the chair, and he was smiling playfully. I could tell that he was glad I had dressed out.

Practice was just about like it had been the last couple of days with the exception of the end. Coach broke us up into groups of three and said we were going to have a three-on-three tournament.

He put me with two girls who could barely dribble and couldn't shoot at all. At first I passed the ball off every time I got it. They kept losing it, and we got behind by three baskets. I asked Dawn, who was on the other team, what we were playing to, and she said five baskets.

The next time I got the ball, I drove left, spun in the lane, and shot a jumper about ten feet from the goal. It went in, and I felt good. Dawn's team missed the next shot, and I got the rebound. I faked a shot and went all the way to the goal for a layup. Dawn helped the girl I had beaten by sliding over in front of me, but since I was at least three inches taller than her, I jumped sideways and made it anyway. "Nice shot," she said.

I wasn't going to lose on the first day of practice no matter who my teammates were. I stole a pass Dawn intended for her post girl and tied the game with a jump shot from near the free throw line.

Dawn said something to her teammates. When she passed the ball to Tate, she cut to the basket and got it right back from her for an easy layup. I told her nice give and go, but I wasn't happy. I wanted to yell at my teammates to play defense. Instead I kept my mouth shut. No one wants to have the new girl yell at her.

We were down four to three. I checked the ball to the defender at the top of the key, but Dawn said, "Wait, I got her." She switched with her teammate in order to guard me. I wasn't sure what to do. The girl that had been guarding me was taller and slower than I was. Dawn was smaller and quicker. If I took her down into the post and shot over her, I would look like a bully. I really wanted her to continue being my friend.

I passed the ball and my teammate dribbled one time and picked it up. I went over and got it back from her. As I pivoted and looked around, I noticed I was on the wing and just outside the three-point line. This was the shot I loved to practice. When I would throw it in to Sarah, she would draw the double team and throw it back out to me for a quick three.

I faked as if I were going to drive, and when Dawn jumped back to stop me, I shot and made the three-pointer. Dawn told me good shot as she and her teammates jogged over to the baseline to run for losing the game.

Coach Bradshaw walked down to our goal and asked what the score was. "It is tied four all," I said.

"No," Dawn said, "three-pointers count for two baskets. You guys win five to four." I tried not to smile too big, but I knew that this first practice had gone very well.

On the bus on the way back to Reydon, Dawn started telling me how well I played. I knew I had, but I didn't know what to say except thank you. She kept bragging on me, and I was getting uncomfortable.

I reminded her about her give and go with her friend Tate. "Yeah," she said, "we do that a lot." That sounded like something I would say about Sarah. Trying not to show my emotions, I looked down at the floorboard of the bus. I reminded myself about what Mrs. Latta had said earlier today and regained my composure.

Dawn's face told me she knew that I was upset. "Are you all right?" she asked. I bit my lower lip, nodded, and fought back the tears. Playing without Sarah was going to be tough.

Lana Calls

L ana called to invite me over to work with the horses. I was glad because I was having trouble with Golden. I couldn't get him halter broke. That is where you can lead the horse by the halter, and it will go wherever you walk without fighting against you.

I knew Lana's horses were all halter broke. I had even seen her horses come up to her because they wanted to be with her. I hoped Golden and I could be close like that. I wanted Lana to teach me how to have that kind of friendship with Golden.

At Lana's ranch, it was so easy to lose track of time. Uncle Patrick had told me to be home by eight o'clock, which would mean I would have to start walking home by seven thirty. I told Lana that I needed her to help me to be sure to get home on time.

I didn't want to give Uncle Patrick any reason to start snooping into my life. If I got into trouble again, he would probably have his buddy Mr. Monroe start giving him reports on who I was hanging out with at school. Also, I knew that if I was grounded again, it would be for longer than two weeks.

I was surprised when Lana chuckled at my request. "What?" I asked.

"Your uncle is a special guy," she said. I had to turn my head so she couldn't read on my face what I thought about Uncle Patrick right now.

"I'm glad you are listening to him. He has taught me a lot over the years. It takes a lot of maturity to know who to listen to and who to ignore."

All of the adults I had met seemed to think Uncle Patrick was some kind of a hero. I bet they would have had a different idea about him if he were trying to pick their friends and control their lives. I wished I could tell Lana what I really thought.

"Come on." Lana motioned. "Let's go see the yearling. He ran through a fence last week, and we need to check his wounds." She talked as we walked, and I learned so much about caring for horses.

She told me that horses are creatures of flight, not fight. "That fact should color everything we do with horses," she said. "For example, when I pull on a horse's halter, he will immediately try to go the other direction to flee. I have to train him to cooperate by using a reward. I hold the pressure on the halter until he stops trying to go the opposite direction."

"How do you reward him?"

"When he stops pulling in the opposite direction, I release him," she said. "Then he learns that when he feels pressure he needs to accept it instead of give in to the instinct to flee." I looked at Lana in amazement. In just a few minutes, she had taught me how to solve my problem with Golden.

Lana changed the bandages on the yearling. He was jumpy when I got close to him, so I moved back to the gate and stood very still. Lana was so gentle, and she spoke softly to him as she put medicine on the cuts. One of the cuts was deep and long. It ran down his neck and onto his chest. It looked really bad.

When she finished with the yearling, Lana asked me if I wanted to go in the house and get some iced tea. When we sat down, I asked Lana if the yearling was going to make it.

"I am hopeful," she answered. "His mother was one of my best horses ever. She is very special to me because I won my first World Championship on her. The yearling is her last foal. I won't breed her back again because she is twenty years old. It will break my heart if we lose him." I could hear the emotion in her voice. I had never seen anyone who loved horses so much.

"There are so many things that can happen to young horses," she continued. "They are very flighty but curious at the same time. The yearling was cut up because he got spooked by something in the night and ran through the barbed-wire fence. I have seen foals that were killed when they ran into a pole fence and broke their neck. Colts are naturally curious. My neighbor had a foal that was chewing on a tree branch. He swallowed a piece of it, and it punctured his stomach."

Lana paused to take a sip of her iced tea. "Last year I had one get colic, which is like a stomach-ache. The problem is it caused her to lie down and roll around. When they do that, it often causes their intestines to get kinked and knotted up. If their intestines aren't straightened out before infection sets in, they will usually die. We didn't catch her condition in time, and the vet couldn't save her."

When she said "in time," I remembered Uncle Patrick's instructions about being home by eight o'clock. "Oh no!" I exclaimed. "What time is it?"

"Eight fifteen. You're late," Lana said with a frown. "Jump in the pickup, and I will run you home." She grabbed her keys.

I jogged to the pickup thinking ahead to what I would say to Uncle Patrick. Lana tried to calm me down. "Don't look so upset. It was an honest mistake. I'm sure he will understand." I wasn't so sure.

Uncle Patrick was waiting on the porch when we drove up. He was always talking about responsibility and keeping your word. I expected him to be mad and probably ground me.

Lana let me out, waved, and drove away. *Chicken!* I thought. I turned and braced myself to take Uncle Patrick's wrath. He was smiling!

"We were talking," I tried to explain. "She was teaching me about horses," I continued. Uncle Patrick just sat there smiling. I wanted to say, "What?

Say something!" but I decided to wait and see what he said.

"Sit down, Lexi," Uncle Patrick began. *I knew it!* Here comes the lecture. "Someday you will have children of your own. When you're raising children, you have to be able to distinguish between childish, immature behavior and direct disobedience. It is similar to working with a young horse like Golden."

He paused for a long time, collecting his thoughts. "Mistakes and poor choices must be corrected but not by harsh discipline; otherwise the child lives in fear and learns to hide everything from the parents even when it isn't even a real problem. Fear is not the goal of discipline or punishment. The goal is to help the object of your love learn that there are consequences for disobedience. This causes him to use self-control so that someone else doesn't have to control him." He asked, "If children don't learn to obey their parents, who they can see, how will they ever learn to obey their heavenly Father, who they can't see?" I could tell he was not expecting an answer, and I was glad because I hadn't understood half of what he had said.

"That is what happened with you tonight. You made a mistake, but you expected to be in trouble in the same way as when you disobeyed and went to the party. The two situations are very different," he said. "Tonight you were late not because you wanted to be your own boss but because you're not ready to be your own boss. That is because you are still immature."

"But Lana didn't say anything about the time," I

objected. I couldn't believe he was telling me I was immature! I knew I could take care of myself.

"Whose responsibility was it to be back here on time? Was it Lana's?" Although I knew the answer, I wasn't ready to lose the argument.

"I guess I could have done a better job of watching the clock. I was just having so much fun talking to Lana about horses."

"If you want people to treat you like a grown-up, you have to take responsibility for your actions." I frowned at him and looked down at the floor to break away from his intimidating gaze.

I could feel the struggle inside of me. I wanted to tell him that he was too strict and way too hard to please. It was my nature to fight back and prove that it wasn't my entire fault. On the other hand, I needed him to see me as mature so he would start letting me have more freedom. The only way to accomplish that was to take responsibility.

"It was my fault." I tried to sound sincere.

He smiled and said, "You just took one giant step toward becoming an adult." By the way he smiled as he spoke, I could tell he was truly proud of me.

I couldn't get over him making me take all the blame. I stayed up half the night fuming and trying to figure out how I could get my mom to come and take me home. Still, there was a part of me that was thankful he hadn't punished me for being late.

Dawn's Best Friend

"All right, girls," Coach Bradshaw said. "Off-season sissy practices are over. Tomorrow is the first after-school practice. I suggest you get a lot of rest tonight."

I looked over at Addey. She and the softball girls had joined us a couple of days ago. They were a little sad that they had gotten beat out in the regional tournament, but most of them said they were ready for basketball season. She smiled and shook her head as if to say, "I've been there before, and he's not kidding."

Usually it put me at ease when Addey smiled at me with those big dimples, but I was too worried. She reached over and patted me on the back. I appreciated the way she was always doing that to people when she saw they were having a hard time in practice. Addey

116

had such a good personality and tried to make things better for the people around her.

In practice the next day, I needed a lot of Addey's encouragement. Coach Bradshaw had told us that we would be in better shape than anybody else we played this year. After this practice, I believed him.

We ran so many sprints that I lost count. It lasted over two and a half hours, and my legs felt like Jell-O. We never practiced that hard back home. I didn't know if I wanted to play bad enough to go through this every day.

In the locker room after practice, Dawn plopped down beside me on the bench. She was a sandy blonde with the most amazing eyes. They were a clear blue color that looked as if you took a blue sky with a few wispy clouds and swirled it all together. She had a slim build but was a fairly athletic girl. I liked playing ball with her because she would set me up for shots just like I had done for my teammates back home. Her smile was pretty, and she always seemed to be smiling.

On the basketball court, she traded her smiling face for one that was covered with determination. When we scrimmaged, she was always talking to her teammates. She wasn't afraid to tell people what they were doing wrong, but she was careful to encourage as well.

"Praise the Lord that is over!" she said. I was hot, tired, and a little bit angry. I didn't see any reason for the coach to work us that hard. Dawn's praising God

when, as far as I was concerned, he didn't have anything to do with it pushed me over the edge.

"Why do you praise God for everything?" I
asked, trying to mask my aggravation with a smile. I
couldn't hold it in. "I mean you act like God is your
best friend or something."

"What do you mean? Of course he is my best
friend," she answered with a smile.

When I realized she wasn't mad at me for asking,
I continued, "You can't see him. You haven't ever met
him. Santa Claus could be your best friend instead if
you don't care that he is never around."

I looked over at Dawn to see if she was still okay
with my questioning her. She just moved off the
bench and sprawled out on the floor with her back
against the lockers. I looked around and saw that we
were the only ones left.

Dawn sighed. "You're right that I have never seen
Jesus like I can see you. At first, I saw him in other
people. I saw him in my Mom when she prayed with
us at night and in my Dad when he asked us to forgive him for getting mad and yelling at the car when
it broke down. I have met him," she continued, "and
I do know him. He speaks to me in my heart. Also,
he teaches me from the Bible and through preachers
at church. Jesus is always around if we are listening
to his spirit speaking to us. He says in the Bible that
it is like he is standing at the door knocking. Who-
ever hears him and opens the door of their heart will
become a friend to Jesus."

Dawn looked me right in the eyes and asked,

"Lexi, don't you see the difference between Christians and those that don't go to church and follow the Lord?"

I looked away. Her eyes were penetrating and made me feel uncomfortable. The question left me confused. I knew there was a difference between Dawn and most of the girls that I called friends back in Chicago. "Yes," I admitted, "but there are a lot of good people who don't go to church."

"Jesus said that no one is good except God. Also, the Bible tells us that the very best we can do is not good enough," Dawn explained.

"Then how can anybody be a Christian?" I asked. I was confused by what Dawn was saying.

"That is why Jesus had to die on the cross to pay for our sins. We couldn't pay for our sins, but Jesus could because he was perfect and sinless."

I felt tears start to roll down my cheeks. I knew I wasn't good enough to be a Christian like Dawn, but I still didn't think I was a bad person. "I'm not sure Jesus would want to be my friend."

Dawn's eyes were teary too. "I felt exactly the same way, but he does. The good thing is that understanding that you are a sinner is the first step to becoming a Christian. The Bible says that Jesus loved us while we were still sinners. He forgave us and died for us before we had ever even sinned one time even though he knew how we would be. That is because he is real love. Accepting his love for us is how we get rid of our sin and become his friend and follower."

I stood up quickly. "Dawn, I am glad we had this talk, but I have to go meet Uncle Patrick before he gets mad about waiting." I could tell from her face that she knew I was making an excuse to get out of there. "We can talk about this some more later," I said. She smiled and nodded to let me know it was okay.

As we started walking out of the locker room, I stopped and looked at Dawn. "Thanks for being such a good person. Please don't be mad, but I am not ready to—"

"It's all right, Lexi," she said with a very serious look in her eyes. "I understand, but let me know when you are ready to talk about this again."

I nodded. I knew she had said that because she didn't want to feel like she was bugging me about it. Secretly, I wished I was ready and hoped Dawn would not stop talking to me about Jesus.

When I got out to the pickup, Uncle Patrick looked concerned. "Is everything all right?" he asked. I could only nod my head yes. I knew he would not be satisfied by that for long, but I was too tired and confused to talk about it right then. I tried turning toward the window so he wouldn't continue, but he wasn't ready to let it go. "Did y'all have a problem in practice?" he asked.

I felt a rage come over me like when my mom would question me about where I had been. "Everything is fine with basketball!" I yelled at him. "That is all you care about anyway. If I wasn't good enough to help the team, you would probably send me back home!"

His response didn't come right away, and when he did speak I was surprised at how quietly and calmly he spoke. "Lexi, I am glad you are here, and I love you. You can stay with us as long as your mom will allow it, even if you never shoot another basket. I am sorry you are upset. When you are ready to talk about it, I will be happy to listen."

I turned and looked at him. He wasn't mad at all. I wanted to say I was sorry, hug him, and tell him how confused I was. I couldn't do anything but shake my head and look out the window. He put his big hand on my shoulder and said, "I bet Jo has some pie and iced tea for us when we get home."

Sweet Sixteen

"Come on! Please, Uncle Patrick, we're going to be late. Lana wants me there early to decorate," I pleaded. He was busy messing with his favorite toy. He spent more time working on that old John Deere tractor than he did using it. It was frustrating when he would tinker around like this when it was time to go.

Uncle Patrick came walking up toward me with a determined look on his face. "Lexi, you are always in a hurry to go, go, go. When is the last time you made a point to stay around here and help your aunt or continue Golden's training? We're glad you are making some good friends and fitting in, but you have responsibilities here as well."

He was right, but I couldn't believe he was bringing it up now. We were supposed to be leaving for Lana's ranch any minute. In hopes that he would drop the subject, I decided to agree. "You're right. I'll start back working with Golden tomorrow."

I was so excited. Lana was throwing a sweet sixteen birthday party for me. The theme was a barn dance. Lana took me to buy my first pair of cowboy boots so that I could dress appropriately.

She told me to wear them for at least a week so they wouldn't bother me during the party. After the first day, I had a blister the size of a quarter on my left foot. It was almost healed up by now, but I honestly couldn't understand why anyone would want to wear something so uncomfortable.

Uncle Patrick finally finished working on the tractor, and we left to go to Lana's ranch. I couldn't wait to get my license so I could have more freedom and wouldn't have to wait around on my aunt and uncle. On the way there, I couldn't help thinking about the plans Sarah and I had made for our sixteenth birthday parties.

I tried hard not to think about it. I wanted to enjoy the party tonight. I still held out hope that they would find Sarah soon. Her birthday was in two months, and maybe we could be together then. I was sure that when she was found my mom would let me fly back to Chicago to see her.

Lana came out of the big red barn just as we pulled up to the ranch. Uncle Patrick let me out and said he would be back later. She waved me over to her and went back inside. I ran over to the entrance of the barn. The huge doors had been pushed back, and country music was blaring from inside the cavernous building.

I couldn't stop smiling when I saw how awesome it looked in the barn. Lana had put several long wooden picnic tables in the center of the barn with red and white-checkered tablecloths on them. Decorating the tables were miniature hay bales, tiny saddles, and painted buckets filled with all kinds of candy. On one of the tables was a mound of paper plates, plastic silverware, and cups.

She had hay bales set up all around the barn so people would have places to sit. A dance floor had been prepared on one end of the barn complete with sawdust on the floor. In one corner, two huge black speakers sat on stands with a sound system set up on a small table.

I was blown away! "Lana, thank you so much. But what did you need me here for? You've done everything already," I said.

She gave me a hug and said sheepishly, "I know. I got excited. We haven't had a good, old-fashioned barn dance here in a long, long time."

"I am so happy. What can I do to help?"

"Come with me to check on the food." She led me toward the house. When we rounded the corner, I stopped in my tracks. Keith was standing next to his dad, who was cooking on a barbecue grill.

I did not expect to see him so soon. I looked horrible. I had come two hours early to decorate and cook. Lana had said I could get dressed for the party in her house after everything was ready.

Wheeling around, I looked at Lana for help. She had to know that I didn't want Keith to see me looking this way. She read the situation quickly and said, "Hi, Keith. I didn't know you had come so early."

"I came to help Dad." He paused and then continued, "And to see Lexi before everybody else got here." I was shocked. He barely talked to me at school, but tonight he came early to see me. This had to be a dream. I looked at Lana and then at Keith. They were both grinning. I smelled a setup, but I wasn't angry. I smiled at Lana and mouthed, "Thank you."

"I have your present in the pickup. Do you want to go with me to get it?"

"Sure." I tried hard to act calm and to keep him from knowing that my heart was about to pound out of my chest.

We walked out to his pickup. I stayed close to him, hoping he would reach out and touch me or hold my hand. We bumped into each other a little once as we both tried to avoid a mud puddle. I was so excited just to have his undivided attention.

He pulled a nicely wrapped package from his pickup. It was the shape and size of a book with a smaller box attached to it by a big red bow. I didn't know what to expect. That was part of the reason I liked Keith. He was totally unique. It was also what drove me crazy about him.

I opened the book first. It was a Bible. I thought, *Who gives someone a Bible for her sixteenth birthday?* I knew Keith was religious, but this was over the top. I looked up at him and grinned like it was the best gift I had ever received.

Next, I opened the little box. It was a beautiful cross necklace with a gold chain and a tiny diamond placed in the center of the cross. "It is beautiful," I said softly. He motioned for me to turn around and started putting it around my neck. "I don't think I'm worthy to wear this." I hoped he would reassure me and say that I was a good person.

"None of us are," he answered. "I didn't know if you had a Bible of your own, so I took a chance. I couldn't think of anything better to get someone, but my mom suggested I also get you the necklace."

The wind caught my hair and blew it in my face. I brushed it away and looked down at the Bible I held with my other hand. "I love them both." I tried not to tear up.

I turned and looked up at him, daring him to kiss me. Our faces were inches apart, and he looked like he just might. I leaned forward and started slowly closing my eyes when I heard a horn honking just a few feet away from Keith's pickup.

It was Uncle Patrick and Aunt Jo. He was waving and smiling with a goofy grin. I knew he did that on purpose. He thought he was so funny.

Just then, Lana hollered, "Lexi, give me a hand with this." *No way! I can't believe this.* Keith turned to see what Lana needed. I told him I would be right back and started stomping off to the barn.

Keith called after me. I stopped and turned around to see what he would say. "I have to go. I came early because I have to work tonight." Of course. We get a little bit close and he bolts. I was so angry, and it must have shown because he said, "I'm sorry to miss your party. Tell me about it tomorrow at school."

I gave him half of a smile and turned to go help Lana. Before I knew it, I was running toward the barn. I flew into the barn and almost knocked Lana down. "Whoa, what's wrong with you, birthday girl?" she questioned.

"For starters, the one guest I really wanted to spend time with just left," I snapped. I wanted to tell her what Uncle Patrick did, but I could see him coming toward the barn. He would be there any second, and I didn't know if I could keep myself from making a scene. "I'm going to the house to get ready."

I passed Uncle Patrick and Aunt Jo, but I wouldn't make eye contact with them. I was so angry that I was shaking. I heard Aunt Jo say, "I told you not to honk like that." I would thank her later, but right then I was too angry.

I was disappointed that Keith left before the party really got started. Sometimes he acted so weird. About the time I thought he liked me, he would do something that told me it wasn't ever going to happen. I had given him every opportunity to ask me out, but he never did. Still, I couldn't get him off my mind.

Dean was just the opposite. He left no room for doubt that he not only wanted to date, he wanted to go out with me exclusively. He wasn't bad looking.

In fact, out of all the guys I had gone out with, he would have been in my top ten. He was tall enough and had a really good-looking face. He dressed well, and I really liked his athletic build.

There were two problems with Dean. One, he was all over me all of the time, and it got tiring. Most girls in Reydon or Cheyenne would have welcomed his flirting. In fact, several girls had told me I was crazy not to go out with him.

That brings us to the other problem: he wasn't Keith. From the first time I saw Keith, I was head over heels. He was the guy of my dreams, the love of my life, and all that other mushy stuff all rolled into one. Why did he have to be so hard to read? I was beginning to think it had something to do with his church. They probably told him I wasn't good enough for him because I got sent out to Oklahoma by my mom. Maybe I wasn't.

I finished getting ready and went back out to the barn. I was uncomfortable in my boots. My jeans were new and not stretched out yet, so I was self-conscious about how tight they were. When I went into the barn, my stomach was churning because of all the people who had shown up while I was getting dressed. Someone yelled, "There's the birthday girl!" I turned red in the face.

Everyone was really nice, and the food was terrific. Dean was at my side from the moment I walked into the barn. He followed me through the serving line and sat down with me to eat. I talked to everyone else around me, but he wasn't going anywhere.

The dancing started, and Dean asked me if I would dance with him. I was still angry with Keith for leaving early. I decided to have a good time with Dean just to spite him. We danced for almost an hour. Just about the time I would think I was going to have to sit down to rest, the band would play a slow song that allowed us to catch our breath.

Dean was talking even more than usual. I could tell by some of the comments he was making that he was starting to get the wrong idea. When he said, "So I guess this means you're my girl from now on, huh?" I didn't know what to say. If I told him I just wanted to have a good time, he would blow up and make a scene. But I didn't want him to tell people we were going out or Keith would never ask me.

I took him by the hand to lead him out of the barn so I could tell him the truth. Outside, I wheeled around to start my explanation and was met by his face coming toward mine. I ducked his kiss and gave him a little shove.

"What is wrong with you?" he complained. "You dance with me like that and then lead me outside away from the others. You're crazy!"

"I'm sorry, Dean. I just wanted to have a good time, and I gave you the impression that I was ready to be your girlfriend," I said apologetically.

"Or at least ready to be kissed!" he yelled even louder than before.

"What is the problem, Lexi?" It was Uncle Patrick, and he had that look in his eye that he only got when he was about to lose his temper.

I stepped toward him, purposefully putting myself between him and Dean. "Nothing. Everything is fine," I said. I was stammering a little, but for the most part I was in control of my emotions.

Uncle Patrick's voice was low, and his words came methodically. "When a young man yells at a young lady because she chooses not to kiss him, he has worn out his welcome. Dean, I suggest you get out of here before I help you do so."

"Whatever. This party is lame anyway. Oh, and, Lexi, you don't have to worry about me asking you out anymore. I'm just glad I found out how much of a tease you were before I spent money on a date." As Dean finished those last few words, Uncle Patrick brushed me aside. He grabbed him by the back of the shirt and the belt loop on the back of his jeans and began pushing him toward the vehicles.

As they got close to where everyone had parked, Uncle Patrick sped up, causing Dean to stumble. Dean was flailing his arms back against Uncle Patrick's huge, work-weathered hands, but he couldn't break free. All of the sudden, Uncle Patrick let go of Dean's belt loop and kicked him in the rear end. Dean looked as if he would fall on his face, but he was athletic and caught his balance.

He turned around, and I could see he was considering charging Uncle Patrick. He thought better of it and decided that cursing him from a distance would be safer. Uncle Patrick turned his back on Dean and began walking back to the barn.

When he got back to where I was still standing

like a horrified statue, he said, "Whew, that took a lot more out of me than it did when I was younger!"

I was so embarrassed that I didn't say anything. I just walked back into the party and told Lana what my uncle had done. She smiled knowingly and said, "That's Patrick. Don't worry about it. Let's open your presents."

I did as she said, and everyone seemed to have a good time. I was glad that no one said anything about what my uncle had done. Several of the gifts were really nice, but I decided that none of them were as thoughtful as Keith's.

The iPod

All of our basketball practices and most of our games were held at Cheyenne. Every day we would hustle out to the bus at the beginning of sixth hour. I usually sat with Dawn on the bus trip over to Cheyenne for basketball practice.

Dawn turned to me and asked, "Do you want to share my iPod?"

"Sure, what songs do you have?" I asked while putting in one of her earbuds.

"Just listen and see if you like it," Dawn replied, smiling slyly as she spoke. "If you don't like the song, just skip it." She continued as she handed it to me. She kept one earbud in her ear to see what songs I would like.

I had never heard any of the songs. At first, I pushed the button to go to the next song as soon as I realized I didn't know it. I knew something was up because Dawn smiled at me each time I went to the next song as soon as it started. After a few songs, I realized I wasn't going to know any of them.

I decided to start listening to the whole song even if I didn't recognize it. All of the songs talked about God, loving other people, or things like that. A couple of them were really good. I liked the beat on the faster songs, but a few of them were too slow.

"I like this one," I told Dawn. She looked really happy and wrote the name of the song down in her notebook. I liked Dawn. She was always pretty happy and listened closely when I told her something. A lot of my friends back home were so stuck on themselves that I could tell they didn't care what I had to say. I also liked how Dawn had included me in everything she could from the first time we talked.

Dawn had asked me to spend the night at her house a couple of times, but I didn't know if I wanted to get that close to anyone here. I knew I would be gone in a year. I thought it would be easier if I didn't make too many close friends. I knew I wouldn't be able to put Dawn off much longer or she might quit trying to be my friend.

Also, I had seen how close Dawn's family was. Her dad was our principal, and her mom was a secretary at our school. They were almost always together and talked to each other more than any family I had ever seen. Part of me thought it was weird, but another part was sad that I didn't have that with my family.

One day a bunch of us stayed after school and went down to the Reydon gym to shoot and scrimmage. Dawn's dad, Mr. Blevins, came down to the gym and worked on her shot with her. I watched to see if she would put up with him telling her how to shoot. Not only did she listen, she seemed to enjoy him working with her.

I felt a wave of jealousy come over me. My dad had played basketball in college and knew a lot about it. We had spent hours in the driveway working on dribbling and shooting. He drilled it into my head that "there is always a place on the court for someone who can handle the ball and shoot." I felt tears welling up in my eyes as I thought about my dad. I went into the locker room to keep anyone from seeing that I was upset.

Later, I asked Aunt Jo what she thought about Dawn's family. "I like them. They are good people. I have heard Mr. Blevins preach, and he can step on your toes with the best of them."

"That explains the music on Dawn's iPod!" I told her about Dawn sharing her iPod with me and how I had never heard any of the songs she had on it. "The songs all talked about God and stuff," I said. "I guess that is because her dad is a preacher."

"I disagree," said Aunt Jo. "Mr. Blevins just fills in preaching in churches when the full-time preacher is not available. Many full-time preachers have children that don't have an iPod full of Christian music. Besides, if Dawn didn't like Christian music, why would she listen to it when her dad isn't around?"

I couldn't stop thinking about what Aunt Jo had said. There was something different about Dawn and her family. I was drawn to them, but I didn't know why. I started wondering what they were like at home. I decided that the next time Dawn asked me over, I was going.

Conference
Tournament

The basketball team was undefeated and gearing up for the conference tournament. The stands were fuller with every game we played. The girls told me that apart from the playoffs, the biggest game of the year would be when we played Hammon in the conference finals. We were the number two seed, and they were number one. Coach consistently reminded us that we had to win the first two games to get to the finals.

One evening at dinner, I asked Uncle Patrick why the girls were making such a big deal about the conference tournament. He chuckled. "It may have to do with the fact that on the girls' side of things the conference champion has played in the state tournament seven of the past ten years."

Uncle Patrick told me that when it came to basketball, our conference was considered by many people to be the toughest small school conference on this side of the state. He added that all of the teams in the conference were in class A or B, and the conference had rarely failed to put a least one girl's basketball team into the state tournament on a yearly basis.

He also told me that the conference final was so well attended that only the schools with gyms that could seat a thousand or more were able to host it. Most of the time the girl's final would feature two top ten teams and the boys' final always had at least one highly ranked team. I was pumped about playing in front of a thousand people.

"You girls are playing really well," he said between bites of Aunt Jo's lasagna. "I have been impressed by how well you have blended in with the team, Lexi. However, there may be a time that you will need to take over a little more."

I cocked my head to the side. "What do you mean? Like be a ball hog or something?"

"No, but there is a time at the end of a quarter or especially at the end of a close game that you need to call for the ball and go to work," he explained.

I thought about what he had said for a while. We hadn't had any games that had been close at the end. I had been able to play about half speed through most of the games.

Uncle Patrick was right. I hadn't been giving everything I had, but there was a reason. Even playing the way I was worried me. I was afraid of scoring too much and making some of the other girls mad.

I already had one enemy. Stacey had let me know that she was not happy with me starting. With the one senior graduating last year, she obviously thought I had taken the spot that was rightfully hers.

Stacey was a senior and a pretty good player. She was a good shooter, but when she drove in the lane, it was hard for her to shoot without getting blocked. She did a good job on defense, and I liked playing with her. I wished she didn't make snippy comments to me and try to make me look bad in practice. I knew she was just trying to get me to back off so I wouldn't play well enough to start. I liked getting along, but I liked staying off the bench even more.

Our first game of the conference tournament was against a team that could beat us. At least that is what Coach Bradshaw had told us in practice. We hadn't played them this year, but the girls said they beat them easily last year.

After Coach's talk, the seniors held a meeting in the locker room. Toren said, "We have to take every game seriously. Last year we almost lost to a team that hadn't even won half of their games because we didn't come ready to play."

Tina hollered, "Let's stay undefeated." Everyone started clapping in agreement. I was excited by the determination on the faces of the seniors. They were becoming good leaders.

We won the first round game by fifteen points. The second round game would be against a really good team. We had beaten them the first game of the year, but they had been short two starters that had been sick with the flu. Coach Bradshaw told us that they would have all their starters back and gave us a game plan.

The night of the game I felt energized. I couldn't put my finger on it, but I knew I was going to have a good game. My legs felt fresh, and I couldn't wait to play.

When Coach announced the starting lineup, I wasn't in it for the first time all year. Stacey started in my spot. Coach hadn't said anything to me about it, and I was numb with shock. I didn't get in the game until the second quarter. I went on the attack, and scored seven points in one quarter.

At halftime, everyone came up and told me how well I had done. I knew I wasn't finished. About midway through the third quarter, Coach put me back in the game. We were down six points. I felt a surge of energy, rage, and frustration. Everything I had been through over the past few months fueled my emotions. I decided to take it all out on the other team.

Usually I can recall specific plays from a game, but I don't remember much about that second half. I just know I cut loose on defense and offense. We won the game by ten points or so. After the game, my uncle came up to me and said, "That is how you need to play all of the time. In the second half, you had seven rebounds, three steals, and sixteen points. It was a remarkable performance."

I started in the finals of the tournament. When the starters were announced, Stacey deliberately refused to slap my hand as I ran out on the floor. She was such a brat. I decided not to let her get to me.

Just as the girls had predicted, we played Hammon. This time I played hard from the opening tip. I looked to score every time I got the ball and still led the team in assists. We played well for three quarters and went into the fourth quarter with a three-point lead.

Before we went out on the floor to start the fourth quarter, Coach said, "This quarter we're going to throw the full-court press on them. With three or four steals, we can blow this lead wide open." He reviewed on his marker board where everyone was to be on the press.

As we walked back out onto the court, I looked up in the stands and saw Keith looking right at me. He smiled. I acted as if I hadn't noticed him, but it was tough not to smile back. Coach would have benched me if he knew I was looking in the stands, especially at some boy. If he only knew that seeing Keith watching me made me play even harder, he might change his mind.

We threw the ball in at the half line to start the fourth quarter. Tina had a girl guarding her that she knew she could score on, so she told Toren she wanted the ball. Toren got the ball in to her on the block, and she scored easily off the backboard. When Hammon took the ball out of bounds, we jumped into our press.

Toren and I trapped the girl who caught the ball in bounds. She tried to get it to her teammate in the middle of the court, but Leisha stepped in front of the pass and started toward the bucket. She shot a layup and scored.

We were into our press again as soon as the ball went through the net. The girl passing the ball in bounds tried to throw it over our heads to the half line, but Tina was ready. She swooped over and tipped the ball just as it was about to hit the Hammon girl in the hands. Kylie recovered the ball and threw it ahead to Toren, who hit me in the corner. As I caught the ball, I saw Tina flashing to the block on my side of the basket. I gave her a bounce pass, and she shot the ball off of the backboard. She missed, but Leisha was there to rebound and put it back.

Their coach called timeout, and the crowd exploded in excitement. I had never played in front of this many people before, and it was awesome. We ran over to the bench, and Coach Bradshaw said, "Great job. Keep it up. We got 'em now, girls!"

We were all pumped. I loved the rush of adrenaline during a tight game. We were up nine points, but we knew that wasn't enough. Leisha told us not to let up because they could score nine points in no time at all. I looked around at the girls. They were all so into it. The girls were all nodding their heads and completely focused on the game.

When we went back onto the court, the Hammon girls were ready for the press. They took the ball out of bounds and proceeded to break our press with three passes and an easy backboard shot on the block. We worked the ball back up the court against their press and set up our offense.

Addey and Dawn had come in the game for Toren and Leisha. Addey had the ball at the top of the key when two of their girls ran at her to trap her. She attacked the one on her right and drove past her opening up Dawn on the three-point line. Her pass to Dawn was perfect, and Dawn made the three-point shot.

We tried to press them again, but all it did was slow them down a little. The good thing was they couldn't figure out a way to stop us from scoring. We were able to keep the lead that the press gave us, but we couldn't pull away from them.

In the last two minutes, they started fouling us on purpose. We were all smiling at each other because we knew that Coach Bradshaw had made every single one of us stay after every practice until we had made one hundred free throws each. All that practice paid off, and we won the conference tournament for the first time in several years.

After the game, the fans were all telling us how great we played. Coach walked by, and I heard Dawn ask to speak to him. I walked over to see what was going on just in time to hear her say, "Coach, that was awesome how you had us wait to press them until just the right time. You really caught them off guard. I see why you made us shoot all of those free throws every day." I looked at her, and she was so happy. She probably didn't play more than a quarter and a half, but she was bragging on the coach.

Coach Bradshaw was smiling at her. Everyone in the crowd was telling the players how great they were, but only a handful of people had came over to him to offer congratulations. I could tell he really appreciated what she had said.

Sarah

t was the last week of school before Christmas break. The girls were all circled around in the locker room. Everyone seemed to be talking at the same time, a few were pointing at something, and some were giggling with excitement. I went over to see what was happening.

When Leisha looked up and saw me, she started beaming. She jumped up and gave me a hug. "Look! We are on the cover of *Vype*. Can you believe it?" she asked.

Dawn handed me the magazine, which said it specialized in high school sports. The picture was of the entire team after we had won the conference tournament a couple of weeks earlier. "This is really cool," I agreed.

"Read the article," Toren said. As I did, a few of the younger girls got dressed and made their way out of the locker room. All of the girls that played at all in the games hung around to talk about the magazine article. What really excited them was that the writer picked us as one of eight teams likely to play in the Big House.

I caught a ride home with Tina, who lived about five miles from my aunt and uncle. Uncle Patrick had told me once that in this part of Oklahoma living that close to someone meant you were neighbors. Tina and I talked about the scrimmages Coach had planned for us over Christmas break.

Coach had told us he was excited because we would be going to Oklahoma City to scrimmage a school called Harrah. They were ranked number five in class 5A. That meant they had about ten times more students in each class than both Reydon and Cheyenne combined.

I was looking forward to the scrimmage because Coach said the bigger schools played more like we did back home. Out here, referees called a lot more fouls. It took me a while to figure out how physical they would let us play. The girls also told me there were a couple of good malls in Oklahoma City. They laughed when I said, "Good. I have been having mall withdrawal!"

I burst through the kitchen door and started hollering for Aunt Jo and Uncle Patrick. I knew they would be as excited as the team was about the article. Uncle Patrick had told me after the first few games that he thought we were good enough to make it to the state tournament. He reminded me constantly how hard it was to get that far in the playoffs and added that it took a little luck as well.

If we were good enough and lucky enough, it would be the first time Cheyenne or Reydon girls had been to state in several years. He said the whole town was talking about it, and I had noticed the crowds getting bigger at the home games. It was exciting to play in front of hundreds of people. Even though my school back home was a lot bigger, nobody came to our games except for the families of the players.

I finally found Aunt Jo in her bedroom kneeling beside her bed. I had found her praying like that a couple of other times but never this early in the day. I called her name, not wanting to wait to tell her the good news. When she turned to face me, she tried to smile.

I could see she had been crying. "What's wrong, Aunt Jo?" I asked. "Is it Uncle Patrick?" I was already getting angry that no one had called to tell me something was wrong.

"No, Patrick is fine," she said. But her eyes showed me that something awful must have happened. She got up and sat on the bed, patting the spot beside her. "Sit, dear, we need to talk."

I sat on the bed with a lump in my throat. "Who is it?" I managed.

"It's Sarah," she answered, her voice breaking as she spoke. "They found her."

"Is she okay? What is it?" I asked.

"No, dear. Sarah is gone," she answered.

The words sunk like a stone to the pit of my stomach. I was numb. So many questions were running through my mind that it was hard to get hold of any one in particular. Finally, I was able to ask, "Where did they find her? How do they know it was her?"

Aunt Jo held me and said, "I don't know all of the details. Your mother called and said that Sarah's mom identified the body."

"No!" I screamed and pushed her away.

I felt sick at my stomach and ran to the bathroom. I had dry heaves. As I knelt by the toilet, I felt my aunt's hand on my back. I turned and sat down on the cold, white tile floor and leaned up against the toilet.

"Surely it wasn't Sarah. It has to be someone else," I said, my heart pleading with her to agree that I was right. "It has been so long. I know it was a mistake. She can't be gone!" I began to sob even harder.

Aunt Jo had tears running down her cheeks. "I think we have to begin to accept that Sarah is gone, dear."

She took me to my room and helped me get under the sheets. Melting into the mattress, I heard the door shut as she left the room. I hugged my pillow tightly, but sleep was not an option.

On the nightstand beside my bed, I saw a magazine. It was one that my mom had sent with me to read on the bus. I had been reading it one night when I couldn't get to sleep. My handwriting was on the cover. I had written, "Go for the gold" with a permanent marker.

"A lot of good that did, Bessie!" I whined out

loud to myself. I started trying to tear the magazine apart. After a couple of puny rips, I threw it across the room in a rage. It hit my dresser and knocked my pink makeup mirror to the floor.

A moment later, I began to yell at the top of my lungs. "Why? It should have been me. It's my fault! I'm the one that talked her into going." I knew her mom would never speak to me again, and I didn't blame her.

Aunt Jo peeked in on me and asked, "Want some company?"

"I think … I … I don't know," I answered.

She came in and lay down beside me. After a few minutes of silence, she began to sing softly. The song was about how we are all children of God. I felt myself dozing off, and when I awoke she was gone.

I didn't get out of the house for the next couple of weeks. I couldn't even go to the funeral. Uncle Patrick offered to pay for my flight home, but I didn't want to face Sarah's mom or our friends. I was crippled by feelings of guilt and grief and sure that everyone back home blamed me for what had happened.

I rarely got out of bed during that two-week period. I also missed the last game before Christmas break, an entire week of school, and the scrimmage in Oklahoma City. I had this overwhelming feeling of emptiness and hopelessness.

I felt tired all of the time and didn't want to eat. Aunt Jo tried cooking my favorite foods, renting movies my friends told her I would like, and having my teammates come over to cheer me up. I was surprised when Keith came over, but I didn't want him to see me looking so badly. Nothing seemed to work. Even though I really wanted to get out of this funk, I just couldn't.

Some days I felt like I wanted to get up and get out of the house. By the time I took a shower and got dressed, I would be drained and that empty feeling would come over me again. Uncle Patrick came in my room every afternoon and read the Bible to me. I enjoyed that and found out there were a lot of interesting stories in the Bible.

Amanda and I wrote a few letters back and forth, and Aunt Jo allowed me to talk to her once a week. That was against my mom's rules that she set when she sent me out here, but Aunt Jo said she felt like it was important that I talk to someone. I appreciated her understanding and caring.

I knew Amanda was one of the few people that could understand how I felt. Even though I was closer to Sarah than Amanda had been, she had been there when Sarah was taken. Amanda was my only link to the time before Sarah was gone. We rarely wrote or spoke about the actual night that it happened. It was too painful. Instead we shared memories about Sarah.

Tough Love

As I continued to grieve Sarah, I was lying in bed in the afternoon and heard Uncle Patrick and Aunt Jo arguing. I had never heard them raise their voices to each other before, so I crept to the door to listen. I wanted to know what the problem was until I figured out it was me.

Uncle Patrick said, "Jo, you know that tough love is causing the object of your love to do what is best for her, even if she doesn't like it or understand it."

"You know that I have always supported you when you felt it was time to be more stern. I just don't know if she can take it right now."

"Sweetheart, it has been two weeks, and we have tried everything else," he said patiently.

He turned and headed toward the door. When I heard him coming, I ran back to my bed. He knocked on the door. "Come in," I said. He came in and sat down on the edge of the bed. I was shaking so badly on the inside that I was sure he could see it. I didn't know if he was going to give me swats or drag me out of the room, but I knew he came in there to give me tough love.

"Lexi, can I pray with you?" he asked.

"I don't care," I said, confused about what prayer had to do with tough love.

"Lord, we love you. You have heard our prayers for Lexi. She is hurting, Lord. Please give her the strength and desire to get up and get moving. Precious Lord, thank you for dying on the cross for all of our sin. You showed us that you have the power to work in our lives when you arose from the dead on the third day. Please, Lord, release your power into Lexi's life so that she might know you, love you, and follow you. In your holy and precious name, I pray. Amen." When he finished praying, he put his hand on my arm and spoke softly. "Lexi, I need you to take care of Golden," he said. "I came to tell you that I will no longer take care of him for you. You are going to have to get out of this room and continue your life."

I was relieved that he wasn't going to yell at me, but I didn't know if I could do it. "I'll try," I said.

Uncle Patrick smiled and got up off of the edge of the bed. "Golden is counting on you to do more than try. I trust the Lord to give you the strength, so I know you can do it. You need to know that neither Jo nor I will be feeding the colt. He is in the third stall in the horse barn." With that, he left the room and shut the door. If I hadn't heard them argue so loudly, I would not have believed that he would actually refuse to feed Golden.

Lying there in bed, I tried to decide if Uncle Patrick would let Golden starve just to get me out of the house. I decided he would, but I couldn't imagine Aunt Jo going along with it. Still, I didn't want to ever hear them argue like that again.

Aunt Jo had to be upset. She wasn't the kind of person that could take yelling and fighting. If I stayed in my room, she would likely break Uncle Patrick's rule by feeding Golden. I would be hurting the one person on whom I could count.

I got up and dressed, deciding against a shower because it would leave me feeling drained. I went out to the feed truck and drove down to the horse barn. Golden was glad to see me. All the farm kids out here were allowed to drive by the time they were thirteen.

Sometimes kids that were close to getting their license would even drive to school after their morning chores. Mr. Blevins never said anything about it. I was allowed to drive around the ranch, but Uncle Patrick only let me drive to school a couple of times. Still, it was the coolest thing about being here.

I found the feed and gave him a bucketful, but he seemed more interested in me than the feed. I went in the stall and started brushing him down. That must have been what he wanted because he started eating almost immediately.

Brushing his golden brown hair and braiding his

blonde mane was one of my favorite things to do. He seemed to enjoy all of the attention. Also, when no one was around, I would tell him all my problems. Golden was a great listener.

I had found out that Amanda was a pretty good listener too. Although our talks were limited to once a week and we weren't allowed to e-mail, we had grown much closer. She acted more calm and mature since Sarah's funeral.

However, something she said on the phone the night before had me worried. She had been very upbeat and said after this weekend everything was going to be better. She kept mentioning this weekend, but she wouldn't tell me what she was going to do. At first, I thought she was going to a party and didn't want to make me jealous. But there was something strange in her tone and the way she said everything was going to better. A party wouldn't make everything better.

It reminded me of how she had talked last year when she took some sleeping pills. We all agreed that she just wanted attention. All the pills did was knock her out for about a day. Still, I was getting worried about her. What if she learned from last time and did it for real this time?

I went to tell Aunt Jo about my concerns. "I need to call Amanda. I am afraid she is going to do something to hurt herself."

Aunt Jo gave me a skeptical look. "What makes you think that?" she asked.

I told her what Amanda had said about this

weekend. I could tell she wasn't sharing my concerns. "I'll have to think about it," she said.

"There is no time to think about it. We have to call Amanda's mom and warn her. School starts after this weekend for Amanda. Don't you see? She is planning to do something to herself so she doesn't have to go back to school and face all of Sarah's friends!"

By the time I finished talking, I was yelling out of fear and frustration. My aunt was getting mad, but I couldn't calm down. It didn't look like she was going to believe me or even consider that I might be right. "I will think about what you said, and we might call her mom tomorrow."

I couldn't believe it! "Why are you choosing now to not trust me?"

She frowned and said, "School starts tomorrow, and I know it must be hard to go back after the long break and the bad news you have had. I think you are overreacting because of all your emotions. After you get a day of school under your belt, you'll feel better about Amanda and everything here as well. If not, we can call her mother tomorrow evening."

I stomped off to my room and slammed the door. I listened for the picture in the hallway to fall, but I hadn't done a good enough job with the door. I threw my school backpack across the room and yelled, "I'm not going anywhere until I know Amanda is okay!"

The Chase

The next morning, I woke up to the most awful sound. For a minute, I didn't recognize the sound. Then it dawned on me that it was my alarm. I had slept in every day during Christmas break. Turning off the alarm clock, I put my pillow over my head.

There was a knock at my bedroom door, and Aunt Jo hollered her usual, "Wake up, sleepyhead." I groaned loudly, and she called out the time. I knew she was taking me to school, which bought me an extra thirty minutes, so I tried to go back to sleep.

This time she knocked heavily on my door and swung it open. "Lexi Elizabeth Turney, get up now," she yelled. I quickly looked at the alarm clock. It read seven forty-five. I thought I had just dozed for a minute, but I must have fallen fast asleep.

The tardy bell was at eight. I wasn't going to make it. I jumped out of bed and ran around trying to get ready as fast as I could. Every few minutes Aunt Jo would yell something from another part of the house. I couldn't understand most of what she was saying, but the message was clear. We were late, and she wasn't happy.

On the way to school, all I could think about was Amanda. By now I was convinced that she was going to hurt herself this weekend. We started back from Christmas break on a Wednesday, but they didn't start until Monday. I would have to leave today to be sure and get there before something happened. After what happened to Sarah, I couldn't live with myself if something happened to Amanda.

When we pulled up to the school, there was no one around. Aunt Joanne pulled up by the front steps that were about one hundred feet from the front door of the school. "Your uncle left early this morning to pick up some cattle. He should be in tomorrow night, and we can all sit down and visit then."

Aunt Jo told me she loved me, but I didn't answer. I needed her to know how mad she had made me by not trusting me about Amanda. As she pulled away, I knew what I had to do.

One of Uncle Patrick's fields was just outside of town. He kept an old feed truck there. It was a flatbed pickup with a feed dispenser on the back. I decided to walk out there, get that feed truck, and head home to help Amanda.

As I walked away from the school, I went back over the trip in my head. I already knew the route. Several different nights I had lain in my bed and tried to figure a way home. At school, I had used the Internet to map the fastest route home. I carried the money Bessie had given me in my purse just in case I ever needed it. Surely three hundred dollars would get me home.

Walking by a house on the edge of town, I saw that all of the lights were still off and figured the owner was still asleep. In the driveway was one vehicle, a new gray Dodge pickup. The feed truck was old, and I was concerned about it making it all the way to Chicago. I bent low and ran as quickly as I could over to the pickup. I looked through the passenger side window and saw the keys were in it.

I stayed low and went around behind the pickup to keep it between me and the house. Quietly opening the door, I slid into the driver's seat and turned the key. The lights came on automatically and shined right into the living room windows. I pushed every button I could find to shut off the lights. Finally, I just gave up and backed out of the driveway.

As I sped off, I looked in my rearview mirror and saw a man running down the driveway. He was barefoot and had on only his shorts. This wasn't going as I had planned in my room all those nights. I knew he would call the cops. I didn't know what to do next.

I decided to drive around in the country and look for another vehicle. I took the back roads toward my aunt and uncle's house. If I stayed off of the main roads, the sheriff wouldn't be able to find me before I found another ride.

The more I drove, the more I realized this wasn't

going well. The only hope I had was to ditch the Dodge and hope the owner couldn't recognize me. I would cut across country on foot and go back home to Uncle Patrick's house. If I were lucky, no one would ever know it was me that took the pickup.

While I was looking for a place to ditch the truck, I saw a brown pickup coming toward me fast. It had antennas all over it, and I knew it was one of the sheriff's department pickups. It was at least a mile from me, so I pulled over and started running across a pasture.

The pasture I was in had a big pond about a quarter of a mile off the road. The pond dam was fairly tall. I thought I could probably disappear on the other side of it. The area I was heading toward was covered in trees and brush.

I ran as hard as I could. When I reached the pond dam, I looked back to see how close the sheriff deputies were. There were two of them crossing the fence, but neither one looked like they could catch me. My heart was pounding, but my legs felt pretty good. I was still hopeful that I could escape without being identified.

I stayed at least a half mile ahead of the deputies. I hid behind a tree or peeked over a small hill when I needed to see how close they were. They weren't running very fast, and they kept stopping.

I crossed a big valley that was full of brush. When I came up the other side, I saw a deer stand. I climbed up in it to rest and watch for the deputies. They came to the far edge of the valley. I saw one talking on a radio or cell phone. They were far enough away that it was hard to tell. How did I get myself into this?

One deputy turned around and headed back toward the road, and the other stood there for a long time looking around in every direction. He didn't seem to know where I had gone.

I decided I had gotten lucky and just might be able to sneak back home. I sat down in the deer stand intent on hiding there until they gave up the search. It was warm inside the stand. There were windows on three sides that enabled me to see if anyone was coming. I could get down to run well before they could make out my face. There were two old lawn chairs and even a couple of magazines with big deer on the cover.

After a few minutes, I got antsy and slowly raised up to peek out the window in the direction of the valley. I was shocked to see the deputy heading straight for my deer stand. I felt a strange feeling, like a jolt of electricity, when I saw him.

I climbed down the metal ladder as quickly as I could, missing the bottom two rungs and falling to the ground. I jumped up and headed toward a long line of trees. I had noticed a lot of these lines of trees, mostly at the edge of fields while checking cattle with Uncle Patrick. I had asked him why there were so many of these. He told me that they were planted because of the dust bowl. He called them shelterbelts and said they were to keep the wind from blowing all of the soil away.

To me, they were a great place to try to lose the deputy. He wasn't fast, but he had gained ground on me while I was hiding in the deer stand. He was close enough now that if I stopped he would be able to identify me or possibly even catch me.

The shelterbelt I was in was along a dirt road. I couldn't decide if I should cross the road, which would leave tracks, or stay in the trees. I tried to see how much farther the trees went, but I could only see about fifty feet in any direction.

Across the dirt road, I could see a stretch of open field that led to a group of trees. I didn't know how far the trees went in the direction opposite the road, but I did see that they spread across the width of the field for what had to be a half of a mile.

By my best guess, the field across the road and the big bunch of trees were in the same direction as Uncle Patrick's house. I decided to chance leaving tracks on the dirt road. I was sure that if I could get to that stand of trees I could get back to the ranch without being seen.

I started across the dirt road when I had a great idea. There was no way I could hide the fact that I had gone that direction, but I could smear out my tracks from my tennis shoes. I had seen lots of cop shows where they used shoe tracks to prove someone was guilty.

As I began to smear out my tracks with a big stick that I picked up in the shelterbelt, I heard the roar of an engine. I looked up and saw two brown pickups coming from opposite directions. They had their lights flashing. I was being trapped between them!

I ran for the barbed-wire fence that was between me and the sanctuary of the shelterbelt that I had just left. The deputy that had followed me on foot was just coming out of the shelterbelt. I turned around to run in the other direction toward the trees I had originally planned to use for cover.

Just as I bent down to crawl through the fence, one of the sheriff department pickups slid to a stop next to me. I got through the fence and started to run, but this deputy was a new one. He was young and skinny. Unfortunately, he was fast too. He caught me by my heavy winter coat before I could get even a few feet from the fence.

He spun me around and looked at my face. I could tell he was surprised at something. "Who is this?" he yelled to the other deputies, both of whom had not even made it across the fence.

The one that had stayed behind me the entire time just shrugged his shoulders. The older one said, "That is Patrick Curtis's niece. We need to keep this quiet for his sake."

The young deputy still had me by the coat. He started laughing. "That will be near impossible," he said, still laughing. "You two boys were on the scanner for the past half hour, and by now the whole county had busted a gut laughing at y'all." He started faking like he was trying to catch his breath and said, "Do you … see her anywhere?"

They all started chuckling, but I thought I was

going to faint. If Uncle Patrick was mad when I went to the party, what would he do about this? Would I go to jail? They said that they would keep it quiet, but from what the young deputy said it didn't sound like that was possible. What had I done?

Choices

The ride to the sheriff's office was gut wrenching. It was different than my dad's funeral or when Sarah, Amanda, and I had that awful night in Chicago. Both feelings were devastating, but sitting in handcuffs in the back of a sheriff's pickup made me feel like a criminal.

I felt dirty and ashamed. I made up my mind that I never wanted to feel like that again. I just hoped that I wouldn't have to be fingerprinted and left in jail. I was afraid Uncle Patrick might leave me in jail for a while to teach me one of his lessons.

The deputies put me in an office and told me that the Sheriff would be in to talk to me soon. Their demeanor had changed, and they were much more serious now that we were at the jail. The sheriff had to duck to fit through the doorway. He looked like a giant. Even though he told them to take the cuffs off of me, I felt like a prisoner in his office. I was so scared that I was shaking.

The sheriff said gruffly, "I don't know how they deal with y'alls little joyrides up in Chicago, but down here folks don't take kindly to having their vehicles taken. What were you planning to do?"

I looked down at the floor and wished I could dig a hole and hide. I didn't want to tell him that I was going to drive to Chicago in the pickup I took. I started to think that a joyride sounded a lot better than stealing a pickup. I took a chance and said, "Officer, I know it was wrong. I just wanted to drive around for a while and think."

He cocked his head to the side, nodded, and grinned as if he were happy with what I said. Suddenly, he turned on me with anger in his face and got within an inch of my face. "I already talked to your aunt and she says you may have been trying to take that pickup all the way home to Chicago. You are lying, little lady, and you aren't very good at it."

I could almost feel the blood drain from my face. I put my head in my hands to cover my emotions, but I couldn't control my sobbing. I was convinced that this guy was going to put me in jail for sure.

He got up and left the room. I heard the door shut and then open again, but I didn't look up until I heard Aunt Jo's voice. "I'm having trouble knowing what to say about this, Lexi."

I looked up, startled to see her sitting where the sheriff had been. I tried to say I was sorry, but I'm sure she couldn't understand me. I hadn't cried this hard at my own father's funeral. That reality just added to my guilty feelings.

Aunt Jo's voice was shaky as she said, "The sheriff got the guy whose pickup you took not to press charges. He says you are free to go. Let's go home and sort out this mess."

I ducked my head and followed her out of the room, through the outer office, and to the parking lot. As we got into her car and started home, I kept peeking over at Aunt Jo, wondering when she was going to start talking to me. "I wish your uncle were here." Except for that one comment, we rode in silence the entire trip home. I knew that was a bad sign.

Once we were in the house, she motioned for me to sit down on her dark leather couch. I sat down on one end, and she took the other. I fidgeted with my fingernails nervously and found some dirt under a couple on my right hand.

"Lexi, I really don't know where to begin. What were you thinking?" she asked.

"It sounds dumb now, but I wanted to go to be with Amanda. I don't know how to deal with what has happened to Sarah." I started breaking down in tears again. I still had not been able to say out loud that Sarah was dead. It seemed like a bad dream. I had turned it into a nightmare by taking that pickup.

Aunt Jo reached over and took my hand. "I knew that must have been your plan," she said. "Did you think about how you would get there without anyone catching you? Did you think of how frightened you would make your mom, your uncle, and me? You are smarter than that. What would you do for money, gas, or food? This just doesn't make sense to me, Lexi." Tears began to fill her eyes and run down her plump cheeks.

"I should have told you, but on the bus Bessie gave me some money. I know I was wrong. I just reacted without thinking at all," I said apologetically. I really felt bad this time, but I didn't expect her to believe me after the party incident.

"Come here," she said, opening her arms wide. I nestled my head on her chest and hugged her for a long time. I wished with all my heart that my mom had hugged me like that even one time.

There was a question that had been burning in my heart since I had heard about Sarah. I couldn't keep it inside any longer. I asked softly, "How did she die?"

Aunt Jo didn't speak for several moments. I looked up at her to see if she didn't hear me. Her lips were moving, but no words were coming out. I gathered that she was praying about how to answer.

She opened her eyes and looked down at me with a loving and tender smile. "Lexi, I didn't know when it would be the right time to tell you," she said. "Sarah was suffocated. The police found her in the basement of an abandoned building."

I felt a calmness that I could only contribute to being in the embrace of someone that I truly believed loved me. Tears did not come. I was numb and exhausted, but I still felt guilty for not crying at the news I had just received.

I laid my head back down on her chest and allowed my body to completely relax in her arms. She held me like a helpless baby. I dozed off for several minutes, and when I woke up I had a new concern to share with my aunt.

"I'm sorry I embarrassed you and Uncle Patrick in front of all the people," I said through my sobs. Aunt Jo was such a sweet person. What I did would make her look bad to her friends and neighbors that she had known for years.

She took me by the shoulders and looked me right in the face. "You listen to me," she said forcefully. "I don't care what anybody else does or thinks. I care about you. I am here to help you. Your uncle and I love you, Lexi. Don't you know that by now?"

In my present state of mind, I wasn't able to soak up her love. "What will Uncle Patrick say?" I asked.

She drew a long breath as if she were deciding how to answer. "He will tell you that you were wrong. He will love you enough to discipline you, and he will not care what one person in this county thinks about what happened. We decided years ago to only worry about what God thinks about our actions. The gossips aren't listening to God, and those listening to him aren't going to gossip."

I wished I could have that kind of self-confidence. What my friends thought controlled my actions much of the time. I could only imagine not letting what others said bother me. Already, I was imagining what Stacey and her friends would say if I were kicked off the team for what I had done. "Will the coach kick me off of the team?" I asked, hoping she would reassure me that it would be okay.

"I have no idea. The real question is have you learned how critical your choices are in this life." I nodded my head in agreement. I had already made one choice in the sheriff's pickup: I would never do anything that was going to make me feel that guilty again.

We sat in silence for several minutes. I could tell she was exhausted from the events of the day. My mind was running through a thousand questions. What would they say at school? Would Lana still like me? How will Keith treat me now?

Suddenly, I blurted out, "My mom will make me come back home, won't she?" I figured that since I had gotten sent here because of what happened at home, she might think this wasn't working out since I had been in trouble here too.

"I already spoke to her. She is really upset and did say that we should send you back." When she said that, I felt my heart leap in my chest. I just wanted to go home and get away from all of these emotions. I didn't want to face anybody after what I had done. "I reminded her that I was her big sister and that she had to listen to me." I frowned. She seemed to know what I was thinking. "Lexi, you need to finish this year. It is important to finish what you start. Also, I can see you growing and becoming a wonderful young lady."

At that, my head snapped around and I stared

at her with a quizzical look. "How can you say that after what I did?" I asked in amazement.

"Call it faith. I have learned to trust in a Lord who can do miracles." Her beautiful smile beamed at me.

I didn't understand what she was talking about, but I liked how her belief in me made me feel. I would need a miracle tomorrow at school and tomorrow night when Uncle Patrick was supposed to come home. I would rather do a million chores at the ranch than go to school tomorrow.

I spoke respectfully, but with feeling. "Aunt Jo, I am still concerned about Amanda. What if she hurts herself this weekend?"

I was surprised when she nodded her head in agreement. "I already called her mother, and she assures me that she will stay with her every moment this weekend. I also urged her to take Amanda to a professional counselor."

I thanked her over and over. She was so special. If only I had trusted her, I wouldn't be in this mess.

The next day at school, everybody had something to say to me about what I had done. Most of them were just joking around about it, but a couple of the girls I had gone to the party with told me how cool it was. That made me feel worse. I knew if I hung around them, I would break my promise to myself not to ever do anything like that again.

I didn't catch the bus over to Cheyenne for practice. I couldn't face Coach after what I had done. He had taken me in on the team and even made me a starter. I knew he had been griped out at least once for giving me Stacey's starting spot.

After school, I went out to get on the bus. Uncle Patrick was waiting in the old blue pickup in the gravel parking lot near the gym. He smiled as I walked up to him. I got in and said, "I thought you weren't coming home until tonight."

"I hear we had some excitement while I was gone," he said.

I dropped my head. I wasn't ready for this talk and hoped he wouldn't be home until I was asleep tonight. I would do almost anything to avoid the combination of one of my uncle's lectures and feelings I had experienced yesterday.

"What did Aunt Jo tell you?" I asked, hoping he would say that she had already told him everything. I didn't look forward to reliving any of that day.

"She told me the basics of what happened. Is there anything that you want to say for yourself?"

I didn't know what to do. If I started talking about it, I might tell him more than Aunt Jo did and get him even angrier with me. If I didn't talk about it, he was sure to think that I just didn't care. I tried to gain his sympathy. "I was so upset about Sarah and worried about Amanda that I wasn't even thinking." I let my eyes fill with tears. *There, that was true and pretty good, if I do say so myself.*

Uncle Patrick cleared his throat. He had given me several talks since I had come to stay with him and Aunt Jo, but he had never started one by clearing his throat. I suddenly felt hot all over, and my mouth was so dry that I couldn't swallow. I quickly conjured up a couple of very believable sobs in order to soften his attitude.

He began talking in his louder-than-usual lecture tone. "Lexi, you should know by now that crying doesn't work on me. Rather than trying to get out of trouble, you should be trying to learn from your poor decision. The only way things are ever going to get better in your life is for you to start making good choices. Life will be much easier on you when you learn to be harder on yourself."

He was always talking like that when he got on to me. Why would I want to be harder on myself? Hadn't I already lost the only two people in my life that understood me? Besides, I knew I had made a bad choice by taking the pickup. I felt horrible about it. I decided it might get him on my side if he knew. "I know taking the pickup was a stupidly bad decision and I feel awful about it," I said seriously and with feeling.

"Whether or not taking someone's property is wrong is not in question here. The real question is are you sorry you did it or are you sorry you got caught? If you had made it to Chicago, would you still feel sorry?"

I pondered that question for a few minutes. At first I thought I knew the answer. I was sorry for what I did, not just that I got caught. But when he asked me about making it to Chicago, it got me thinking. I would have been happy. I would have bragged to Amanda and my other friends.

Seeing myself as a thief who was not sorry for stealing made me feel even worse. I was a bad person. I didn't ever think of myself as a bad person before this moment. Was there any hope for me?

Uncle Patrick interrupted my thoughts when he said, "We have a meeting with Coach Bradshaw in fifteen minutes. I suggest while you're sitting there thinking, you figure out what you are going to say to him."

This was worse than I thought! Not only did I have to listen to Uncle Patrick's lectures, now I would have to face my coach. I had already thought about what he would do to me. I was sure he would kick me off the team.

Coach was no nonsense. He didn't have any patience for players who broke the rules. He had made those two girls that kept forgetting their clothes at the first of the season get out of his class completely.

The meeting was in the coach's office. It was a little small for the three of us. Earlier in the year, I had been in the office and admired all of the coaching awards he had hanging on the walls and the cool posters with motivational sayings with which he had decorated. This time I was looking straight down at the tile floor and trying to count the number of dots on each tile while we waited for Coach to get off the phone.

He hung up, and I glanced up quickly and back down in an attempt to gauge his mood. He started speaking first. "That was the OSA in Oklahoma

City. They set the rules for our games and the play-offs. I wanted to make sure how your five-game suspension would affect your eligibility in the playoffs. They said that you would be eligible to play after whatever suspension is served."

"Coach, you're the boss. Lexi will serve any suspension you set and do whatever running you see fit. Isn't that right, Lexi?" Uncle Patrick said.

I was in shock but I managed to answer. "Yes, sir, and I am sorry for the way I have embarrassed the team and you." It felt as if I were dreaming. Five games was a lot, but I would be allowed to come back to the team. Stacey would probably take my spot for good now. I wondered if he would put me in the games when I came back, but I didn't dare ask.

"Do you have any questions?" he asked. I looked up at him, and he actually looked more sympathetic than angry. I wondered if he felt sorry for me because of my stupidity or because of the loss of my friend.

"What do I do during the games while I'm suspended?" I asked meekly, avoiding eye contact with him.

"I expect you to dress nicely and sit on the end of the bench. You are to be at all five games and support you teammates," he stated calmly.

"Thank you, Coach Bradshaw. I won't let you down again." He stood up to walk us out of the office.

Back in the pickup with Uncle Patrick, I was feeling sad, but I knew it hadn't been as bad as it could have been. I wanted to know if that was the end of my punishment, but I didn't dare ask.

We rode in silence all the way home. As we went in the kitchen door, he told me to wait at the table. I could hear him talking to Aunt Joanne in the other room, but I couldn't make out what they were saying. In a few minutes, they both came into the kitchen and sat down with me at the table.

Uncle Patrick began saying, "Lexi, what do you think your punishment should be?" I could not look at them. They obviously believed that I needed to be punished more, but I had hoped the five-game suspension would be enough.

Aunt Jo said, "The suspension has nothing to do with our discipline. The coach's decision was in response to how your actions reflected on the team and the school. We are responsible for helping you learn about the consequences of bad choices. Also, you caused the man you stole from to miss work, and you caused him stress that he didn't need. We are all blessed that he did not press charges."

I knew there was no sense in arguing. If anyone was going to help me out, it would be Aunt Jo. It was clear that she agreed with Uncle Patrick. I was a little surprised and thought about calling my mom for help. After what Aunt Jo had said last night, I knew my mom would never side with me against her sister.

"What is my punishment?" I asked flatly. I was not prepared for what came next.

Uncle Patrick said, "If you don't come up with a better plan, we both feel that you should do some work for the man that owns the pickup. Also, you will only be allowed to go to school, basketball, and home until further notice."

I expected the grounding, and my mom had said until further notice a hundred times before, but I was not going to work for some stranger. "I don't want to work for that guy. I'm sure he hates me, and I wouldn't feel safe. I understand the grounding, but I don't think I can do the other part of the punishment."

Uncle Patrick got up from the table and walked out of the room. I looked at Aunt Jo, and she didn't seem surprised. She leaned toward me and spoke quietly. "Your uncle would never put you in a bad situation, and it made him angry that you would think he might. He has known Carl, the owner of the pickup, for twenty years. He is a good person and dropped the charges in part because of all the help your uncle has been to him over the years. You are going to have to learn to think before you speak." She sat back and continued in a conversational tone. "There is one other thing, and we can take care of that right now. You must call your mom and tell her what you did."

That was good news to me. Surely she would listen to me and talk to them for me. This was not fair. I didn't care if Uncle Patrick knew him or not; I couldn't go work for some guy who I didn't know. What if he was some kind of a creep or treated me like a criminal? I was happy to call my mom.

My mom answered, and I began to tell her everything as fast as I could. I wanted to hurry up and get to my complaints. She let me talk for five minutes or so and then she interrupted me. "Lexi, what you did was worse than anything you have ever done here. Maybe you think going out there isn't working and that you would be better off back here."

"Yes! Thank you, Mom," I exclaimed.

"Well, that is not going to happen," she snapped. "You are going to finish your year out there, and you are going to do whatever your aunt and uncle say to do." I couldn't catch my breath to argue. How could I have been so dumb as to believe that she would actually side with me? She had said all of that stuff about coming home just to be mean. She continued, "Don't think that any amount of trouble you decide to get yourself into is going to change my mind. You had better straighten up and do what is right or face the consequences."

"Fine!" I screamed into the phone and slammed the receiver down so hard I thought I might have broken it. I ran out of the house and didn't stop until I got to the horse barn. Golden was waiting patiently for me as always. At least he would listen to me.

Coach Bradshaw

The next day at school I was miserable. As the hours passed, I dreaded going to practice. Toren and Tina told me that Stacey and a couple of other girls had gone to Coach and asked him why he didn't kick me off the team. I don't know what he said to them, but I had noticed that he didn't let people tell him what to do.

Coach told us on the first day of practice that he was the only one who would run the team. At the parent meeting, he told them the same thing. He also told them that during the season he did not talk basketball with parents of his players.

Coach Bradshaw was quieter than my coach last year, but when he got fired up about something, he would let us have it. Sometimes he would joke around with us before or after practice, but during practice or a game he was all business.

A few years ago, in seventh grade, our coach drove us nuts because he acted crazy on game day. He would get mad at things that he laughed about the day before and give us big speeches about how important it was to win. He didn't care about us, and we could tell.

I didn't get that feeling from Coach Bradshaw. If anything, being around him calmed me down about winning and losing. He always told us that all he cared about was how hard we played and how well we listened to what he taught us. I had learned so much about the game of basketball from him. Disappointing him crushed me.

We had been having a great season so far. Although I would have to miss the next five games, I knew we were good enough to keep our undefeated record. The article in *Vype* had all the girls pumped. I hoped that my suspension wouldn't mess up everything. On the other hand, if they did fine without me I would feel bad as well.

The first three games of my suspension went well. We were so much better than those teams. We all celebrated when we would beat a team bad enough that all the subs got to play. Coach seemed to relax a little in those games as well. It was fun once in a while, but he said we needed to be challenged more.

The challenges came in the next two games when we had to play Sentinel and Hammon. They were ranked number seven and eight in our class. Coach said that if we won those two games, we would be ranked in the top eight in the state and that was important in the playoffs.

"How does that help us in the playoffs?" Tina asked Coach.

"The top eight teams in the rankings get to play easier teams early in the playoffs. If you have to play the best teams early in the playoffs, it is harder to make it to the state tournament."

After the next two games, which we lost by double digits, I was feeling terrible about my idiotic choices. I watched helplessly from the bench as we looked out of sync in both games. Stacey had started in my spot. She played terribly and was benched for talking back to Coach.

They were both good teams, but I knew that had I been able to play, we would have won. My suspension had cost us the chance to have an easy road to the area tournament and that could cost us a trip to the state tournament and the Big House. I made up my mind that if I got the chance to play again, I was going to make sure we won.

The Playoffs

We started the playoffs ranked number ten because of the losses to Hammon and Sentinel. I consoled myself with the fact that number ten was close to the goal of being in the top eight. I made the mistake of mentioning it to Uncle Patrick one night at dinner.

"The people who make up the brackets for the playoffs only protect the top eight teams," he said. "We will have to face a top-ranked team in the regional tournament now because of those losses."

I could tell he was not happy about it so I decided to change the subject. "How was Golden today?" I asked.

He frowned, and I knew I had made another mistake. "He misses you, Lexi. When is the last time you spent any time with him?"

"I feed him every day," I said, defending myself with an exaggeration.

Aunt Joanne looked up at me quickly and said, "You might want to rethink that statement."

"Well, most of the time anyway. Thank you for helping me with him, Aunt Jo," I said, hoping she would jump in and smooth everything over for me.

"Lexi, the foal was a gift and a test all rolled into one. You did well with it until the new wore off, but lately you have neglected Golden. Horses are social animals. You bonded with him, and now he needs you to care for him with more than just food."

I knew she was right, and I had felt bad about neglecting him. I told myself it was because I was so busy with basketball, friends, and homework. I wanted to tell my aunt and uncle that I didn't ask for the responsibility, but something told me that wouldn't go over very well. I decided to just agree with them and go on until I remembered the phrase Aunt Joanne had said, *a gift and a test*. My competitiveness kicked in, and I found a new determination to pass this test.

I stood up quickly, almost knocking my glass of iced tea over onto my aunt's beautiful flower arrangement on her immaculate table. They both looked up at me in expectation. From Uncle Patrick's expression, I gathered that he expected an argument. "If it's okay," I said, "I'm going to see Golden." My announcement was met with approval. I heard Aunt Joanne saying what a good girl I was as I went out the kitchen door.

Golden whinnied to me as I walked up to the horse barn. I felt like someone kicked me in the gut. He was just waiting on me to make up my mind that he was important enough to visit. He was so beautiful and loved me whether I did the right thing or not.

It reminded me of how Dawn described Jesus to me that time in the locker room. I shook my head to clear those upsetting thoughts and focused on brushing Golden. I told him all about the suspension, the losses, and the upcoming playoffs. He seemed very interested.

○

Uncle Patrick printed the playoff brackets off the Internet. My uncle didn't even use e-mail, but if it had to do with basketball, he was all over it. He called me into the living room to show me the bracket. I asked him about how the playoffs worked.

He told me that every team in the state plays in a district tournament. We would be hosting ours at Cheyenne, and he showed me that the two teams we would be playing had losing records. I asked him what happened after districts.

"The district champions and the runners-up go on to the regional tournament," he explained. "Looking at the bracket, I expect we will play Leedey in the regional championship game. Both of those teams go on to area, but the loser of that game will have to win three games to go to the Big House, and the winner will only have to win one. If you don't win all three games in the area tournament, you don't go to the state tournament."

"Well, we will just have to win that game," I said, almost promising a victory with my tone.

"Let's do it!" he agreed.

We won the district tournament easily and went into the regional tournament on the winner's side. Just as Uncle Patrick said, this set up a game against Leedey, the third ranked team in the state. Coach said, "Leedey has a great basketball tradition. We will have to play one of our best games of the year to come out on top. The good news is that if we win, we will be in the area tournament with two chances to go to the state tournament. If we lose, we will still go to area, but we will have to win three games in a row."

We were super nervous before the game. The seniors tried to calm all of us down, but they were almost as jittery as we were. The Leedey girls didn't act nervous at all. In the first quarter, we turned the ball over against their press and got behind by ten points. Once we settled down, we got their lead down to seven points, but we never could catch up with them.

On Monday, Coach went over the bracket with us. We would have to win three games in a row, and he said one of them would be against either Hammon or Leedey. Those two teams would play on Friday night, and the loser would play on Saturday in the area consolation championship.

Coach said that everybody in the area tournament was good. We would have to be focused and get lots of rest. After we watched film on our next opponent, he went over the game plan with us. Our first game was on Thursday night. The team we played was much easier than Leedey or Hammon. They had won twenty games during the season, but they must not have played as many tough teams as we had. We won by seventeen points, and lots of people got to play. We were excited to be going on to the next game.

We played the early game on Friday afternoon. Just before we lined up to run out on the court, Coach told us that if we won, we would all watch the Leedey versus Hammon game together. "If we don't win this game, we won't get a shot at either of them," he said. The seniors told Coach that we were going to win. They looked calm and confident. We always won when they acted like that.

The team we played had an awesome point guard, so we couldn't press them at all. Every time we tried, she would dribble right through us. Fortunately, they didn't have anyone who was good enough to stop Tina in the post. She had twelve points early in the game. We had an eight-point lead before their coach put his team into a zone to stop her.

At halftime, Coach told us to stop their point guard from driving into the lane so much. Then he looked at several of us guards, pausing to make eye contact, and said, "Did y'all see that zone they're playing because of Tina? Start bombing the threes!"

We poured out of the locker room fired up and

believing we were about to win. Coach started four three-point shooters and Tina in the second half. By the end of the third quarter, we had made six three pointers and led by sixteen points. They tried to mix up their defenses in the fourth quarter, but we were rolling. I hoped we could play this well the next night.

The Leedey versus Hammon game was fun to watch. They were both really good. I was pulling for Hammon because we had beaten them earlier in the year, and I thought we could do it again. They were ranked number six in the state, but that could easily have been us if I hadn't been suspended for our game against them.

In the end, Hammon upset Leedey on a last second shot by their sophomore star Libby Unruh. We were all surprised and dejected until Coach made an important point. He called us all together and said, "Girls, we beat Hammon, and they just beat Leedey. I figure we are all three about dead even in talent. What is going to be the difference between winning and losing is how hard you are willing to play."

I hadn't thought of it that way. Looking around at the frowns turning into smiles told me that the other girls hadn't either. His talk had cheered us up and gotten us ready for the game the next night. We were convinced we were just as talented as Leedey. We knew from living through Coach Bradshaw's practices that we would be able to play harder than them.

This time we were ready for Leedey's press and actually led at the half. The second half was back and forth. We led with two minutes to go and went into our stall game, forcing them to foul us. I missed my first two free throws, and they got within two points of us. We got the ball back, and since I had missed before, they started fouling me every time. I was able to make my next six free throws, and we pulled out the win.

Everyone was so excited! The students came down out of the stands and were giving all the players hugs and high-fives. Stacey went straight over to Keith and gave him a long hug. When he finally pulled away, she looked at me with a devilish grin. I stared straight through her as if she wasn't even there. The joke was on her. Keith would never be interested in someone who did hateful, petty things like that.

After the celebration, Coach walked into the locker room and everyone settled down to listen to what he would say. "We're going to the Big House!" he exclaimed. The room erupted in excitement. After allowing us to celebrate for a few minutes, Coach held up his hand to get our attention.

He began to yell, "Are we done yet?" We didn't know how to respond. He yelled again, "Are we done yet?"

Leisha yelled out, "No!" Then all of us began yelling no as well.

Coach started smiling and said, "Girls, we go into the state tournament even with everyone else. One loss knocks anybody out. We are all in the same boat. Now that we are going to the Big House, why don't we just go ahead and win the whole thing!"

The locker room exploded again in enthusiastic cheers, and someone started chanting, "Take State!" Before I knew it, we were all chanting and stomping in unison. It was awesome!

The next week we went to the state tournament. On the day before our first game, Coach was able to get us into the Big House. It was huge. None of us girls had ever played in a gym as big as the arena. Coach had played there, so he knew what we were going through. He walked us all over the arena. We stood on the floor while they turned the huge overhead game lights on, and we all got goose bumps.

Coach emphasized that the gym floor was the same size as the one at home. He pointed out that the free-throw line was still fifteen feet, and the three-point line was the same distance as all the other places we had played. "When I played here, I decided to forget about all of the people and the atmosphere while the game was being played. I figured there would be time to enjoy all that other stuff while we were getting our medals for winning."

I was wishing I had the guts to start our "Take State" chant again right out there on the court, but I was too nervous. I looked at the other girls. They looked nervous as well. Spontaneously, Dawn did the silliest and bravest thing I had seen in a long time. She started doing cartwheels right there on the court in the Big House.

At first the girls were in shock, and then they started giggling nervously. A few of us looked at Coach to gauge his reaction. He just smiled in amazement at her. Somehow her actions loosened us all up, and we started talking a little. Toren started the "Take State" chant, and we all joined in enthusiastically. Coach even joined in with us. I knew we were going to win the next afternoon.

The first game was against Lookeba-Sickles. They were the champion of another area tournament and ranked number five in the state. We went into the fourth quarter with a small lead. Tina and Leisha were in foul trouble, so Coach said, "We're going to slow it down and keep the ball in our hands for the first few minutes of the quarter."

Our opponent came out trying to press us and make us play fast. Their plan caused them to foul a lot, and we started shooting free throws. Shooting free throws was one of our strengths, so we were able to build the lead up to six points.

Coach said, "If they're going to put us on the free throw line, we're going to win. Keep holding the ball." We made eleven of twelve free throws in the fourth quarter. Despite some dangerous three pointers by Lookeba, we won by four points.

The girls were so fired up that we got very little sleep that night. Our game the next day was at nine in the morning. Our opponent was Schulter. They were an athletic team that liked to press. It didn't go very well. We started the game the same way that we had against Leedey in the Regional tournament. Their press put us behind by seven points in the first quarter. We never recovered. We fell short of our goal for a state championship, but after the initial disappointment, we were all proud of our accomplishment.

Over the next few weeks, we were honored several times. The Cheyenne steak house fed all of us and our families for free. A huge rally was held at the courthouse, complete with a dozen roses for each of us players. Finally, we all celebrated as our banner was hung in the gym next to the one Coach had earned as a player. We stood in awe as each of us read our names on the banner.

Church Camp

t had been two and a half months since we played in the state tournament. My days of working for Carl, the owner of the pickup that I stole, went well, but I was glad they were finished. He was nice and didn't make me do much work. Mostly I cleaned his house while he was at work.

I decided not to try out for slow-pitch softball, but Uncle Patrick allowed me to go to most of the home games. I wanted to support the girls and be with my friends. On game days, I wished I had gone out for the team.

Golden and I had been spending a lot of time together. He was getting big. I had decided to leave him at the ranch when I went back home. If I took him with me, I would have to put him with a horse boarder.

Over the past few weeks, I had become very close to Dawn and Toren, who were in the youth group.

Uncle Patrick let me drive to church on Wednesday nights for youth group meetings. He said I had earned the freedom.

At Wednesday night youth class, it was time to sign up to go to summer church camp. "You have to go!" Toren exclaimed for what felt to me like the millionth time. "It's awesome!" I figured Toren was trying to help her mom, who was the youth leader, get more people to go.

I began to think of excuses. "I don't know if my aunt and uncle will let me go. I am still not allowed to go to town with anyone. Besides, I don't know exactly when I will be going back home this summer." I hoped they would buy at least one of my excuses and drop it.

Dawn said, "Don't you think Patrick will want you to go to church camp?"

I just shrugged my shoulders, but I knew he would probably let me go. The problem was that I didn't know if I wanted to go. I figured all they did was sing church songs and listen to preachers. "What is it like there? I mean, what do you do?" I asked doubtfully.

Everyone turned to look at Keith when he started to speak. He didn't talk much, but when he did, people wanted to listen to him, at least I did. "Church camp is the most amazing place I've ever been. It is up in the mountains. When you drive in, it's like going into a little city. There are lots of things to do during the free time in the afternoon. The best part is the praise and worship music, and they have some of the best youth speakers in the world."

While he was talking, I could feel my attitude change. Keith was going. Why didn't someone tell me that? Free time in the afternoon with Keith would be worth listening to a bunch of boring speakers anytime. Of course, Keith probably wouldn't even care if I went or spend any time with me, but it was worth a chance. If we were there together for a whole week, he would have to talk to me.

While I had been thinking about Keith, Patty had been talking. I brought myself back to reality just as she said, "Remember, you have to sign up by next Wednesday night to go to church camp." We prayed and were dismissed.

As we walked out of the youth room, I felt a hand on my shoulder. I turned around and looked into the eyes of the guy of my dreams. Keith said, "I hope you can go to church camp."

My heart melted, and I couldn't do anything but smile. *I am so there!* I thought to myself.

The day came to leave for camp, and I had mixed feelings. I had little interest in listening to preachers and didn't enjoy most of the music that Dawn had in her iPod. On the other hand, Keith was going. Besides, it would be boring around the ranch, especially with all my friends being at church camp.

We loaded our bags in the little U-Haul trailer hitched to the church van. I had one objective. It was to sit with Keith on this trip even if I had to throw somebody out of the seat. If I didn't get to spend time with him this week, I was going to be ticked.

When Keith got on the bus, two junior high

boys were on his heels. I couldn't understand why he paid them so much attention. They were immature. I stepped between Keith and the boy who was closest to him. He looked at me and then at the boys. I gave him a smile and pushed his shoulder to get him to sit down in the green vinyl seat of the church van. Sitting down next to him on the aisle side, I effectively blocked him from getting past me.

The boys sat down in the seat across the aisle and started jabbering. I turned to Keith and said, "I was hoping we could talk about some things on the way to camp."

"Really? I couldn't tell," he said teasingly.

We talked most of the trip to Oklahoma City, where Patty had said we would stop and eat. She pulled into a Walmart parking lot that was next to several fast food places so we could have choices. Keith asked me, "Where do you want to eat?" I was so happy. We were having a great time.

"I don't care. Tacos or burgers are all right with me," I answered. He put his hand on my back and moved me toward the taco place. He said something about Mexican food, but I was so excited about how close we were that I couldn't concentrate.

The rest of the trip was great. I was pleasantly surprised with how this was all turning out. We talked about everything. I even found out that he was nervous about going to college next year. I wouldn't have guessed that he was ever nervous about anything.

When we pulled into the camp, I was amazed. It was huge. There were kids walking around everywhere. The church bus could barely get down the narrow roads because of all the people. It took forever to get to the cabin.

Our cabin was not a cabin at all. It looked like a two-story house. I was glad that it looked nice on the outside, but I wondered about the sleeping areas. The inside of the cabin was simple but nice. The girls' dorm was on one side of a large meeting room, and the boys' dorm was on the other side. There was a snack bar near the stairs in the meeting room. The kitchen and dining area took up the entire upstairs.

The girls all went to the dorm to choose a bed and put up our bags. I hurried so I could find Keith. From the trip up here, it looked like we were going to be spending a lot of time together this week. When I came out of the dorm, I looked all over the cabin for him.

There was a large porch outside the front door. There were benches and a couple of Ping-Pong tables on the porch. I looked everywhere for Keith. I asked Dawn and Addey, but they hadn't seen him. I even checked with the junior high boys, but he was nowhere to be found.

I didn't see him until supper several hours later. "Where did you run off to?" I asked, trying to act like I didn't care that much.

"Sorry," he said. "I went to the prayer garden and walked around some with some of the guys. I heard that you were looking for me."

I could feel my cheeks blushing, so I looked away. I didn't want him to think I was following him around like some lost puppy dog. However, I had noticed that had worked for the junior high boys. I decided right then that I didn't want his sympathy even if that meant I couldn't have his attention.

"Who told you I was looking for you? I just wanted to tell you I was going to hang out with Dawn and some of the girls so you wouldn't wait around for me," I lied. I wanted him to do at least a little of the chasing.

He didn't bite. "Okay, well, I'll see you later," he said. I couldn't tell if he wanted me to follow him around or leave him alone. He was so confusing. I wheeled around and headed to the stairs. I ran down the stairs and into the dorm. It was all I could do to hold back the tears.

Fatherless

The first night, we had to go to the sanctuary to listen to a preacher. The sanctuary was like a gigantic church. It would seat all the people in Cheyenne and Reydon with lots of room left. The stage was almost as big as my aunt and uncle's house. At first, all I could do was look around at all of the kids that were there. I saw Keith sitting a few rows from the front between two girls who were dressed like they were going on a date.

I was so jealous that I wanted to get up and leave. We had been warned that if we skipped any of the services it would mean kitchen duty all week. I tried to calm myself down. After the way he had been with me on the bus ride earlier, I thought Keith was more into me than he was showing now.

Finally, everyone started singing the praise songs, and I was able to get my mind off Keith. The band was really good, and I got into the singing. I loved it! I wondered if Dawn had these songs in her iPod. Looking over at her, I saw she was singing with her eyes closed and hands raised. I wondered why so many people had their hands raised in the air.

As the preacher earnestly began his sermon about how Jesus was a father to the fatherless, my mind latched onto the word *fatherless,* and I struggled to contain my rising emotions. *What was it with crying and church? Everybody cried all the time, including me!* I bit my lip as hard as I could stand, but it didn't help. The tears still flowed, smearing my thick mascara.

Not having a father around made me different, and I resented that like crazy. Even when people didn't ask questions, I knew they were thinking about asking them. *Where are your parents? Why do you live with your aunt and uncle?* I wanted to stand out on the basketball court, but I didn't want to draw attention to myself otherwise. Glancing quickly down the row, I saw my fellow group members staring intently at the preacher as he read from the Bible. His words began to drift away as my mind dredged up bittersweet memories.

○

The basketball slapped mercilessly against the driveway backboard and almost smacked me in the face. I grabbed it and slammed it against the concrete driveway with all my might. It bounced back up and slid soundlessly through the hoop. *Two points for me,* I thought sarcastically.

"Great shot, kiddo," my dad said with a wry smirk and one eyebrow lifting as he came down the front steps with practiced ease. Exhibiting the graceful movements of a former athlete, my dad always stood out in a crowd, and not just because he was taller than most dads.

Those years up and down the collegiate basketball court seemed to have given him an innate confidence. I was proud just to stand beside him when we were in public. He loved me and I knew it, mostly because he told me so often, but also because he took time to be with me. Basketball was our common ground, and I loved that sport just as much as he did.

I smiled halfheartedly at him and began to fix my ponytail, tugging hard with erratic gestures. "Stupid trick shots are the only ones I can make today. My shot is so off, and I can't figure out what I'm doing wrong," I moaned. I slammed the ball against the pavement with sharp, crisp movements.

Dad laughed at my overdramatizing and shook his head. "Okay, let me see what you're doing here." He slapped the ball out of my hand with a simple flick of his wrist, and his long fingers palmed the ball in his right hand and put it right in front of my face, gently smashing my nose.

I made a noise of mock protest and tried to slap at it. He merely lifted the ball high over his head, turned, and executed a perfect jumper, his shoes well behind the three-point line. The ball arched beautifully with perfect backspin and kissed the net as it shimmied through. My dad's wrist was flexed, his arm extended high, *hand in the cookie jar,* and he was staring at me, not even watching his shot hit home. He laughed out loud at my consternation and proceeded to lope after the ball. I caught his bounce pass and took a small dribble and sent up a jumper. Same result. *Off the stinking backboard again!* "See, Dad! I just can't get it!" I complained mournfully.

"Slow down, Lex Luther. You are shooting from too low, just like you did when you were younger. You have the strength now to shoot from your shoulder. Arch the ball and follow through. Let's just catch and shoot. No dribbling right now, okay?" He looked directly at me as he spoke, slightly bending close to my height and speaking calmly.

○

I wish I had that strength now.

Pieces of
My Heart

The next day I felt as if I were sleepwalking through breakfast and the morning Bible study. The junior high girls wouldn't be quiet last night. They talked until two in the morning when one of the sponsors woke up and came in to quiet them. The sponsors told us they would be sleeping in our dorm from now on, and I was glad.

Leisha wrote me a note during the Bible study asking me whom I was going to walk around with tonight. I gave her a quizzical look. She looked perturbed that I didn't know what she meant. She wrote that everybody gets a date and walks around the streets of the camp for about an hour after evening services.

I wrote back to her that the only guy I wanted to date was Keith. I bravely added, "You know he is the love of my life, and I am going to wait until he asks me out." She wrote me back saying that I was too stubborn.

She leaned in and said, "He doesn't ask anyone out. Every year girls come to our cabin looking for him, and he goes and plays Ping-Pong with the junior high boys."

"Yeah, what's that about?" I asked sarcastically.

She shrugged and said, "He told Toren once that they are young and homesick so he cheers them up by hanging out with them."

Every night while all the others were walking around on dates or looking for dates, I found Keith in or around the cabin hanging out with the younger kids and making camp fun for them. I asked him, "Are you going to be a youth pastor some day?"

He cocked his head to the side and said, "Maybe. I'm praying about it."

I admired him for caring more about the younger kids than himself or dating. I liked hanging around the cabin with him, but I could hardly handle all of the girls that came by to see him. I asked him, "Did you date any of those girls?"

"They're just friends. I met them over the years at church camp and church events," he said. Surely, he knew every single one of them wanted to go out with him. For someone who was so smart, he could be clueless sometimes.

There were only two nights of camp left when Keith finally asked me if I wanted to get a Coke at the concession stand. I was proud to be seen walking with him. I was floating down the street beside the most awesome guy. We began talking like we had on the bus, and I felt so close to him. I thought that every girl who saw us was probably dying of jealousy. A few of them must have been, as they seemed to stare at us as we walked by them.

I got caught up in the excitement of having the attention of the guy I had thought about all year long. I was so happy that before I thought about, I reached up and kissed him. He didn't kiss me back. I looked into his eyes to see what the problem was, but I couldn't tell what he was thinking. He didn't seem mad or happy, just surprised.

We walked for a few more minutes in awkward silence. Keith stopped and took both of my hands in his. He looked me in the eyes and said, "Lexi, I have committed myself to save all of my kisses for the person I know I am going to marry. I really like you, and I can see that God is working in you. That is what really matters. I hope you understand." I nodded my head in agreement so he would drop his uncomfortable gaze, but I didn't understand.

We dropped our hands and walked for a little while. "Lexi, you are beautiful, and I want to kiss you. But wouldn't you like to share all of those special things with only your husband someday?"

My mind started racing back to my past. *That is not possible for me!* I had kissed lots of guys, and I had done things with guys that I regretted. Every time I had broken up with a guy, I felt like he took a little piece of me with him. This idea of Keith's was brand new to me, but it didn't matter because it was too late for me.

I made it back to the cabin and into the dorm before I let the tears start pouring. I shared with Dawn what had happened. She told me that she heard a youth speaker talk about starting over in the area of kissing and touching. "That means that you ask for forgiveness for all of your mistakes and start fresh today."

My first thought was that this starting over talk sounded too good to be true. It seemed like I would be lying to myself and the guys I dated, pretending that I had never done anything with anyone. I told her what I was thinking.

"God forgives and gives us a new start. Besides, what will you do when you don't have any more pieces of your heart to give away? What will be left to share with your husband? How will you be able to bond with him the way you want to if your heart is strung out all over the place?"

She said it so sweetly and with such feeling that I knew she wasn't putting me down. I lay on my bed for a long time just thinking. The more I thought about what she said, the more I wanted to know about starting over in my heart.

I whispered to Dawn, "Tell me more about what the youth speaker said about starting fresh." When she didn't answer, I listened quietly and heard her regular breathing. I was all tied up in knots, and she was sleeping peacefully. I was so jealous of her calm assurance. *I want that so bad!*

Bubble Wrap

On the last night of camp, Patty Wright taught the evening devotion. She was Toren's mom. I had been to her Wednesday night youth class several times, but she hadn't taught a lesson during our week at church camp. She was always interesting, so I looked forward to listening to her.

Patty gave everyone a piece of bubble wrap about the size of a quarter. She told us that sin, even one, is enough to keep us out of heaven. Once we had sinned, she said, we could never do enough to fix it. She said the only way we can be made whole and forgiven is by believing in Jesus, which means accepting his sacrifice for our sins.

Patty told us all to pop the bubble wrap at the same time. Then she challenged us to fix it back to exactly how it was before we popped it. We all looked at each other knowing there was no way we could do it and wondering if someone else had figured out the secret to fixing it. When we all realized she was making a point, she continued with the lesson.

"Don't answer out loud," she said. "But have you ever committed even one sin?" I knew I had sinned many times. She continued teaching. "If you realize you have sinned, and everybody's guilty of sin, then your bubble wrap is already popped. The good news is that Jesus can take away your sins and make you right with him tonight."

From what Patty had said, I knew I needed Jesus to make me right. I could feel something stirring inside of me. It was as if God was tugging on my heart. I felt sorry for my sin, but not like when I got caught drinking or when I ran from the sheriff. Instead I felt hopeful. I believed I could be made right and forgiven, but I didn't know what to do next.

Patty closed the lesson by praying for us. Then she said if anyone wanted to talk, she would be available. I started toward her, but Sheila got there first. She was always crying at tabernacle and devotion. The first day I felt bad for Sheila, but it had been four days of the same old thing. I told Dawn at lunch one day that I thought she just wanted attention all the time.

I didn't want everyone to see me standing there waiting for Patty, so I turned and went out on the front steps of the cabin. As usual, a couple of boys were playing Ping-Pong on the porch. I sat down on the old, saggy couch with Toren. Dawn followed me out and sat down beside me.

Dawn looked over at me and said, "What is it?" All I could do was look away. "Did you want to talk to Patty?" she asked. I found the strength to look her straight in the eyes, but I still couldn't say what I was thinking. She took me by the hand and led me back to Patty.

Sheila was gone, and Patty was cleaning up the snack counter. When Patty looked up, she smiled so big and bright that I knew she was aware of what I wanted. I was relieved that I wouldn't have to explain what I wanted to do.

The three of us sat down on a bed in the girl's dorm. I began to cry. Patty and Dawn's eyes started welling up with tears. Patty asked me what I wanted to do. "I don't know what it is called, but I'm like that popped bubble wrap. I need Jesus to fix me," I said between sobs.

"Can you tell me what sin is?" Patty asked.

"I can name some. I have lied, cheated, and stole a pickup," I admitted.

Patty chuckled and put her hand on my knee. "Yes, those are sins. They go against God's commandments. The Bible says that if we break one commandment, we have broken them all," Patty explained.

"That is why Jesus had to die on the cross to pay for our sins," Dawn added.

"I understand that part. It is like the song we sing in the tabernacle about how he paid a debt he did not owe and we owed a debt we could not pay," I said. "But what do I do now?" I asked.

Patty smiled a big, bright, beaming smile. "You have already done it. You have seen that you, like all of us, are a sinner and that only Jesus can fix you. That means that you believe he can set you free from your sin and the consequence of sin, which is separation from God in hell forever."

"Okay, but I didn't do anything," I said. I was beginning to think she wasn't going to understand what I meant.

"Exactly! Jesus does it all," Patty said. "Let's read Ephesians 2:8–9."

Dawn opened her Bible and read it out loud. It said that we are not saved by what we do; it is a gift of God.

Patty explained, "Through faith means you believe in, cling to, and trust in Jesus to forgive and save you. You see, Lexi, if you could do anything to fix the broken bubble wrap of your life, then why would Jesus have come to earth to die?"

I was relieved when she didn't wait for me to answer. "Are you ready to pray and make your decision to accept and follow Jesus official?" she asked.

"Yes, I'm ready," I said. At that moment, I felt like when we used to have chicken fights in the pool and the person on my shoulders fell off. I was so relieved.

"Repeat after me," Patty said. "Now, remember, these words are not magical." I nodded my head. I was ready. She continued, "Jesus saved you the moment you believed in him. This is just a way to verbalize what went on in your heart. Ready? Dear Jesus, I believe you are God's Son. I believe you died on the cross to pay for my sin and rose from the dead the third day. I turn away from my sin to follow you in a new life. Please come into my heart and teach me to live for you and not for myself anymore. Thank you for my home in heaven. Amen." I know I repeated every word, but I don't remember it exactly. I just remember feeling so peaceful and relieved.

We all hugged, and I felt so happy; it was beyond happy. "I want to feel like this all the time!" I exclaimed.

Dawn said, "That feeling is real joy. The only thing that gets in the way of this joyful feeling is sin. When we sin, it hurts our friendship with Jesus. He can't stand sin." She paused and then said, "Let's go tell everybody!"

Before I could say anything, Dawn was pulling me out of our dorm and into the meeting room where everyone was hanging out. "Guess what, everybody?" she yelled.

One of the boys said, "You want to go out with me!" It was Will. We all knew that he had a crush on Dawn.

She grinned and then turned to me. "Tell them," she whispered.

I could feel the blood rushing to my cheeks. "Lexi wants to go out with me?" Will joked. I was glad he did because it took everyone's eyes off me for a minute.

I managed a smile and said, "I, uh, I chose to follow Jesus tonight." The whole group started clapping. My head was spinning. Lots of kids and all of the sponsors came up to me and gave me a hug or said they would be praying for me.

Later as we lay in our bunk beds, I whispered to Dawn, "I'm so glad y'all talked me into coming here."

"Y'all?" She laughed. I hadn't even realized I said it, but it made me laugh too.

"I'm so happy!" she whispered back.

"You're a great friend," I said.

"Tonight was awesome!" she said a little too loudly for one of the sponsors who shushed us. We just giggled like little girls, and I knew we weren't going to be getting much sleep.

The next morning it was time to clean the cabin and head home. I didn't want to leave. Church camp felt like the safest and most peaceful place in the world. I was afraid that when we left I would lose this feeling of happiness and closeness to God. I told Patty I was scared about leaving.

"I know how you feel. I never want to leave camp either. But you have to remember that it is God's Spirit speaking to you and working in you that is making you feel all those good and special feelings. His Spirit can speak to you anywhere if you will listen. It does seem like it is easier to hear him at church camp. I—"

"Why is that? Is it the mountains being closer to God?" After I said it I knew it sounded dumb, but I really wanted to know how to keep this feeling.

Patty didn't laugh at me or even smile about my question. She answered, "Lexi, I think it is because up here we don't have all of the distractions we have allowed into our life at home. Instead of watching movies or television, we are singing praise choruses and studying God's Word. Also, there are people all over the state praying for us up here at camp. Prayer is so important in our lives as we fight to stay close to the Lord."

"I hope they keep praying for me. I am going to need it." Patty promised to pray for me every day and told me that I could call her anytime I needed to talk. I knew she meant it and that felt good.

We loaded all of our bags into the little trailer and got into the church van. I was still feeling worried about how I would live right when we got back home; I hadn't even thought about sitting with Keith.

I sat with Dawn. She started talking to me about the week and all of the people we had met. I quickly forgot all of my worries and joined in the conversation with her and the rest of the kids. We drove for hours, but it flew by because we were talking and singing some of the songs that we had learned during praise and worship.

We drove into Oklahoma City, and we all started discussing where we wanted to eat. Patty pulled into the same Walmart parking lot that was near several fast food places. That made us happy because we could choose the one we liked. She told us to all stay in groups of three or more and meet back at the bus in forty-five minutes.

I looked over at Keith to see if he would try to join our group. He came over and said, "Lexi, I'm so glad about your decision last night." I smiled and told him thanks.

"So where are you going to eat?" I asked.

"Let's all go get a burger together," he answered.

We started walking, and I realized that Dawn had moved to my other side so I could be next to Keith. I playfully pushed her on the shoulder and we laughed. We had a good time, but Keith's attention didn't feel as important to me as it had a short time ago.

When our group got back to the van, we had five minutes to spare. It didn't matter though because Will and a bunch of the guys had walked about a mile down the road to CiCi's Pizza. They were twenty minutes late, and Patty was not happy with them at all.

We finally got everyone in the van and Patty said, "Only two more hours and we will be home." Then it hit me. Home. My year of exile in Oklahoma was up next week. My aunt and uncle had said that I could stay as long as I wanted, but I didn't know what I wanted. I missed my friends. I even wanted to see my mom. However, it would be so strange to be home without Sarah.

In our letters, Amanda had told me that a couple of girls on the basketball team were talking about me. They were saying it was my fault about Sarah and that I had left because I was too scared to face them. Amanda said they had lost most of their games, and when she told them how well the team I was on out here had done, they were ticked.

They told her that if I came back I might as well not play because if I did they would quit. Amanda said that most of the group saying all of that weren't even starters. I wished I didn't care what they thought, but I did. How could I go home and face all of those people?

I started crying. I tried to stop. I didn't want to ruin the good time Dawn and the others were having, but I couldn't help it. This week had been so amazing and now, before we had even gotten off the van, I had started freaking out.

Dawn put her arms around me and whispered in my ear, "What's wrong?" I just shook my head side to side. I couldn't speak. She prayed in my ear that God would comfort me and help me calm down. Immediately, I felt the peace I had felt at church camp.

I turned and looked up at her. She was smiling so sweetly. I said, "I am supposed to go back home, but I don't know if I should."

Tears began to run down her face. "Do you want to go back?" she asked.

"I'm not sure. I like it here, but that is home. And my mom … we have a lot to work out. Amanda needs me, but I know if I hang around her I won't be strong enough to follow Jesus like I should. In some ways, I feel better here with all of you."

Dawn's eyes brightened up. "Remember the preacher who talked about what to do when you had two choices and neither one was a sin?" I couldn't remember right then so I shook my head no but gave her an expectant look.

"He said that is why being a Christian is a relationship and not a religion. God is always with us. We can talk to God and he will answer us like a friend does. He is our best friend. Let's pray and ask him to tell you what he wants you to do. If you do what he wants you to do, then everything will work out the way it should."

We bowed our heads and Dawn began to pray. She asked God to tell me if I should go back home or stay here. It was so strange because I could hear her, but there was another voice speaking to me on the inside. I knew it was Jesus, but I couldn't explain how. He told me he would be with me wherever I was. He told me that he loved me.

I looked up when Dawn finished praying, and I couldn't quit smiling. "What is it?" she asked. "Did he tell you already?"

"No, not yet," I said. "But I do know one thing. Whether I go back home or stay here, he told me he would be with me." Dawn hugged me. When we stopped hugging, I looked at Dawn and said, "Jesus is so good! I get it now. There is no guy on this earth that could make me feel this—"

"Joyful?"

"Yes, that's the word," I exclaimed. "Jesus is the love of my life!" Aunt Joanne had said she hoped coming to stay in Oklahoma would end up being a blessing to me. I couldn't wait to tell her how God had answered her prayer.

THE ART OF

SECRETS TO UNLOCK

EXECUTIVE

LEADERSHIP PERFORMANCE

COACHING

NADINE GREINER, PHD

PRESS

ATD Press is an internationally renowned source of insightful and practical information on talent development, training, and professional development.

All names, characters, places, or incidents references in *The Art of Executive Coaching: Secrets to Unlock Leadership Performance* are fictional, and any resemblance to actual persons, entities, places, events, or incidents is coincidental. Further, *The Art of Executive Coaching* summarizes the perspectives of the author and contributors only and does not constitute the opinion, policy, approval, or endorsement of ATD.

ATD Press
1640 King Street
Alexandria, VA 22314 USA

Ordering information: Books published by ATD Press can be purchased by visiting ATD's website at www.td.org/books or by calling 800.628.2783 or 703.683.8100.

Library of Congress Control Number: 2018947182
ISBN-10: 1-947308-79-3
ISBN-13: 978-1-947308-79-4
E-ISBN: 978-1-56286-550-4

ATD Press Editorial Staff
Director: Kristine Luecker
Manager: Melissa Jones
Community of Practice Manager, Senior Leaders & Executives: Ann Parker
Developmental Editor: Jack Harlow
Senior Associate Editor: Caroline Coppel
Text Design: Shirley Raybuck
Cover Design: Faceout Studio, Lindy Martin

Illustrations by Amber June Cross
Printed by Versa Press, East Peoria, IL

I dedicate this book to you.

*May you summon the courage to learn something new,
and may you build the resilience to sometimes fall,
pick yourself up, and learn even more.*

CONTENTS

FOREWORD

IN MY 30 YEARS OF FORTUNE 500 consulting experience, I've often served as a coach—it's unavoidable. When projects are initiated and plans implemented, key people need coaching in how best to garner support, delegate work, and assign accountability.

All too often, the traditional view of "coaching" is remedial: Someone isn't measuring up, so they need help in the form of an expert—the coach. However, the traditional view is wrong, because that's the minority role of coaching. I equate it to flying on an airplane primarily to enjoy the food, rather than seeking a safe, on-time arrival where you intend to go.

If you consider people at the top of their game, yesterday or today—Frank Sinatra in song, Meryl Streep on film, Denzel Washington onstage, Tom Brady on the football field, Jack Welch at GE—they all had or have coaches. Strong people realize there is constantly a need for new ideas, diverse suggestions, and outright improvement. The best seek out coaching, because they're usually head and shoulders above the competition to begin with. (And, sometimes, there *are* some dysfunctional behaviors that accompany highly positive ones, which should be culled.)

As of late, having a coach has evolved to possess a caché. Thus, we have "coaching universities" (who certified the certifiers?) and "life coaches" who, presumably, coach anyone about everything. After all, life doesn't come with an instruction book.

In a volatile world, such coaching is more important than ever, largely because we tend to default, if we don't understand coaching, to the remedial, instead of helping those who can help us most—the all-stars!

Nadine Greiner is the perfect person to help coaches to fulfill these vital roles. She doesn't hold "certificates" of completion from a pseudo-university, but rather quite real PhDs in organization development and clinical psychology. (That's what certifies the certifiers!) She has been a CEO, a clinician, and a consultant. She grew up in a war zone, so she can certainly handle the boardroom.

This is a rare book oriented toward improving coaching with an exclusive look at the traits and skills required to help people to help people. It is neither mercenary nor aimed at marketing (I know this because I'm the one who wrote *Million Dollar Coaching*). This is a special book for specialists. It is undiluted and not diverted by a focus on other specialties or helping professions.

With all my experience, I learned by reading it. That's because I know I need a great coach, too. With *The Art of Executive Coaching*, you now have one as well.

—Alan Weiss, PhD
Author, *Million Dollar Consulting, Threescore and More,*
and More Than 60 Other Books

PREFACE

ARE YOU A PRACTICING executive coach? Do you want to become one? Are you a coaching consultant who wants the new, exciting challenges of helping executives deliver transformative results? If you are, you've come to the right place. This book was written to inform, entertain, and inspire you. Through the nine stories presented here and the practical advice sprinkled throughout, you will follow an experienced coach as she guides her clients through the challenging process of change. Some of these clients are high performing and brilliant, lined up for their next promotions. Others are struggling in one way or another, in danger of being fired or disliked by their teams, and a few have placed their entire enterprise at risk.

You will see these individuals struggle to change their personal and leadership styles—and triumph. You will watch as they overcome their resistance, illuminate their blind spots, and adopt new ways of relating and managing. And you'll see how these personal changes affect entire departments and even whole organizations.

By the end of the book, you will understand *why* coaching works so well—why it is able to achieve such dramatic results in a relatively short time. And you will begin to learn *how* coaching works—techniques that are most effective in bringing about a positive outcome.

What Does an Executive Coach Do?

Even for those with experience working with executives and coaching others, it's important to clarify the purpose of executive coaching—and how it differs from the everyday coaching that occurs between co-workers or between managers and direct reports. Simply put, executive coaching is an on-target, tailored, expedited, and effective way of boosting leaders. It is a formal engagement in which an executive coach works with a client in a series of confidential and dynamic meetings designed to establish and achieve clear goals.

Similar to other executive and leadership development processes, there is no one-size-fits-all approach to executive coaching. There is no step-by-step procedure that will work, without fail, for each new client. Intuitively, that makes sense. While executives might share some traits or habits, they and their work are unique. The challenges they face are unlike those of another executive at the same size firm, in the same industry, down the same street. That's part of what makes the business of executive coaching thrilling—but also increasingly in demand. No executive is perfect; there's always room for improvement—improvement that can have impressive effects on the business, its employees, and its customers.

Because of the essential individuality of executives, I've written each chapter to present the story of a client who is experiencing a different type of challenge at work. Each story demonstrates the different approaches you can employ in working with your clients. That said, there are certain processes and procedures that any executive coach should consider deploying and can enable anyone with a passion for coaching to become a more effective executive coach.

While my own clients often appreciate the immediate value I add (having held the most senior positions within an organization myself), a coach need not necessarily have held a particular position to be successful, especially if you follow a structured process as described here. As an expert in human performance, I designed a process of executive coaching that has four distinct steps. This scope of work or contract can be applied to most executive coaching engagements: assessment, goals, implementation, and review.

1. **Assessment:** Before you can suggest advice or create a development plan with a client, you must compile information, such as a 360-degree feedback assessment. This process involves interviewing the client's colleagues about the client's strengths and areas of potential development. Assessments can also include psychological and business profiles and other such tools.

2. **Goals:** Based on the assessment's results, you will set goals with your client. These goals are built around developing certain competencies, such as developing and operationalizing strategy, executive presence, confidence, critical thinking, problem solving, project oversight, setting priorities, managing through systems, team building, and interpersonal ease. In situations where appropriate, they might then forward the goals to a superior.

3. **Implementation:** During your sessions, you will use coaching solutions to help the client meet their coaching goals. Such solutions can include encouragement, reflective listening, questioning, exploration, guidance, reframing, compassion, challenging thinking, and support. There will be homework, of course. Tools for attaining goals might include reading, learning new skills, course work, practicing new skills, rehearsing or role-playing, viewing video of the coaching client, and shadowing.

4. **Review:** Before you can tie a bow on the coaching engagement, you need to compile any post-coaching results

and feedback to make sure the client achieved all their coaching goals. This is also an opportunity to provide final recommendations before you part ways.

An important aspect of executive coaching is confidentiality. The goals of the coaching engagement are often sent to the manager or the board of directors, but how we obtain those goals and everything else we discuss is strictly confidential between the coaching client and coach. I usually work with the client actively for four to six months—they have unlimited access to me during that time—and the contract specifies a set project fee.

Who Am I?

You might be wondering about my background, or what makes me a person with secrets worth sharing. Well, I am an executive coach with doctorates in organization development and clinical psychology, and I teach in master's and doctoral programs. I've held high-level positions in private and publicly traded companies. I first served as a CEO at the age of 38, so I understand the experience of leadership in a very intimate way.

This unique combination of psychology, business, and executive leadership has contributed to my success. I believe we are placed in this world to learn from one another. I have been blessed with powerful mentors, and I am eager to share my knowledge and secrets. During my 30 years of executive coaching, I've helped more than a thousand clients become more effective and fulfilled in their jobs. I also prepare a very select few individuals to become executive coaches themselves, and they in turn change the professional lives of many more executives.

Business books can be long and wordy. I wanted to offer a short book packed with solutions—and I expressly wanted to write a business book that was an enjoyable read with plenty of tools, techniques, tips, and secrets for the reader. I learned long ago that people learn best when they are relaxed and having fun.

What's in This Book

In these chapters, you will find:

- A short, animated description of the coaching client and their challenges. The executive coach is referred to as Alice Well; however, this is a fictional name, as are the names of the coaching clients.
- Examples of the four distinct phases of coaching: assessment, goals, implementation, and review. Each phase has a distinct set of tools and processes, laid out in a simple, easy-to-follow fashion.
- A diagnostic picture based on psychological profiles and interviews with colleagues.
- Coaching goals formulated with the client along with remedies and homework.
- A "Tips for the Reader" section, with activities and approaches that are known to yield positive results.
- A review of the coaching engagement's results.
- A "Why Coaching Matters" section, in which coaching clients speak directly and openly about the impact of coaching.

The Art of Executive Coaching presents a number of remarkable success stories. If you enjoy being inspired by happy outcomes to troublesome situations, you will enjoy this book.

The Power of Coaching for the Coaching Client

Do you find yourself baffled by a colleague? Or surprised at how you react? Could you use some tips on how to navigate the culture at work? Perhaps you want to provide value within your company?

Most of us work in some kind of organization. We might have taken training and earned degrees to prepare us for our jobs. But nobody taught us how to handle some of the personalities we come across at work or how to conduct ourselves in puzzling new situations. Through dramatic situations and humor, this short, entertaining book illustrates how you can be more effective and happy at work.

The coaching tips, tricks, and goals you're going to read about have proven results. Each chapter provides secrets that will help you stay in control of your job, your career, and your future. In addition, they'll each give you a leg up in handling different personalities and difficult situations at work. So, this book is written for anyone who wants to learn how to navigate more skillfully through challenging situations in the workplace.

It will also be of interest to managers at all levels who want to learn more about executive coaching. Coaching is a hot topic these days, and there are good reasons for this: A *Public Personnel Management* study shows that when training is combined with coaching, individuals increase their productivity by an average of 88 percent, compared with just 22 percent with training alone (Olivero, Bane, and Kopelman 1997).

The benefits of successful coaching, however, are not limited to the individual being coached; they can apply to their entire department and, by extension, the whole company. Numerous studies have shown a return on investment of 500 to 800 percent on the cost of coaching, in addition to substantial intangible benefits to the business (Anderson 2001; ICF et al. 2009; McGovern et al. 2001). The stories in this book reveal these dramatic collateral benefits as the executives change their leadership styles.

Your Journey

I can't promise you will always have your dream job for the rest of your life. But, whether you are an executive coach or not, I can prom- ise you that you will increase your choices and your chances of being effective and happy at work by using the secrets, methods, tips, and tricks presented in this book. And I promise you will smile when you read about the fascinating personalities in each chapter.

To summarize, this book will do three things: inform you about executive coaching, provide you with tips and insights on how to negotiate difficult situations in your workplace, and entertain you with inspiring stories.

ACKNOWLEDGMENTS

I HAVE SOME DEAR people to thank. Firstly, thank you to my mentor Sandra Boeschen for believing in me wholeheartedly, and for developing me step by step. And thank you to Alan Weiss for shaping my career. Sam Case, Vineeta Hiranandani, and Lisa Earl, your rigorous feedback encouraged me and shaped this book; thank you. Melissa Umeda, Kevin Nerius, and Charles Cao, my Zumba tribe, I appreciate you for supporting me, mind, body, and soul. The Association for Talent Development shaped my early development and that of my team, and continues to be a joy to work with. Queen of Everything, I owe it all to you. And finally, thank you to the love of my life, mon Petit Prince.

All proceeds from this book go to the protection and love of animals.

1

THE BULLY

Even immensely successful sales directors need coaching. Tom, a sales director for a hospitality and tourism company in the United States, was known for tripling sales during his first year on the job. Although Tom outperformed his peers thanks to his single-minded focus on results and the company benefited tremendously from this success, he had some aggressive behaviors that hurt people—and himself. Dr. Alice Well's task was to soften Tom's behaviors while allowing his high performance to continue.

TOM CALLED ALICE UP one day and said he'd like to work with her. His colleague in marketing had gone through her coaching process, made changes, and gotten promoted. Managing West Coast sales for a hospitality and tourism firm, Tom had done well for himself, but he too wanted a promotion. He aspired to become the global vice president of sales. Perhaps Alice could help him get there.

Week 1: Focus
Tom's secretary showed Alice into his office.

"He'll be right in," she said.

One of the walls was decorated with framed photographs, large and small. Some were of racing cars, others of men dressed in racing gear. One was autographed: "To Tom. Follow that line! Shel McGuire." Alice recognized the name from a Ford commercial.

Next to it was a large photo of what looked like a cross between a sports car and a racing car.

"That's one of five," said a voice behind her.

She turned to face a tall, tanned, fit man who smiled and stuck out his hand. "I'm Tom. And you must be Dr. Alice Well," he said. He had thick, dark hair and nice features, but there was a certain hardness to his face.

She took his hand and smiled back. "One of five?"

"That's an Aston Martin 419, 1992. They only made five prototypes. Never took it into production. They should've. I took it down to the track last Sunday. Sucker did 150 on the straights."

Nodding, Alice racked her brain for any tiny bit about auto racing and classic sports cars. She'd never been into cars or shop growing up, but having worked with many übercompetitive male executives, she'd picked up bits here and here.

"Have you ever raced?" she asked.

He sighed and shook his head. "Should've started when I was a kid. Big regret. I'd love to be part of a racing team. Would you like to sit down?"

He motioned her to a low-backed chair and went to sit behind his large, uncluttered desk. The desk—and all the furniture—had an air of expensive chic. Alice couldn't help noticing the large mirror on the desk as well.

"What attracts you to racing?" Alice asked, settling in.

"That's easy," he said. "Excitement, teamwork . . . and focus."

"Focus?"

He pointed to the autographed picture on the wall. "I asked Shel what his secret was—how he's won 57 races—and he said, 'Focus. You've got to be totally focused when you're driving.' I haven't raced, but I've driven tracks at some pretty good speeds. When you're totally focused, everything else goes away. It's just you and the car and the track."

Sensing an opportunity to link racing to the matter at hand, Alice prodded, "You've been driving this sales department for a few years, and I understand that you've done very well. Is this the same focus that you're talking about?"

"Absolutely. It's my job to stay focused on the numbers and to keep everybody else focused. That's why sales have doubled in the last four years."

"That's very impressive. Could you say more about how you achieve this focus?"

"Sure. I'll give you an example. I just had a meeting with one of my sales team—Annie. Now, I like Annie, and she's usually one of my top performers. But over the last two months, her numbers have gone south, so I called her into my office and told her that she had to bring them up. She said there was a personal matter, and I said I don't get paid for listening to personal matters. I get paid—and she gets paid—for focusing on sales. That's what I mean by focus."

"OK. Thank you for that. Now, an important question: What do you hope to gain from our work together?"

In cases with a client who reached out to her directly rather than a company that requested she coach an executive, Alice liked to hear what the client wanted from the coaching engagement. That way she could measure the difference between what her clients wanted at the outset of coaching and what they ended up needing after the assessment. Self-awareness can vary widely in executives.

"I told you about my friend, Steve, who worked with you. He's a VP now, and he credits you with helping him get there. I want to move ahead too." He paused. "And there's something else. I don't know, I've had a lot of wins here, but I feel I'm missing something."

"OK, moving ahead and discovering what you might be missing," Alice confirmed. "In a couple of weeks, we'll focus on a few more specific goals that we can work on together. Right now, I'd like to go over with you what the coaching process entails."

Weeks 2-3: No Bonus

As she approached Tom's office, Alice could hear him cursing and swearing behind the closed door.

"What's going on?" she asked as she stepped in.

"Those suckers! I *creamed* the competition! They don't even see that! How can they not give me my damn bonus for Q4?"

"Would you like to explain? I thought the numbers were up for Q4."

"They are. They *are* up!"

"Then I don't understand."

Alice, now seated, reached for her notebook in her briefcase and winced; she'd scraped her hand after taking a fall in the parking lot. She noticed a little blood smear on the corner of the notebook. Tom did, too.

"Don't touch that chair," Tom ordered, not missing a beat or offering to get her a napkin. "They say my comp level was set so high that I missed the bonus."

"Who set the level so high?"

Tom blew out a bunch of air like a tire going flat and collapsed in his chair, defeated.

"I did," he said. "It was meant to be a challenge. Nobody got their bonus. The jerks should give it to me anyway. The numbers are up, the competition is down. . . . Damn!"

Alice had experience coaching sales executives and knew the compensation structure all too well: Tom had arranged it to benefit the top performers, with everyone competing against one another. Unlike other departments, in sales all boats don't rise with the overall increase in productivity. Tom had been caught by his own creation, and he didn't like it one bit. Alice made a note to talk about this compensation structure later, when he'd had time to cool down.

Up to this point, Tom had been nothing but upbeat about his work situation, despite passionately targeting the promotion he felt he deserved. Today, Alice witnessed firsthand what people had said about Tom's bad temper and his lack of compassion. His response to her bloody hand was not concern, but a gruff order to keep it off his fancy chair.

All this and more came out in the assessments, the first phase of the coaching process. As part of the 360-degree assessment, which happened during week 2, Alice had interviewed 10 people around Tom about his leadership style, personality, and competency. In addition, she had conducted a psychological profile, an evaluation of how he dealt with conflict, and a self-assessment.

According to those interviewed for the 360-degree feedback, Tom was mean and bad tempered. No compassion. He came down hard on people in the Monday sales meetings if their numbers were down, wanting only "winners" to work for him. Mixed in was some admiration for his ability to increase sales, particularly from the CEO; but mostly, resentment and animosity at the way he treated his direct reports and those who reported to them. Unsurprisingly, turnover was high in his unit due to his take-no-prisoners attitude.

By the time of their fourth session, Tom had read her writeup of the assessments, including the 360. They were ready to discuss next steps.

Week 4: Management by Volume

When Alice came into his office, Tom was gazing out the window. He didn't respond to her greeting, so she sat down, got out her notebook, and waited.

"People don't like me, Dr. Alice," he said finally, still looking out the window. "That 360. . . . They say I don't care about them, I don't have any compassion, all I care about are the numbers."

Turning to face her, he continued, "I didn't think I got paid to care about them. I get paid for one thing: to make this company the top seller. I mean, here they've got great jobs, bonuses, perks—and they want compassion? I don't get it. I just don't get it."

He shook his head. "They say they hate Monday mornings. But I have to tell them who's behind and who's ahead. I'm the ass-kicker here. And if they don't like the way I do that . . . well, shit! I'm not here to coddle them. They need to grow up, get real."

Alice leaned forward. "I'd like to focus for a few minutes on your personal history. I understand that you worked for your dad in his bakery when you were a boy. How was that?"

"My dad was OK, but he expected the whole family to get up at three in the morning and work. I had to go to school too, of course. The bakery—it was just something you did. It was the family business. Nobody questioned it."

"Then, when you were 17, you went to work for an electronics firm?"

"Yeah, I learned about electronics and I learned about how business works."

"How would you describe the management style of your boss there?"

"Oh, I would say his style of management was essentially . . . yelling."

"Yelling?"

"Yeah. If he wanted you to do something, he'd yell at you. If you didn't do it right, he'd yell louder."

"Management by volume," she smiled.

"When I was a young guy, I thought it was kind of cool," he said, walking over to the window. "You yell, and everybody jumps. But he was a mean son of a bitch. He thought everybody was trying to take advantage of him."

"How much of your management style do you think you absorbed from him?"

Tom looked back and nodded. "I think I probably swallowed the whole enchilada. But now it's a part of me and I don't think I can get rid of it. I mean, it would be nice if people liked me, but this is who I am, and it's probably not going to change."

"I think you're going to be surprised," she said. "But right now, I do see the resemblance. Your first boss, always an influential figure, was totally adversarial. He saw everybody as potential enemies, even his own staff. You have the same tendency. You say competition is to be 'creamed,' your sales team needs to be yelled at if their performance is down, your superiors are against you because they didn't give you your bonus last quarter. . . ."

"But the thing is, it works! I've doubled sales since I've been here. You can't argue with success."

Yes, you can, Alice thought to herself. More than once she'd been called on to help a company where a new manager had come in and made a lot of changes that initially looked good, but left a lot of wreckage in their wake. And the toxic culture they'd created sometimes lasted for years.

Out loud, she said, "For starters, your homework this week is to seek out three managers whose style is more low key and inclusive, and describe what types of results they get. When you were 17, your first impression of what leadership and management was all about came from this electronics guy. There's no blame there. We all get things laid on us when we're young, but we don't want to be held back by the past. If you really want to move into another way of doing things, we can work on that, and I think you'll find your success will continue."

Weeks 5-7: Coaching Goals

Over the next three weeks, Alice and Tom worked to set and draft three goals. Although his original list was a collection of to-do items and tasks, he quickly grasped the concept of competencies. They reviewed the 360-degree assessment comments and discussed the profiles again with an eye to creating goals for their next phase of coaching work together.

The goals they landed on were straightforward but ambitious:

- Improve interpersonal skills.
- Focus on customers.
- Build effective teams.

Improve Interpersonal Skills

Tom could be aggressive and results oriented, with little awareness of how he affected people. And, because he had been so successful, he believed his way was the right way.

Remedies and homework included:

- Avoid knee-jerk reactions and keep composure while listening. Then, with an understanding of the situation, form a conclusion, communicate a plan, and act on the plan.
- Practice active listening. At the end of a meeting, close by using language that shows you heard what the other person said and ask for affirmation. (For example: "So what you're saying is . . ." or " . . . Did I get that right?")

- Adapt communications to audiences. Mentoring a direct report and presenting at a speaking engagement, for instance, demand different styles of communication.
- Build a purposeful rapport with colleagues at all levels.

Focus on Customers

Tom had to start by building his listening skills; he was often "too busy" to listen.

Remedies and homework included:

- Spend time in the field with sales staff, build rapport with the team, listen to customers' business needs, and learn to anticipate future needs with the team.
- Diagram the links or processes between employee and customer engagement. This could result in new training and tools.

Build Effective Teams

Tom didn't reward individual members of his sales team in an effective way. Because he had a focused mindset, he was only now learning to foster open dialogue and manage process.

Remedies and homework included:

- Engage the team in building common goals and mindsets with a game plan.
- Instill the practice of anticipating customer needs and employing innovation and process improvement to meet those needs.
- Mentor and promote two managers.

Executives might offer reason after reason for why they can't move ahead: too much work, it's not the right time, they don't know where to even begin. Tom fit the same mold, but he embraced his goals and committed to doing his homework.

Weeks 8–10: Star Performers

Tom was in a good mood. He had flown to North Carolina for a NASCAR race over the weekend and was full of talk about the event. His guy, Shel, had come in third, but Tom talked only about his great performance, the speed of the pit crew, and the near-disasters.

When he slowed down a bit, Alice jumped in. "I'm curious. Suppose your guy had a losing streak. Would the owner and the sponsor get on his case—tell him that his job is on the line?"

"No, they would never do that, not on this team. That's not their style. Everybody supports everybody else, from management on down. Also, it might not be him. Maybe they got a new car. Maybe the car chief made some bad decisions about the engine or the tires. Maybe Shel's just having a few bad months. Drivers are like any athlete. They can have a bad day, or even a bad year. Or, like they said about the Chicago Cubs, 'Anybody can have a bad century.'"

They both laughed, and Alice rejoiced at the laughter. Laughter always makes everything go more easily with clients, and it's a sign that they feel comfortable. Up to now, she had shared few laughs with Tom.

"Besides," he continued, "they wouldn't come down on him because he's their star. You don't come down on your star."

Alice leaned forward. "It seems to me that there are a number of stars around here. The members of your sales team are your drivers. They're the ones who make it all work with your guidance. In the world of sales, both you and your team are stars. Your performance over the last four years is star quality."

Tom paced behind his desk. "You're suggesting that maybe I shouldn't come down on people so much. But what about consequences? There have to be consequences if you have a bad quarter. They have to know that I'm not pleased with them. They have to know their performance is shitty."

"But you say that a losing streak for a driver might come from several different things. Your team's performance might be affected by other things too, like new products, competitors, or personal things. You told me Annie had a bad quarter. At that time, her son was in the hospital with spinal meningitis. He almost died."

He stopped pacing and looked at Alice in surprise. "Aw, damn! Why didn't she tell me?"

"She tried, but you didn't want to hear it. She didn't pursue it because she didn't think you cared. She's afraid of losing her job like everybody else. She was afraid that if she told you that she was spending more time with her son and was afraid he might die, that you might let her go, and she needs this job."

Tom gazed out the window for a long time. Finally, he turned back to Alice. "You've given me a lot to think about."

She nodded. "I know. But you're handling it. I want to commend you for the work you've been doing. You've been moving ahead rapidly on the goals we set. And you're doing it all at the same time you have this demanding job."

He gave her one of his rare smiles. "Thanks for that, Dr. Alice. I needed that."

From day one, when Tom talked about the racing team, Alice knew she had something she could use. Her approach to coaching was to be open to using whatever interests or habits she discovered to help guide clients in the direction they wanted to go. The way she saw it, she had some key things going for her:

- the racing team—the teamwork and the way they supported one another, and Tom's admiration for them
- Tom's ambition for a promotion and more recognition
- his goal to discover what was missing in his life
- her skill in helping clients work through their blind spots.

On the challenging side, they had:

- The model of his first boss. The impact of that example was still with him 25 years later.
- Tom's resistance to change. He feared that he would become a different person.
- Ironically, his success in doubling sales. Because this had been accomplished before Alice started to coach Tom, he feared that changing his personal style would negatively affect his performance.
- His uncertainty about how to move ahead.

Also on the positive side were Tom's intelligence and ability. Most of Alice's clients were very accomplished people; if she could get their talents and abilities working for change—and she usually could—she knew the outcome would be a good one.

Over the next two weeks, they discussed ways to achieve Tom's goal of expanding his presence in the community through public speaking. They discussed the best venues, how he might present himself given his new insights, and what topics to speak on. Ultimately, he decided to wait until the coaching was over before pursuing speaking engagements.

Weeks 11-14: As If

By week 11, Tom and Alice were back to interpersonal matters. Tom was still worried that if he changed his style with his team, their performance would suffer. He pointed out that they became the best in the industry when he was his old aggressive self. Alice acknowledged his concerns, but assured him that she had never seen performance go down as a result of changes made from coaching; usually, it went up.

But Tom was also worried that any attempts to become "Mr. Nice Guy" would ring false—that he would come across as phony. That's

Tips for the Reader

Do you recognize one of your coaching clients in Tom? If so, per-haps encourage your client to act *as if* until the client can develop a more authentic tone or manner. Ask them to talk like, and adopt the behaviors of, a more considerate and kind person (maybe even a role model) until it becomes second-nature to them.

But what if the past is holding your client back, like how Tom felt hamstrung by his experience being ordered around by his first manager? Encourage your client to experiment with *responding* instead of *reacting*. You might say, "Don't go with your first in-stinct; instead, take a few seconds to consider your many options of how you might respond. And, if you can't think of a good way to reply, you might want to keep your contribution to a minimum until you can."

Encourage your client to see their customers as partners, not as conquests. Executives and senior leaders have important busi-ness and perhaps sales goals and are motivated to meet them; but the key to long-term success is partnering with customers to better understand and predict their needs. This will ensure your coaching client is ahead of product or service development, and it will make for very appreciative customers who enjoy the partner-ship and the attention to their needs.

If your client works with people who behave like Tom, en-courage your client to be a team player because success builds on success. Encourage your client to boost their colleagues' sense of self and to collaborate in a way that makes the colleague look good. Their colleagues' self-image is fragile, despite that learned harsh manner; if your client can reassure them, your client might be better able to partner with them. Most coaching clients work in ecosystems, and changing the coaching client internally is not sufficient for success. Helping the coaching client set the tone of interactions, and hence the internal dynamics of a colleague, is a great goal.

when Alice introduced him to the "as if" strategy. For the next few weeks, in the privacy of his office, he would practice saying things like, "Can I help you?" or, "Sorry," or friendly things like, "How was your weekend?" He would say them *as if* he was really concerned; then, after a while, he would begin to sound authentic, and finally he would begin to feel authentic. She assured him they would rehearse until he felt ready to take this out of the office.

Week 15: "Please Do More"

Alice had watched Tom rehearse his interpersonal skills in the privacy of his office. Soon, he had begun to use them out in the company environment.

On the way up to Tom's office, she passed Annie in the hall.

"Hi, Dr. Alice," she chirped, smiling.

"Hello, Annie. How's your son?"

"He's much better. Doctors say he can go back to school next week."

"That's wonderful!"

Annie moved closer and lowered her tone. "You know, somebody else asked me about Ethan yesterday. It was Tom! Tom stopped me in the hall and asked how my boy was. And he was really asking—not just being polite." She touched Alice's arm. "Whatever you're doing with Tom, please do more. It's working."

Weeks 16-20: Part of the Team

By week 16, Tom's practice on interpersonal skills, with Alice's encouragement, was already beginning to bear fruit.

When she came in for their next session, Tom was all smiles—a big departure from his usual impassive expression.

"OK, Dr. Alice, I just accomplished one of my goals. I just realized what it is I've been missing—that nagging feeling we've talked about.

"For years, I've been wondering if I should just chuck all this and join a racing team. I've seen the way that Shel works with his team—everybody knows their job, and they all support each other, from the pit crew to the management. I thought, *What a great thing to be part of a team like that!*"

He shook his head in disbelief. "Now, I'm beginning to see that I can be part of this sales team. I've been using the stuff we've been practicing, and it's actually working. People respond to me differently. So yesterday at the meeting, I suddenly realized, *Oh, this is what I've been missing. This is what I want!*"

"This is wonderful, Tom. This is a big win!"

"What gets me is that it was so close all the time. All I needed to do was shift the way I relate to people, and suddenly I'm not the bad guy anymore. I'm part of the team. A couple of times, I got annoyed at something, but then I remembered what you said—that I have a choice of how to respond. So, instead of getting pissed off, I responded more calmly. I still disagreed, but without getting all riled up."

Over the next few weeks, with Alice's help, Tom continued to hone his interpersonal skills. He watched videos on how to recognize other people's body language and how to be aware of what his own body language was saying. He also began to employ his hard-won skills to improve his relationships with customers and his sales team.

Tom had thought of customers in terms of predator-prey. Alice reintroduced the concept of customers-as-partners: listening carefully to what they need and what issues they have, then showing them how your products can help them deal with those issues. This involves a constant give-and-take; but in the end, it results in loyal customers who view the company as a helpful partner and collaborator. Of course, this wasn't all new to Tom—he had simply chosen to dismiss it as an ineffective, less impressive way to make a sale.

In addition, Tom began to work with two members of his sales team on developing their leadership skills. Alice had pointed out that mentoring these new leaders would help him enhance his own leadership skills. It also worked to ease his tendency to micromanage and allowed other managers to take some of the burden, freeing him up to do other things.

With things going well for Tom, Alice suggested they bring the coaching engagement to a close. She reassured him that if he needed support, reminders, or advice on a particular matter, as her former clients often did, all he had to do was call.

Week 21: Blind Spots

Alice had one final session with Tom.

"Dr. Alice, I'm a smart guy, right?"

"Yes, everybody knows that."

"Well, how come I didn't see what I see now? Now, I feel like part of the team instead of just being the ass-kicker. Do you know people actually smile when they see me now?"

"And that feels good, doesn't it?"

"Yes, it does. But how come nobody told me this before? It seems like such an obvious thing."

She smiled. "To borrow a favorite phrase of somebody I know, 'They don't get paid to do that.' I'm the one who gets paid to do that. And, to answer your first question about why you didn't see what you were doing, people have blind spots. I've worked with some super-smart people, including you, and a lot of them had blind spots. I find those blind spots and set up strategies to work through them."

He shook his head. "With some people, you have to start from scratch . . . like with the interpersonal stuff."

Why Coaching Matters

At the end of each coaching session or engagement, it's helpful to ask your coaching clients, "What stands out to you about our time together?" This can enable you to gain more understanding about their experience and what you can do to refine the process as an executive coach.

For example, to Alice, Tom mentioned that he felt bad for having been a jerk to his team over the years. Now, he wants to see them grow. Through coaching, Tom seemed to have developed greater self-awareness of how he came across to his team and, as a result, had some guilt and remorse. This was a good sign and helpful as a moral compass, but he needed to continue to apply these newfound skills to be a better leader and forgive himself for the past. Alice made a mental note to check on that if they stayed in touch.

"You never gave up on me," Tom said to Alice. "Life is strange and short, and people who stick by you are rare." Some executives and leaders grow to feel isolated as they climb the corporate ladder, with fewer people to lean on for support and more looking to use them for their own advantage. While Alice did find herself frustrated at times by Tom's insensitivity, she hung in there with him, like any successful executive coach needs to. He felt that, and it mattered to him. You'll find yourself working with many clients who are struggling with some personal or professional baggage, so you almost need to have a soft spot for leaders like Tom.

"Yes, you worked hard on that. You worked hard on everything; that's why you're in a different place. Some things seem obvious now, but they didn't a few months ago. Where you are now is due to months of work."

Tom did indeed call Alice up and email her a few times, but it was mostly to report good news. The practice of treating customers as partners was strengthening connections with the company's customers—

and this partnership approach to customers was the executive coach's secret to Tom's success. The mentoring of new leaders was enhancing Tom's own reputation as an accomplished leader, and the new managers were contributing their skills. He was doing more public speaking and including some of the themes they had worked on together. This was another case of a client who sought coaching for one reason, but was able to advance in several areas while enhancing the company's performance.

With Alice's help, Tom was more enthusiastic about work again, about his team smashing their performance record in the last quarter, than about getting a promotion. The joys of coaching lie in sticking with clients through the difficult coaching process and never giving up on their potential.

Summary

Tom got high marks for his performance as sales manager, but very low marks for his interactions with people. Although Tom was sometimes doubtful that he could change, he worked hard at reaching the goals he set with Alice. During their time together, Tom grew in self-awareness and made significant changes to his leadership style. He began to treat customers as partners instead of targets to take advantage of, and he learned more effective ways of engaging, leading, and rewarding his team—all of which ultimately increased sales.

Takeaways:
- As a result of skilled coaching, people with extreme behaviors can change, even when they doubt they can.
- In addition to making the workplace more pleasant, personal shifts often result in improvements to the bottom line.

2

THE INTROVERTED COO

Madeline was the chief operating officer (COO) in a small tech company. Her performance was excellent, but her employer, a large venture capitalist (VC) firm, wanted Alice's help to learn more about her: Who was she? What were her talents? Where would be the best place for her? To the VCs, she was a woman of mystery. Alice, armed with her evaluation tools, set out to discover more about this enigmatic person. While the evaluation was for Madeline's employer, Alice had seen the benefits of coaching extend beyond its original purpose—and even result in a promotion. Unfortunately, Madeline didn't see it that way at first.

"WE DON'T KNOW WHAT TO MAKE of this lady, Alice. She's obviously got talent, but how do we optimize that talent? Right now, she's COO in one of our smaller companies and she's doing fine, but I wonder if she's reached her ceiling or if she's got more to offer. The thing is, she's kind of—uh—understated. She doesn't speak much in meetings and she's not real forthcoming in general. So we need to know the who, what, and where of this person."

Vince, a partner in a large VC firm with a portfolio of growing tech companies, often called in Alice when he needed executive help. In the past,

he'd asked her to assess the whole management team of a company his firm was looking to invest in. In these cases, often it was just the CFO and Alice working together; the CFO reported out on the money portfolio, while she evaluated the talent portfolio and recommended where to place that talent.

This task was different. Vince wanted an assessment of a specific person in a company his firm already owned.

While Vince and the other partners were familiar with most of the management team, as Vince said, they were having trouble figuring out who Madeline was, what specific talents she possessed, and where to place her. In stepped Alice.

Week 1: A Rocky Start

An administrative assistant knocked and let Alice into Madeline's office. It was their first meeting, and Alice had emailed Madeline to outline the nature of the coaching engagement.

Sitting behind a desk cluttered with papers and folders, Madeline pointed to a chair in front. Alice sat down. She prided herself on reading body language, but anybody could have noticed that Madeline wasn't pleased to have her there. Madeline was maybe in her late 40s, medium height, brown hair, and attractive, although it was evident that she spent very little time on her appearance. The sparsely furnished office looked a bit shabby. She sat stiffly in her chair with a stern expression on her face.

"Did you get my email?" Alice asked.

"I scanned it," Madeline replied briskly. "Look, I do my job here and I do it well. I don't see why they want me to take all these tests and have me 'evaluated.'"

"I understand your concerns, but I think I can explain. . . ."

"It's an invasion of privacy." Madeline's annoyance couldn't have been clearer.

"I'm here for you as much as for the VCs," Alice started. "They want you in a position that matches your skills. This evaluation will benefit them, of course, but it will also be good for you. It's possible you'll have the opportunity to move to a new position that would be a better fit. You'll be working at the top of your game and using your best talents. This can be a real win-win situation."

Madeline considered this. "So, you'll talk to me and give me some tests, and then. . . ." She paused.

"Then I write up a complete assessment and we talk about it. We can go over all the profiles and the assessment in detail. You'll have copies to keep. Then, finally, I give the assessment to the owners."

"And they'll decide where I should go?"

"They'll present you with options and negotiate with you. This whole thing is never out of your hands. You'll have input at every step."

Alice knew that many executives resist coaching because they fear losing control of their situation. They want to be reassured decisions won't be made for them, overtly or covertly, particularly by an outsider. This last statement seemed to mollify Madeline. She was silent for a while, then nodded. "All right, I think I see the bigger picture. What's the procedure now?"

Alice breathed an inward sigh of relief. "Here's how we'll proceed. I'll forward you some confidential profiles for you to take when you have some uninterrupted time, and I will set up times to interview some of your colleagues."

Weeks 2-4: A Woman of Mystery (and Talent)

Over the next few weeks, Madeline participated in the evaluation—grudgingly at first, but less so as time went on. Occasionally, Alice had clients ask endless questions and voice countless concerns at the first meeting. It is human nature, on some level, to push back against having to adjust your regular routine. As an executive coach, Alice had to quickly find what issues might exist and address them up front, positively and fully.

This sometimes required that Alice show a coaching client some final reports of previously assessed executives to secure buy-in. While it's rare for clients to outright refuse to start the engagement, Alice had heard horror stories from colleagues at industry conferences. For the most part, she could overcome their ambivalence by helping clients see the upside, and how it might improve their overall standing.

Alice prepared various assessments for Madeline, including a psychological profile, an evaluation of leadership skills, and a self-assessment. Meanwhile, Alice set out to interview Madeline's co-workers. By the time of their next meeting, Madeline had read the results of the tests and the 360-degree assessment.

"So, Dr. Alice, I'm a woman of mystery. An enigma to all and everyone."

"What are your reactions to learning this?" Alice replied, smiling. She noted that Madeline now appeared interested and engaged. "How does this make you feel?"

"Mixed. On the one hand, I *am* a very private person. On the other hand, I don't want to appear aloof or cold, like some people said. I know that I'm an introvert, as the psych profile confirmed, but that doesn't mean I have to be unfriendly, does it?"

"No, it certainly doesn't. Many of my clients are introverted. They enjoy a few select people over crowds, but most have great social skills. One of the things the psych profile helps with is determining what kind of position would be best for you. For example, an introvert might not be the best choice for sales or business development."

Madeline nodded. "I was pleased that the respondents saw me as a skilled administrator and said I know how to deal with disputes. I've never been afraid of conflict. If there's a conflict, I'll find a way to resolve the issue. I think that's one of my strong points."

"Indeed, it is," Alice replied. "Another one is your inclusivity. The people on your team say that when you build a new product or process, you get input from everybody involved. They also say that you've mentored, developed, and promoted team members and recognized personal and professional successes. The VCs are lucky to have you in their company."

"Thank you for that." She smiled. "You know, I've always been a bit of a mystery to myself, too. One of the perks of doing this assessment is seeing myself more clearly—my strengths and weaknesses, personal as well as work related."

"That's wonderful! I'm happy that you're getting extra benefits. You know, in terms of strong and weak points, I'd like to make a suggestion."

Madeline raised her eyebrows.

"I know an excellent firm that specializes in public speaking. Would you be open to that?"

She cocked her head. "Hmm, yes, I know it came out that I don't like to speak in meetings or in public, but it's something I have to do occasionally."

"If you got better at it, you might enjoy it more. And you'd be more likely to engage the audience in your ideas."

"Well, you know, that's true." She nodded. "All right, I'll do it."

Week 5: A "New You"

During the next week, Alice put together a report for the VCs: the full 360-degree assessment, the profile assessments, and a recommendation.

Tips for the Reader

Introverts can face unique challenges in the workplace—even accomplished introverts in leadership roles, such as Bill Gates, Warren Buffett, and Mark Zuckerberg. Here are two challenges when working with introverted clients.

The first challenge is that they are often misunderstood. Introverts are usually relatively quiet, reserved, and low key. They might refrain from voicing their ideas in public forums, preferring one-on-one discussions instead. Because of this, they are sometimes thought of as "shy" or lacking personality, or overlooked entirely. The truth is that introverts are just as skilled in social interactions as the rest of the population; it's just that they recharge their batteries either alone or with one or two people close to them. Coaching techniques should be adjusted accordingly.

The second challenge is that introverts are often underutilized. They tend to undersell themselves and be less recognized than extroverts. This is a big loss to the workplace and work teams, because introverts are just as skilled as other people—sometimes more so, because many of them are studious by nature.

You are bound to see many introverts as you build your executive coaching experience. When you do, try to make a point of enabling others to better understand them. Introverts are the world's best-kept secret.

Madeline had seen everything except the recommendation, so Alice sent her a copy before their last meeting.

Madeline was on the phone when Alice arrived. She paused before a small painting of a radiant, blond young woman holding a large, fluffy cat.

"My two loves," said Madeline, hanging up.

She patted the recommendation folder on her desk. "Well, I'm in the right job according to your recommendation, Dr. Alice."

"Yes, internal operations suits you well. I think COO is the perfect position for you, but possibly in a larger company. I could see you using your skills to build a solid infrastructure in a midsized firm."

"Interesting," Madeline mused. "I think I could imagine that." She shook her head. "I've been feeling a bit like a new person with all the insights I got from the assessment. A new job would be the culmination of our work."

"Would you like to go even further with the 'new you'?" Alice ventured. Having coached other executives in the tech industry, Alice understood all too well the pressures women face at all levels in the start-up culture—they're often held to lofty standards while their male peers get a pass, and struggle to grapple with this challenge. Unfortunately, these standards extend beyond performance to appearance. Alice had an idea to help Madeline establish her executive presence.

Madeline seemed intrigued. "I could go further?"

"You're a contemporary professional, but you're not using your executive presence as one of your strengths. Suppose I directed you to a professional shopper?"

She sighed. "I've been aware that my professional image isn't all that it could be. I think, as an introvert, my style has been geared to fading into the background. You're suggesting that I step out more."

"It can be challenging," Alice agreed. "But I'll refer you to someone I trust. You mentioned that you don't want to seem cold or aloof; I think you would appear more accessible to people with a little intention."

Madeline shook her head. "I'm dizzy from all the changes—you've helped me define a whole new outlook on being an executive. I'm excited by the new possibilities in my career and in my life, and I thank you for that. Why *should* I be self-effacing or apologetic?!"

Alice received an email from Madeline a few weeks later. Madeline was very involved in her public speaking class, and delighted with her new look. "Such a difference!" she wrote. "I can't understand why I didn't do this sooner. I'm finding my own personal look that fits who I am."

Alice also met briefly with Vince a few months after the engagement. The VCs had found a position for Madeline in one of their midsized firms, and she had accepted it. The new COO role came with a boost in pay and greater responsibilities. After reading Alice's full report, they had no doubt that Madeline could fulfill those responsibilities.

Vince summed it up. "We have a real winner here, Alice, but we never would have known it without your report. We almost let her get away."

Summary

In this instance, Alice's job wasn't to coach Madeline—a high-performing COO in a small communications firm—but to evaluate her skills for her employer. Nevertheless, Madeline benefited from a new view of herself afforded by the evaluation tools. With encouragement, she started taking a public speaking class and enhanced her professional appearance. Her employers were very pleased with the evaluation and found Madeline a position as COO in one of their midsized firms.

Takeaway:

- There are often unexpected benefits that manifest during the coaching—or evaluation—process.

3

TROUBLE IN THE OR

Warmhearted and kind, Dr. Yelyuk was celebrated in her field for her clinical leadership and avant-garde techniques. However, she had begun to blend her online business and her family into her work at the hospital, and the lack of separation was overwhelming her. The doctor was increasingly short tempered and indecisive, and her drive to perform more and more surgeries placed her colleagues and patients at risk. She needed help honing her leadership, teamwork, and stress management skills. Alice's challenge was to effect change before there was a disaster in the operating room.

"This is where I hang out with my family," said Dr. Yelyuk, indicating the hospital cafeteria where she and Alice sat. "This is our living and dining room."

"Family?"

"Oh, I consider my team my family," she said, smiling. "Isn't that wonderful, to have a second family in your workplace? Ah, there's one now."

She motioned to a young woman in scrubs. "Mai Lee, come over here!

"Mai Lee, this is Dr. Alice. She's my job coach. I'm so excited that I'm going to be working with her."

Turning to Alice, she added, "Mai Lee is my daughter's godmother and one of my best friends!"

They shook hands as Mai Lee blushed slightly at the doctor's effusiveness.

"Mai Lee, Alice is going to observe a procedure tomorrow. I hope you'll take special care of her and make sure that she gets to see everything."

"Yes, certainly, Doctor."

After Mai Lee had departed, Alice asked, "Are you sure you want me to observe a surgery?"

"Oh, absolutely," Dr. Yelyuk replied. "You're my job coach. You have to see me on the job!"

Weeks 1-2: Complaints From the OR

Alice stood in a 10-square-foot room, looking down on four operating rooms; she could watch the surgeries through the windows or on one of the four monitors that gave close-up views. With no place to sit, and dressed in scrubs, a hat, and gloves, she examined the OR. Mai Lee stood next to her, readying instruments on a tray for the next surgery.

On monitor number one, Alice could see Dr. Yelyuk performing a complex battery change for a pacemaker on a 74-year-old man. "They're going to have to stop the heart while they put in a new device," said Mai Lee. "They call it a battery change, but it's really a whole new device combined with a battery."

Alice watched as Dr. Yelyuk worked on the patient's chest, the techs handed her instruments, and the nurse monitored vital signs. Dr. Yelyuk would pull out the old device, put in the new one, check to see that it was working properly, and start up the heart again. Alice was impressed at the speed and efficiency of this life-giving procedure. A speedy ballet, with each dancer moving in rhythm to some unheard music.

"I have to go next door to talk to the nurses," said Mai Lee, exiting to another small room where several patients lay on gurneys waiting to be wheeled in for their surgeries. Alice knew that this was one area of concern; there had been complaints that some of Dr. Yelyuk's patients were waiting too long under anesthesia.

Alice discovered there actually were quite a number of complaints—from Dr. Yelyuk's surgery team, the nursing staff, and the anesthesiologist. These all came out during the 360-degree interview process. Although most people held warm feelings for the doctor, they were concerned about changes in her behavior over the last two years. She had become more rushed and irritable. She was indecisive, and changed her mind about things without involving the techs or nurses in her decisions. And she had begun to ask the nurses to order meds—something only a doctor should do.

The anesthesiologist, a small, Vietnamese American woman, was especially distressed. "She tells me to anesthetize the patients, but sometimes it'll be 45 minutes before they go into surgery. Should be 10 minutes max. This is not good—my malpractice insurance is already through the roof." She left Alice to imagine what dire things could happen if a patient woke on the operating table.

There was more. The nurses complained that she didn't listen to them about the timing of surgeries. Instead, she would barge ahead, going from one surgery to the next with no breaks, exhausting herself and her staff. One time, she even took a selfie in the OR—something the surgical staff found deeply alarming. Consequently, the team would try to guide her into the correct sequence of surgeries without her knowledge; they would slip things by her and trick her into doing the right thing.

Week 3: Clinical Success, Management Failure

Dr. Yelyuk was not happy with the 360-degree assessment. "I didn't expect this from my family," she said plaintively. "We've known each other for years. They come to my house every holiday season for a special dinner. Everybody brings a special dish. They love my cabbage rolls. . . ."

"Your team is concerned about you," Alice said. "They want the best for you and for your patients."

"I don't think of myself as pushing too hard. I just see it as working hard and doing as much as I can."

"Your colleagues say they can always count on you to fill in for them or to shadow for them if they need another hand. I wonder if you sometimes do too much because you don't want to refuse them."

She sighed. "It's very hard for me to say no to a colleague."

Unlike the techs and the nurses, the other surgeons were pleased that Dr. Yelyuk always stepped in when they needed her. They were also happy with the number of surgeries she performed. The surgeons were part of a group that contracted with the hospital in a fee-for-service arrangement; this meant that the more surgeries performed, the more money earned by the group and by the hospital. In the eyes of her colleagues and the hospital administration, Dr. Yelyuk was a top performer. Alice guessed this was one of the reasons they'd proposed coaching to her as opposed to making a referral to the Quality Committee.

The phone rang before Alice could respond. Dr. Yelyuk talked for several minutes about problems with a website and some shipping issues with the person on the other end. She was frowning by the time she hung up.

"The website for the store is acting up. We're going to have to hire someone to work on it."

To Alice's surprise, Dr. Yelyuk had a side job: She ran an online business reselling vintage items from Givenchy, the French fashion line. In her sparse spare time, Yelyuk took calls from the staff filling orders.

"I wonder if running the store is a bit much in addition to your hospital work," Alice ventured. "Would it be possible to hire a full-time manager?"

"Oh, but I love the products so much! And it's a nice diversion from surgery."

Alice struggled to keep from rolling her eyes. Not only was Dr. Yelyuk running the online store, she also had a husband, three kids, and two dogs—and all this was in addition to her demanding surgical work. An overloaded schedule and inability to delegate were common challenges for a high-performing executive.

"When you were in medical school, were there any courses in management skills? Courses on teamwork, leadership, delegating responsibilities, that kind of thing?"

Dr. Yelyuk shook her head. "There were lots of different clinical courses, but nothing on management."

As Alice had expected. "When you came to this hospital, did you go through an apprenticeship with an experienced surgeon?"

She shook her head again. "No, nothing like that."

Surprisingly, most medical schools do not include the basics of management in their training. This is beginning to change; some schools now offer a joint MD-MBA degree. But there had been no such programs in Dr. Yelyuk's school. Similarly, most hospitals do not have an apprenticeship program. For Yelyuk, this meant she went from residency and fellowship directly into the hospital operating room.

Dr. Yelyuk had always kept up her continuing education, and she was an active member on the board of the surgeon's group. In addition, she was recognized for her innovation and incorporation of new techniques. She presented at conferences and was a tremendous resource to other surgeons across the country. But although she was very accomplished on the clinical side, she simply wasn't aware of her shortcomings on the management side.

Alice faced the challenge of finding a way for Dr. Yelyuk to learn the management ropes while on the job. Her first idea was to set Yelyuk up with an apprenticeship with the department's medical director, on the assumption that doctors like to learn from other doctors. She was soon disabused of that notion, however, after consulting with a few nurses; the director's management skills, they advised, were worse than Dr. Yelyuk's.

Alice next reached out to HR and the COO, but they didn't have any orientations or apprenticeships; there were no training programs on day-to-day management for surgeons, though such a program might be something for the chief medical officer and the COO to consider.

OK, Alice thought, *the goals for this coaching assignment are coming to light.* Dr. Yelyuk needed insight around leadership behavior and hands-on training to manage teamwork and handle stress. To sum it up, their work would focus on those three things: leadership, teamwork, and managing stress.

Week 4: A Leader Who Doesn't Lead

"I don't understand. Why shouldn't I let my patients know that Roberto and Mark adopted a baby girl? Why shouldn't I hug Mai Lee and tell everybody that she's my best friend and my daughter's godmother when I'm at work?"

"I have a new name for you," Alice said, smiling. "I'm going to call you 'Dr. Why.'"

They were in the initial stages of setting goals, but had already encountered some difficulties. For example, Dr. Yelyuk simply didn't see why she shouldn't treat her staff as friends and family.

"Are you aware that people look up to you?" Alice asked. "As a doctor, you have a great deal of power and influence. Everyone on your surgical team looks to you for guidance."

This brought Yelyuk up short. She shook her head, a puzzled expression on her face.

Alice continued. "If they don't get guidance from you, then they have to improvise. And they start secretly guiding *you*. You read what they said in the 360."

"Yes, but . . . you mean. . . ."

"Like it or not, you're the leader around here. If you *don't* lead, other people will fill the vacuum."

"Hmm," she said. "I never saw it like that. I haven't thought of myself as a leader. But why can't I still be friendly and treat people like family?"

Alice shook her head. "These people you call your 'family' are actually your staff. It doesn't mean you can't be friendly, but your first duty is to be a leader to them—to manage the day-to-day operations so that things get done smoothly and optimally. This is what they want and need from you most of all."

Dr. Yelyuk was silent for a time. "I guess I don't know how to be a good manager. That's not one of my skill sets. And there are so many things to consider. . . . "

Alice could see that Dr. Yelyuk was beginning to feel overwhelmed. When her clients started to count all the issues the assessments had brought to light, Alice tried to reframe the coaching engagement into WIIFM: What's in it for me, the client?

"We're going to work on management skills," Alice reassured her. "That's why I'm here. And you'll find that you can get a lot of help from your staff if you ask for it. You have a great staff, but you haven't been asking for their help enough."

"Why don't I know these things? I'm 44 years old and I'm an experienced surgeon. I present at conferences. People ask me for advice." She threw up her hands in frustration.

"You don't know these things because you didn't learn them in medical school, and you didn't serve as an apprentice. But we're going to work together on the things you need to learn. I want to assure you that this is very feasible."

A secret skill of the executive coach trade that doesn't show up on a resume is reassuring people. Change can be a scary thing; because Alice dealt with it all the time, she'd become skilled at encouraging her clients and keeping them on the right track. In terms of techniques for providing reassurance, Alice spoke warmly and from the heart. Some clients, like Dr. Yelyuk, needed this more than others. From Yelyuk's interpersonal profile, Alice understood her very high need for inclusion; this meant that anything that seemed to threaten her relationships with her staff (her "family") triggered anxiety. This time, at least, she was able to take in Alice's reassurance.

"I feel like I did when I first came to this country from Ukraine," she confessed. "Scared, unsure of everything . . . but I learned, and pretty soon things didn't seem so strange. Like you say, this is doable. I can do this."

Week 5: Blind Spots

Before Alice and her coaching client set out to formulate any goals, the client has to acknowledge that there are problems. Often, the problems are obvious—and if not, they show up very clearly in the 360-degree assessment. The opinions expressed in the 360 lay out the things that need to be dealt with; and because her clients are smart, perceptive people, they usually see that changes are necessary. Yet sometimes, there are blind spots that need to be talked through. Dr. Yelyuk's main blind spot was that she wasn't aware she lacked management skills; another was how barging ahead with surgeries one after the other affected her staff and created potential danger for her patients.

"Eleven surgeries in one day? No, I can't believe that I ever did that many."

"According to the nursing staff, and they keep careful records, on February 18, you performed 11 surgeries. The last one was at 10 at night. The staff was exhausted, and you were exhausted. Can this be good practice?"

Dr. Yelyuk took a deep breath. "Sometimes, I just get going and can't seem to stop. But no, this is not good practice."

"The staff also says there is often no downtime between surgeries. They have to rush to get ready for the next one, without even time to sit down."

"Why haven't they told me these things? Why is it all coming out now?"

"They say you've been short tempered during the last two years and basically unapproachable. You've been overstressed with all you've been trying to do."

This last statement made her tearful. "Yes, I have been stressed. But I hate it that my wonderful family has been suffering because of me." She wiped her eyes and sat up straight. "We need to make some changes," she declared.

Weeks 6–7: Coaching Goals

Once they had illuminated her blind spots, Alice and Yelyuk were able to move ahead rapidly on formulating her goals in three areas:

- leadership
- teamwork
- managing stress.

Leadership

Dr. Yelyuk had little concept of how to manage her staff. She called them her "family," and had developed close, interpersonal relationships with them.

Remedies and homework included:

- Develop an understanding that she was the leader of her team and they needed her management and guidance. This involved an acknowledgment of the structure and her role in it, as well as the culture she had created.
- Practice relating to her staff as a leader instead of as a family member. This involved employing more professional language.
- Learn basic management skills like giving direction, delegating responsibility, and including the staff in decision making. This meant planning, coordinating, and communicating instead of spewing off-the-cuff reactions.

Teamwork

Dr. Yelyuk tended to delegate by expecting people to read her mind. She didn't ask for enough input from her team, trusting that somehow everything would magically fall into place.

Remedies and homework included:

- Redefine the different roles played by her team and get their input. The nurses, for instance, knew how to arrange the best timing and sequence of surgeries. Patients with severe dietary restrictions or diabetes, for example, needed to be scheduled first thing in the morning.
- Learn that part of being a good leader is not making unreasonable demands on your team. This included scheduling a reasonable number of surgeries and leaving time

between surgeries so that the team has a chance to rest and prepare for the next one.

- Schedule same-day surgeries only in emergencies. This meant learning how to say no to any colleagues who asked her to step in immediately. It also meant that her staff would have time to schedule and prepare for surgeries to be performed the next day.

Managing Stress

Dr. Yelyuk maintained a grueling surgical schedule. In addition, she was managing an online business and had a husband and three kids.

Remedies and homework included:

- Practice the homework for the first two goals. The measures for reducing stress for her staff would also reduce her own stress.
- Reorganize her online business. Alice suggested she hire a full-time manager to relieve her of the day-to-day operations.
- Spend more quality time with her family at home.

Weeks 8–16: The Joys of Delegating

Alice met every week with Dr. Yelyuk for two hours—an intensive schedule. Part of the time, Alice was instructing her in management techniques, so their meetings took on the air of a classroom. Yelyuk was an excellent student, inquisitive and appreciative. They also talked about ways to relieve her perpetual stress.

"OK, Dr. Alice, I did it; I hired a full-time manager for the business. She's an expert at selling online with a great resume. And she loves the Givenchy line. I've been realizing from all the things I've been learning that delegating is a just a smart thing to do; you tell the person what you want to accomplish, and they do it! And they usually do it better than you could, because they're experts. So I thought, why not delegate to an

Tips for the Reader

Do you recognize your coaching clients in Dr. Yelyuk? Are they sometimes too familiar with people, or unskilled at management? If so, encourage them to explore how to get their interpersonal needs met outside work. Perhaps discuss the human resources risks of being too revealing about their personal lives and asking too much about co-workers' personal lives. You can help them prepare for meetings with their colleagues by developing meeting agendas and sticking to those agendas when they get together. Avoiding overly personal information will enable everyone to feel comfortable while also respecting their time.

Your clients might also have too much stress in their lives and be struggling to cope with it. As a coach, this is an opportunity to help them prioritize their tasks and time. This might start with composing a list of superfluous things and cutting those things back. They can try stepping back and thinking about their life mission and values, and ensuring that their weekly activities are aligned with them. They can also consider delegating some tasks.

Sometimes clients get caught up in activities that are not aligned with their values, are unnecessary, or are undesirable. However, as leaders in their organizations, they should be looking out for the stress levels of their peers and direct reports. You should remind your coaching clients that sometimes a quick infusion of positivity can help them and their colleagues. Your clients should not dwell on or try to fix others' stress; tell your client: "Be bright, be brief, be gone!" They cannot change others' lives, but they can manage their own work, tasks, and attitude.

expert online person? She'll probably do it even better than me. And then I won't have to fret about it."

"I'm happy that you can use what you've been learning for your side business, too."

Yelyuk smiled. "I've been using it for my family!" she said. "*Lana, please take the dogs to the park this afternoon. Sophia, please watch over your little brother while I'm on the phone.'* Pretty soon, I'll be able to just kick back on my sofa and eat chocolates!"

Alice and Yelyuk shared a laugh. "The joys of delegating," Alice said.

One of the most gratifying things about executive coaching is seeing clients take what they've learned and start applying it in their personal lives. Dr. Yelyuk was using her new skills to reorganize her business and her family.

Week 17: Success

After an intense four months, Alice and Dr. Yelyuk were nearing the end of the engagement. Yelyuk now had a grasp of basic management techniques and had begun to use them. She was scheduling fewer surgeries and leaving time for breaks and lunch. Her stress level was down, and her mood was upbeat. In addition, her leisure time had increased, which allowed her more quality time with her family at home.

Typically, to bookend the initial 360 assessment, Alice interviewed the executive's staff post-coaching. In this case, things were a lot better—a lot more structured and much more collaborative. Staff members were doing their own work, not hers, so they were happier and more productive—plus, they were taking breaks and able to eat their lunch. The flow of surgeries had improved greatly, and patients were no longer languishing on the tables outside the OR.

On the final day, Dr. Yelyuk and Alice held a sharing circle in a big room with all her staff. The doctor had prepared a letter, which she read to the group; she let them know that even though it hurt her at first, she did appreciate the 360 assessment and saw the truth in it. She talked about all the things she'd had to learn that she wasn't trained for in medical school—like building a culture of teamwork, having boundaries at work, authority, process, standard work for patient safety, and how to be a leader. She concluded by telling them that she was grateful for their concern and cared about each of them, and thanked them for taking great care of the patients, one another, and her.

Each team member then had two minutes to talk about how they had experienced the journey. One spoke about watching Dr. Yelyuk make new decisions; several said that they were learning to speak up for themselves. "You know," remarked one of the techs, "in the future, if something's up, I feel I can talk to you directly now—that I'm not going to hurt your feelings." A number of people were enthusiastic about the improvements in scheduling, in safer patient care, in more break time, and in better communication.

It seemed to Alice that the staff now felt they could co-create their own culture. They had overcome their learned helplessness and no longer held the idea that this was just the way things were; they didn't need to resort to manipulation to accomplish the right thing.

That last meeting was very tearful—coaching engagements tend to bring emotions to the surface. Alice excused herself when they started hugging and talking about all they had been through.

A gratifying aspect of executive coaching is seeing the ripple effect on the people around the client. A client's changes can affect the culture of an entire department: Tension levels go down, communication improves, and people feel a greater sense of well-being.

Dr. Yelyuk called Alice a few weeks later to say that things were continuing to go well at the hospital. "Less is more!" she enthused. "Less micromanaging, less worry, less anxiety—and more happiness!"

Summary

Dr. Yelyuk was a leader in innovative surgical techniques. Yet during the past two years, she had become increasingly short tempered with her surgical team and was performing too many surgeries, ultimately

Why Coaching Matters

"The anesthesiologist and lead tech have turned into strong team leaders," Dr. Yelyuk wrote in a follow-up email to Alice. She was happy for them, but mentioned that she regretted how she had been holding them back. Many executives rise to their level because of their performance history, not because of how skilled they are at developing the people they've managed. As a coach, you have the opportunity to open their eyes to the power of developing and growing others.

After going through the process, Dr. Yelyuk decided that she wanted to have another child. While surprising to Alice at first, it made sense based on Yelyuk's assessment profiles and feedback, which showed a strong inclination to take care of others . . . and now that she had more balance in her life, she could indeed expand her family. You never know what unexpected results executive coaching might yield!

placing her patients at risk. For several months, Alice instructed her in management skills, and they discussed ways of relieving her stress. She learned to delegate responsibility, communicated better with her surgical team, and adopted a reasonable schedule for her surgeries (to the great relief of her team). In addition, she hired a manager for her online business and began to spend more quality time with her family.

Takeaways:

- The collateral benefits that can result from coaching are often dramatic. In this case, the benefits extended not only to the doctor, but also to her surgical team and her family.
- An entire organization can benefit from the coaching of just one of its key people. In this instance, the hospital benefited from the reduced risk to patients.

4

MISTAKES

Alice received a call from an exasperated vice president at a nonprofit. Rebecca explained that she had two major gift officers who were both highly successful and integral to the fundraising efforts. The problem was that they didn't get along with each other, and it was affecting fundraising.

"I DON'T KNOW WHAT the issue is. Madison and John are both reasonable people and great fundraisers, but they just can't seem to get along with each other. I need them to work as a team on some projects, but they won't collaborate. I'm concerned that this will affect our overall fundraising."

The speaker was Rebecca, vice president of philanthropy at a midsized nonprofit. Because Alice had experience as a trained mediator as well as an executive coach, she was sometimes called in to facilitate or enhance communications between clients—and this seemed to be one of those cases.

"They're polite . . . they don't yell at each other, but when they talk to other people, they run each other down—their work, their communication style, anything," Rebecca told Alice. "I get the worst of it; they're always telling me how awful the other one is, and I'm really sick

of it. It's unprofessional and it's divisive. And it reflects badly on me, too: People think I can't manage my team."

Week 1: The Pulse of the City

Alice decided to meet with Madison and John individually. Later, the three of them could meet and talk through things, but first, she needed to establish a relationship with each person, build trust, and conduct the assessments.

She had her first meeting with Madison.

"Hello, Dr. Alice. So nice to meet you! Come see my latest blog."

Madison led Alice over to her desk, where the screen showed a bright display of new niche restaurants and, as she scrolled down, dog fashion shows and fee-free days at museums.

"Looks like you've got your finger on the pulse of the city," Alice remarked.

Madison laughed with delight. "One of my followers said that I *am* the pulse of the city. I've got 10,000 active followers now! And I've just started a Monday-morning vlog to link what's going on around town with the mission of our organization."

They sat down, and Alice got out her notebook. Before she could begin with her questions, however, Madison started in with her own.

"Tell me about your coaching. How long have you been doing it? Do you find it rewarding?"

Alice hadn't expected this; most of her clients are too preoccupied with their own situations to ask about her. By the time she had a chance to ask anything, a picture had emerged of an exceptionally intelligent young woman in her early 30s, funny, pretty, creative, and active in the community. Madison was enthusiastic about the assessment process.

"Bring it on!" she said.

Weeks 2-3: Assessments

The next two weeks were spent conducting assessments for Madison and John. Alice met briefly with John the second week to get acquainted and explain the coaching process, and met with him again after the assessment results were in. In cases involving conflict, Alice liked to take the time to fully understand the individual's approach to conflict using 360-degree interviews and profiles. The coaching client's self-assessment and self-reflections were helpful because they offered Alice a chance to help them build their skills in any capacity needed.

Week 4: The Cary Grant of Nonprofits

John was a handsome fellow in his mid-50s, very dapper and suave. He had an air about him that was reminiscent of Cary Grant. Rebecca had told Alice that John's appearance and demeanor were very pleasing to prospective donors—particularly the older women.

"I appreciate stability," he told Alice. "I've been with this organization for 20 years."

John's profile revealed a man of high values and integrity, with close, long-standing one-on-one relationships. He was a slight introvert and preferred actions over words. His approach to conflict (or anything unpleasant) was to avoid it altogether. If push came to shove, however, his backup approach was to assert that it was his way (the *right* way) or the highway.

John's 360 was overall very positive as well, although Alice was told that at times he could seem a little aloof, almost superior. In their meeting, he talked quite a bit about his personal life and home projects. As Alice was leaving, he picked up several cucumbers and carrots from his desk. "Here," he said, putting them into a paper bag, "I grew these in my urban garden."

Week 5: Nothing in Common

Madison's profile revealed an inclusive, optimistic extrovert with streaks of superb organizational skills. She had a keen ability to abstract and make connections between concepts and people. Her memory skills were exceptional, as was her use of language. Her approach to conflict was to handle things straight on, discuss them and look for a compromise; her backup style was to become competitive and get her own way.

Madison's 360 was overall very positive. At times, colleagues told Alice, she could be so involved in her own activities that she might be oblivious to other goings-on in the room, but she would quickly snap to and join whatever was happening.

Alice and Madison put together coaching goals that involved tuning in to people and her surroundings more quickly and finding a greater work-life balance. In addition, Alice suggested Madison could make a goal of meeting with John to start to work out their differences. Madison seemed surprised at the thought that anything should change in that regard.

"Why would I want to meet with John? We have almost nothing in common."

"You're both top fundraisers, and Rebecca would like you to collaborate on certain projects."

"Rebecca hasn't spoken to me about that. Look, I've raised more than 3 million dollars this year—and the year's only half over. I have all kinds of donors, all professions, all ages."

"But John. . . ."

"John appeals to the older ladies. He charms them, and they write checks. It's as simple as that. I can't imagine any project we could work on together."

Week 6: Completely Unreasonable

"Madison is just an unreasonable person. I've tried to work with her, but I've given up on it. She's too emotional."

Alice and John were discussing his goals, which involved being more aware of his body language, connecting more quickly, and coaching a new major gift officer. But when Alice spoke of the possibility of creating a new relationship with Madison, he rolled his eyes and bemoaned how difficult she was.

Instead of letting this slide, Alice decided to take a different tack with John. "I understand that the two of you have had some differences, but you're both very capable, intelligent people who want the best for this organization. I've worked with a number of people in conflict resolution. Perhaps with a little goodwill. . . ."

"I've never experienced any goodwill from Madison," John countered. "I've experienced her talking behind my back, disparaging my work to Rebecca, avoiding me at gatherings . . . I really don't see how any good could come from a meeting."

Week 7: Isn't It Obvious?

At this point, Alice needed to meet with Rebecca. Through her discussions with Madison and John, she'd discovered that Rebecca had said nothing to either of them about improving their working relationship—and speaking with her now, Rebecca seemed somehow offended that she would have to communicate her expectations to them.

"This is why I hired you," she said to Alice. "I mean, isn't it obvious that things need to change?"

"It might seem obvious to us," Alice acknowledged, "but not to them. My experience has been that coaching succeeds better and faster when the manager sets the expectations around employee collaboration."

"Well, this manager doesn't see it that way. This is up to you. You're the expert."

Weeks 8-12: Fix My Direct Reports

Alice continued to work with Madison and John because they both benefited from coaching and seemed to enjoy the time, insights, and work; however, she was beginning to realize that the better client from the outset would have been Rebecca.

Now Alice was in the sticky situation of John's and Madison's interpersonal skills surpassing Rebecca's (except for them getting along with each other). Meanwhile, Rebecca was starting to behave less and less managerial. Alice's relationship with her was getting a little fraught, as she was still under the impression that coaching was her way out of having to do any "fixing" herself.

At a later meeting, Alice revisited the topic of Rebecca setting out expectations to Madison and John. This time, Rebecca told her that she had a "hands-off" management approach; in addition, she was concerned that if she pushed them to work things out, their productivity and funds would go down . . . or, worse yet, she would lose one of them.

A lot of executive coaching is about helping clients see problem situations in a new light. Alice tried to help Rebecca consider how much more funds could flow into the nonprofit if John and Madison collaborated, and demonstrated teamwork with donors and employees. That didn't work; Rebecca simply continued venting about their faults and inability to communicate.

"Why, just the other day, we had a small event, about 20 people, and they managed to avoid speaking to each other the whole time. It makes me wonder if they're in competition for my job. I'm probably going to retire in two or three years. That would explain why they run each other down so much—especially to me."

She launched into another tirade about the John-and-Madison conflict. Alice was at her wit's end.

Week 13: What Went Wrong?

Alice spent the week reviewing the coaching engagement and realized she had made several mistakes. She'd made certain assumptions when she began the relationship—one was that the executive who called her in would support the coaching work with the senior leaders. Alice needed Rebecca to communicate her expectations to Madison and John about working through their differences and collaborating when necessary.

Another assumption Alice had made was that Madison and John would try to improve their situations, that they would *want* to relate to each other better (at least on a superficial level) and would make at least some effort to work on their communication—an issue that negatively affected the performance of their nonprofit.

While these were reasonable assumptions for Alice to make, she should have placed more emphasis on her role in the dynamic. Even though the engagement contract and the scope of work had clear bullets that she and Rebecca had agreed to, Alice should have kept referring back to them with Rebecca as soon as she realized that Rebecca was not being accountable. Alice had seen foot dragging and hesitation to address an issue, but rarely outright refusal for very long. All three individuals were refusing to move ahead and act in the best interests of the organization.

A couple of months went by; then one day, Alice heard from Madison. She had been successfully recruited into a major role as the director of corporate responsibility at a well-known retail company. She attributed this step up partly to her new glow; she wanted to finish her coaching at her new job with a focus on getting along with everybody and successfully resolving any differences or conflict.

Madison told Alice that John had accepted a position at a university fundraising department as director of planned giving. A while later, Alice received an update from him on social media; he wanted her to do some team building with his new staff. He also was eager to work on getting along with everybody.

Well, Alice thought, *at least the clients had made good progress in their individual coaching.* And because all executive coaches need to learn from their mistakes, she did not propose that John, Madison, and she meet to put things to rest between them, even though she wanted to. Executive coaches by nature often must be peacemakers, but sometimes Alice diagnosed things that people simply did not want to address.

It took a couple years before Alice heard from Rebecca. Filling in the details, Rebecca said she'd been removed from her position due to the departures of some high-profile members of her team. She was having a hard time retiring, and wanted some career advice about how to slow down working while still contributing to the community. This gave Alice the chance to apologize for her own mistakes, but Rebecca shrugged it off and said that often in her life she'd had to learn the hard way, and that it probably would not have mattered because she had not been ready for coaching at the time. As it was, Alice was happy to reach some sort of closure with Rebecca—and with John and Madison.

Sometimes an individual will think or say they are ready for executive coaching, but they are not quite ready to make the commitment or the changes required. This becomes obvious as the divide between what they do and say grows (as with Rebecca). In this case, it is best to confer with them about a better time . . . and perhaps you can schedule a check-in later.

Tips for the Reader

It's always important to learn something from your mistakes. In this case, you can also benefit by reading about Alice's missteps.

Alice's first mistake was to take on the assignment without ensuring that Rebecca had communicated her expectations to the coaching clients. Any good coach, consultant, salesperson, doctor, or parent will tell you that the presenting problem is not always the actual problem. You can probably relate to this in your own work, whether you are currently working as an executive coach or as something else. Alice forgot that important truth in this instance. She should have asked more questions like, "What led to this?" "What brought you to this conclusion?" "What have you tried previously?" "What would success look like?" and "How shall we approach this together?" These questions would have revealed that the goal of having the two employees get along better was a management goal as well as a coaching goal. In addition, they would also have probably revealed the implications of a hands-off management style. Alice could then have discussed these implications at the time and negotiated for Rebecca to communicate expectations before accepting the assignment.

The second mistake was that Alice became more invested than Rebecca, Madison, or John in resolving their conflict. Has this happened to you, where the other person's needs are obvious and you really, *really* want things to be better for them? As coaches, we are responsible for our part, and the coaching clients for theirs. Each coaching client has many choices; as a coach, your role is to invite clients to consider the consequences of their choices and enable them to reach their own conclusions. Alice fell into this caring trap because she wanted to see the team function at its highest potential.

The third mistake was that Alice misdiagnosed who the client should have been. Maybe this happens to you at work, too—the one who seems like the customer is not always the customer. This would not have happened if Alice had caught mistake number one earlier; she could have shifted perspective at that point and realized that Rebecca was the best candidate for coaching (at least at first). She then compounded this mistake by approaching Rebecca about coaching. One might argue that this was the right thing to do no matter what the outcome, and that the only mistake was not doing it sooner. However, in hindsight, there were clear signs that Rebecca was probably not going to agree to coaching for herself.

Summary

Madison and John, both major gift officers at a nonprofit, didn't get along. According to their boss, Rebecca, the discord prevented them from working together—which affected fundraising. Rebecca hired Alice to coach Madison and John with the goal of working through their differences so they could collaborate. However, several weeks in, Alice discovered that the two coaching clients had no interest in or intention of meeting with each other. She also learned that Rebecca was unwilling to set expectations for her subordinates. This unearthed the realization that the person most in need of coaching was Rebecca. However, when Alice proposed this to her, she took offense, and the engagement soon ended.

Takeaways:

- Even skilled coaches occasionally make mistakes. In this case, Alice should have made sure that Rebecca was willing to back up her efforts before the engagement started.

- Coaching can have successful outcomes even when the primary goal isn't attained. Although the main goal of this coaching endeavor was never reached, John and Madison both benefited from the coaching. In fact, they asked Alice to continue their coaching at their new jobs. Even Rebecca requested coaching a couple of years later—which was a successful engagement.

5

AMBUSHED!

Maricel had been hired as director of finance and operations at a fast-growing tech company. Her job was to establish the necessary infrastructure and controls for the company to go public—to complete an IPO. However, her attempts to introduce these changes were met with fierce resistance from the employees. "Culture eats strategy for lunch," as they say. Maricel was in danger of losing her job when Alice was called in. While Alice's work often entails working with high potentials and high performers to hone a new skill, she didn't shy away from helping "last chance" or poor performers get back on track, as many executive coaches do. Her human resources, mediation, and psychologist qualifications enabled her effectiveness. They had just three months to win over the resisters and meet the goal.

"SO, ALICE, HERE'S OUR SITUATION. A few years ago, we were just another startup with a few good ideas and some talented people. Then our software products began to take off, and suddenly we're growing like gangbusters."

According to Jeffrey, the CEO, his small tech company had some growing pains. Like many tech executives, he was young—no more than 35.

"When we were just a few offices, everybody was in shouting distance. We could meet at lunch and talk things over. Now, with the headcount way up and multiple new offices, suddenly managing isn't so easy.

"We need to get this management thing down—but besides that, we want to go public in maybe a year or two. We need the money from the IPO to expand, but, as you know, going public opens the door to a whole lot of new issues."

They had brought on a new hire, Maricel, as director of finance and operations to set up internal controls and procedures . . . but then the whole thing exploded.

"Maricel is an expert in her field, but she doesn't know how to work with our people. These tech workers, they're a breed apart; they're independent, creative, and they don't like following procedures and controls. So they rebelled, and suddenly we've got this big brouhaha with people taking sides, derailing, and stonewalling. I called Maricel in, and I said, 'Look, we've got to let you go. We can't handle this.' And that's when she suggested hiring you to work with her."

"OK," Alice said. "Let me give you an idea of how I work and what I'll be doing."

Week 1: At the Center of the Storm

Alice relished the challenge of working with small companies struggling as they grew larger, but this case was more dramatic than any she had seen. There were noisy arguments in the hallways and the cafeteria, sullen faces, and angry emails.

She met with Maricel the day after meeting with Jeffrey. Maricel was Filipina American, and older than most people in the firm—probably around 40. She wore glasses and a harried expression.

"I understand you're at the center of all this controversy."

"Oh gosh, I had no idea what I was getting into when I came here. I've always worked in more mature firms with more . . . uh . . . mature people. This looked like a simple, straightforward job—just introduce some internal control structures, some Sarbanes-Oxley governance. I've done this several times before, with good results. That's why they hired me."

"You've *got* to have them these days," Maricel continued. "Whether you go public or not, you need to create the kind of standards and procedures that SOX focuses on. Even privately owned firms are doing this. You need the visibility and accountability. And if you don't do it, you get higher insurance premiums and more civil liability, plus low status with investors and customers."

"Have you tried to communicate these things?"

"Well, I thought they basically knew. I mean, that's why they hired me. But I've come to see that even the top guys don't really have a grasp of this. They just know that they need funding to expand. And they're thinking of their own holdings, too, how they'll grow with an IPO. Some of them think it would be easier to go with VC funding, but even the VCs want the SOX structures these days."

Alice nodded. "I have a few ideas. But first, I want to administer a few tests and do a 360. This is how it works. . . ."

Week 2: "We Don't Need Her!"

Alice administered some standard tests related to conflict, interpersonal needs, career inventory, and communication style. She also interviewed the people Maricel worked with most closely in 360-degree-feedback format, reserving about 30 minutes with each. Particularly in this volatile situation, she wanted to keep the questions simple and results oriented: *What are Maricel's strengths? In what areas could she improve? What are three things she should consider doing?*

For the first interview, Alice sat down in the main conference room with the director of product development, Tonya, who got straight to the point.

"Maricel is clearly very bright and well intentioned," she said. "But I've been here since the beginning. Why does she think she can just come in here and change everything?"

Other responses in the 360 were equally vehement: "I work hard at my job. I don't have the bandwidth to fill in all the stuff she wants us to do." "Look how the company's grown just doing what we're doing." "She didn't even ask for our input. Like I don't feel she's even interested." "We don't need her! We can do it ourselves!"

Alice interviewed some of the executives, too. They didn't protest as loudly, but she saw that Maricel was right: They didn't really grasp what she was trying to do. They knew it had to be done to get the investment capital they needed, but they didn't understand the details.

Maricel's profiles showed a balanced, slightly extroverted systems-thinker with a tendency to want to include groups and create a structured environment; she had a strong interest in math and science, but also social causes and the arts. She had a preference for compromise and collaboration, with a slight aversion to conflict but not to the point of avoidance.

For the infrastructure to be accepted and adopted, Maricel needed to understand and leverage the culture. If anybody could turn around this company culture, Maricel could; the profiles depicted a mature, superbly intelligent leader.

Alice couldn't help but wonder how much of the reaction was due to Maricel being a Pacific Islander American woman. This was a culture of boys with lots of toys. Their brand-new building had a movie theater and high-tech games everywhere; they had free on-site concierge services for dry cleaning, food, and massages; they even had a clinic.

It was clear that Maricel had to learn the lingo and the cultural norms, and would need to hold off on tightening controls until she better understood the environment. She had gone in guns blazing, saying, "This is the way it's going to be"—and, of course, they thought they didn't have to listen to her. She was just the new girl. Maricel needed to backtrack and consider what kind of change management to employ in this situation.

Week 3: Planning

At their next meeting, Maricel looked less harried and more thoughtful. "I read the 360," she said, "and I think I know what the next step is. We have to educate the employees and the frontline managers. We have to show them the what and the why of all this. They don't have a clue what I'm trying to do."

"Yes, that's clear," Alice said, noting the shift in Maricel's outlook. She had started to say "we," indicating that she was already envisioning the leadership team working together. That's the secret about leading change: It is a team effort.

"I had no idea that what I did was such a mystery," continued Maricel.

"That's because you've been working with it for 20 years—and in organizations that understand its value. The people here have been working with a narrow lens on computer software, and for some, that's their whole life."

"So, what I think I should do," Maricel said, "is write up some talking points for team leaders about what needs to happen and why. Then, maybe I can give a few talks with visuals and interesting stories."

"Those are good ideas," Alice said. "We can map out an organization chart showing where our support is and where the resistance comes from. And I think it would be helpful to include Jeffrey in our plan, because we need him to show that he owns these changes."

Weeks 4-5: Coaching Goals

Over the next two weeks, Maricel and Alice put together three goals:

- Learn organization dynamics.
- Improve presentation skills.
- Build a cultural experience.

Learn Organization Dynamics

Maricel was an excellent leader and an expert in finance and operations. She was intelligent, even tempered, kind, and modest, and she brought clarity and simplicity to any process. However, Maricel had never before faced a closed culture like this one, and had to learn how to lead change in a new way.

Remedies and homework included:

- Avoid taking resistance personally. Maricel had to set aside her personal feelings; the resistance, although initially aimed at her, was more a rebellion against any change (especially against transparency).
- Map out an organization chart of the advocates, sponsors, influencers, derailers, and gatekeepers, then formulate a plan with the CEO to engage these people strategically and individually to bring about changes in the infrastructure. This would also bring the CEO into greater ownership of the changes.
- Prepare presentations and talking points for leaders to present in their team meetings. Some would enthusiastically support the message, some would simply carry the message, but all of them would make changes in their own team's processes to include the reporting and structure needed to go public.
- Take care to offer something when asking for something. Because some relationships are built on exchange and equity,

Maricel needed to demonstrate the benefits of the new system to the employees at the same time she asked them to make changes.

- Arm her own team with change management training; help them to understand the psychology of change and overcoming resistance.

Improve Presentation Skills

Maricel was extremely well organized and well spoken. However, this was a tougher-than-usual crowd that required even more polished and targeted presentation skills.

Remedies and homework included:

- Learn to place the catch up front, along with the ask. Maricel was comfortable with financial and operations details, but she had to learn to use the kinds of images and metaphors in her presentations that employees could relate to (great slides, great story).
- Learn to read and respond to nonverbals. Frowns, fidgeting, zoning out, and checking the time are all possible signs of trouble. She might need to adapt the conversation, ask how they are doing, or ask for questions or a process check.
- Get around. Maricel might need to use mobility during presentations, but she especially needed to walk around the buildings every day. Making herself visible and personalizing the mission could bring big returns, especially if she included open and honest discussions about the journey, what it required, and how she and her team could help.

Build a Cultural Experience

Because Maricel was the outsider, she had to learn how to create her own cultural experience in this ecosystem.

Remedies and homework included:

- Zumba! Maricel taught a class twice a week at the gym near her home. She would consider replacing those classes with a noon and after-work class at work.
- Partner with human resources on the Best Idea awards; sign up to be a judge and create the process behind the selection.

Weeks 6-7: Strategy

Maricel and Alice were very busy over the next couple of weeks. First, they mapped out an organization chart showing the sponsors of the new infrastructure, the advocates, and the resisters. They then met with Jeffrey to plan how to strategically engage the company to bring about the necessary changes. Maricel drafted an email and sent it to Jeffrey with a note: "This is what you have to say to make way for me so I can be successful in my job at your company."

Jeffrey sent out the following statement to all employees:

Maricel was brought on to help us set up a new infrastructure. This structure is needed as a company of our size gets to the next level. We need processes, controls, and governance to show our potential investors, lenders, and other stakeholders that we are a company that takes accounting procedures and financial reporting seriously. We need to listen to her wisdom in setting up this new structure. Please give her your attention and engage with her. This is top priority. All this work is needed if we want to get future investors and is a requirement to go public. As owners of this company, this is something you all should want to ensure our success and protect your future equity.

Following the memo's release, Maricel held a meeting with the team leaders in which she explained the new infrastructure—what it was, why it was necessary, and how they could educate people about it.

In the meantime, Maricel was beginning to walk around the buildings and spend time in the cafeteria and game rooms. Because she was outgoing and had a pleasing personality, she was able to engage with people socially and sometimes direct the conversation to the changes she was trying to make.

Finally, Alice helped Maricel put together a presentation that she would give in the main auditorium.

Week 8: What's in It for Them

There were about 150 people in the auditorium for Maricel's presentation—a very good turnout, considering the initial hostile reaction to her program. The theme of her talk was visibility. She started with a description of the Sarbanes-Oxley regulations and how they promoted visibility in an organization. She explained how they were enacted in response to some high-profile business failures—Enron, WorldCom, and several others—that stemmed from a lack of visibility in reporting. When Congress passed the Sarbanes-Oxley Act in July 2002, the new regulations essentially said that every public firm had to have internal control structures and must demonstrate that they're effective, visible, and monitor all business processes and procedures.

A young man in the front row raised his hand. "That's what everybody's been complaining about," he said. "We don't *want* to have to monitor and report every transaction."

"I understand," said Maricel. "It's a pain at first. All I can say is that it gets easier as you get used to it."

Another man raised his hand. "It all seems so negative," he said. "You've just got to do these things to keep from getting busted. I think we want to know what's in it for us."

Maricel and Alice shared a quick, knowing look. "I was getting to that," she said. "There are actually a lot of things about the SOX regulations that benefit the company and you individually—besides needing to do them to go public. For one thing, complying with them provides the kind of visibility and tracking a business needs. These are all things that we need to know. If I can find the owner of a process or track a work flow with a few clicks, we are that much further ahead—and so are you, because this makes your work much simpler and faster, and more valuable to our customers." Maricel was bringing home the WIIFM (what's in it for me) by pointing out the benefits of the change.

"When the company was small, everything was visible. As it grows, however, it takes more effort to get the kind of visibility and accountability we need. This is a shift in culture. We need this transparency to make sure the business can continue. What's in it for you is being part of a growing firm that's on the right path. In addition, as an owner, you want to ensure that your company is following proper protocols so that the IPO is a success." Maricel was publicly naming the culture change, and there would be many discussions about culture change throughout the company in the ensuing months.

Week 9: Zumba!

Maricel's presentation got very good reviews—so good, in fact, that she had to schedule another for those who had missed the first one. In the meantime, Maricel warmed up to Alice's idea for holding a Zumba class at the company.

Zumba, a dance-fitness program performed to music from all around the world, is naturally inclusive and joyful. *It could be a fun way to bring people together and let them see me in a new light,* thought Maricel. *It's hard to hold grudges when you shake, shimmy, and sweat together!*

Tips for the Reader

Do you recognize your coaching clients in Maricel? Are they new in a job? They might need your help to learn to read the culture. Coach them to watch for both the spoken and hidden rules. How are decisions made? Who is linked to whom and how? During their first 90 days, your clients could benefit from meeting with key people individually to start a relationship, and from listening and learning more than talking or acting. Encourage them to learn about the company's past, and to refrain from making big decisions or trying to implement changes.

If they are new, were they brought on to spearhead changes in the company? Perhaps you could approach the leaders to decide on the four Ws together: what needs to be done, by when, with whom, and why. You will need to ensure the coaching client and leadership are aligned before heading out with the message and call to action. The best outcomes are usually achieved when executives present the business case, and managers translate that into "What's in it for me?" to employees. Your client should make sure that advocates and supporters get recognized, and should set up individual discussions with derailers to get to the heart of their resistance or fear.

If your client works with people who are in Maricel's situation, encourage them to be an advocate for themselves, their colleagues, and the company, and offer to help. A mature leader like Maricel is rare and can easily become a target due to her position and the culture.

Learn about how cultural transformation and change management is handled within your client's company. There can be a gap between what the business needs and what its culture can deliver, even when the workforce has the right skills. Executive coaches with expertise in these areas are a great resource to help individuals at all levels execute on new corporate initiatives; they can make it easier by helping people become aware of barriers, and they can provide tools to change mindsets.

Weeks 10-11: Success

The Zumba classes took off immediately. People loved them, and they had the desired effect of presenting Maricel in another light.

In addition, between her presentations and the support of the team leaders, the employees were beginning to accept the necessity of the new controls and procedures. They were even getting excited about the prospect of doing an IPO.

Week 12: Tying It Up

Maricel was on-site in the Utah offices, so Alice connected with her online to review the changes that had occurred. Virtual coaching meetings are not always as productive as in-person meetings, but Alice appreciated the ability to keep in contact with her clients despite their busy schedules. Maricel was in a good place now, and the company was on track to instituting the necessary changes; it was time for Alice to move on.

"I've learned an important lesson," Maricel told her. "You can have the best program in the world, but nobody is going to listen if you don't present it in a way they can relate to. Thank you for walking me through this change management process."

Alice also held one last meeting with Jeffrey a few days later to wrap up the coaching engagement. He was pleased: Not only did he now have a process that would position and protect his company, but he'd retained a valuable employee in Maricel. And he admitted that her presentations and talking points had helped him better understand the new structure.

On the way out, Alice passed the cafeteria and caught a glimpse of Maricel having an animated discussion with half a dozen employees. She smiled and thought to herself, *Just three months ago, no one would have thought a scene like this would be possible.*

Why Coaching Matters

Maricel told Alice, "I understand 'Culture eats strategy for lunch' in a whole new way. I've also come to appreciate this less-formal culture—where else could I bring Zumba into the workplace? This is *my* culture too now!" Maricel was right—she had not only adapted to the culture, but also adapted it to her.

Knowing what to change and what not to is an essential element of the process. If your coaching clients are trying to change too many things at once, they might encounter extreme resistance, as did Maricel. By helping clients become better at change management, you're equipping them with skills that will serve them for the rest of their career.

Going through the coaching process can be an eye-opening experience for the client's leaders. The assessments—and implementation and practice of coaching goals—exposes them to their own unconscious biases and how they might be affecting their work. In this case, Maricel was later selected by HR to explore the unconscious bias experience within her company and develop awareness training. Coaching, and all the learning that comes with it, can position leaders to take on more active roles with training and developing the entire organization.

Alice heard from Maricel several times, always to report new successes. Among other things, she wrote that the Zumba classes were bringing people together across all levels of the company; people were forming new friendships and getting in touch with their feelings. And Jeffrey emailed about a year later to say that the company was ready for its IPO—which, he wrote, wouldn't have been possible without Maricel—or Alice.

Summary

Maricel was in danger of losing her job. She had been hired as director of finance and operations at a fast-growing tech company, and her job was to introduce the necessary infrastructure and controls for the company to go public. However, her attempts to introduce these changes had been met with fierce resistance from the free-thinking tech employees. Alice and Maricel worked with team leaders, enlisted the active support of top management, and planned how Maricel could engage with employees in positive ways. She gave several presentations about the new infrastructure that were well received, and began to teach a popular dance-exercise class. In the end, Maricel was promoted to chief operating officer and, a year later, the company launched a successful IPO.

Takeaways:

- Coaching can facilitate a well-planned change management process.
- While many coaching engagements are focused on personal change, this one was focused more on strategy: Maricel needed to find ways of reaching the employees and overcoming their resistance.
- Sometimes, nontraditional methods can make a difference. For example, the employees saw Maricel in a new, positive light when she taught an exercise class.

THE RIGID PROJECT MANAGER

Jay was a senior project manager with long tenure, and despite Jay not being an executive, the company valued his contributions. Jay was good at his job and extremely dedicated, so when the vice president of engineering called him into his office raging about an email concerning a problem on which he and the CEO had been copied, Jay took this very seriously. He explained his reasons for sending the email and exited the VP's office, pleased that he had clarified matters. However, Jay lacked interpersonal skills and had failed to pick up on the VP's reaction. The next thing Jay knew, he was in sitting in front of Alice, his newly assigned coach.

Week 1: Chess

"Do you play chess?"

"Uh, no, I never learned."

"Why not?"

It was Alice's first meeting with Jay. They had just introduced themselves, and Jay had gotten the first word in.

"Why are you interested if I play chess?" Alice asked.

"Because it's easier for me to talk to people who play," he asserted. "We share a language and a way of looking at the world."

"What do you like about chess?"

"I like that it's all strategy and tactics. The only interaction you have with your opponent is trying to figure out what he's going to do. No talking, no distractions."

Jay's clipped, unemotional tone stood in contrast to his appearance. He had the face of an angel, with full lips, wide eyes, and curly black hair, but he was not a warm guy.

Alice described how their work together would proceed; when she'd finished, he shrugged. "Sounds like a complete waste of time, but corporate wants me to do it, so I'll humor them. But it'll take time away from practicing for my next tournament."

In cases like this, without proper buy-in, many coaches would terminate the coaching assignment. Alice decided to regard this interaction as another piece of the assessment—the protest, the compliance—and the curiosity he expressed as he leaned in and asked, "When are we meeting up next?"

Weeks 2-3: Assessment

Jay's assessment showed a man with low interpersonal needs and almost no need for inclusion. He didn't avoid conflict, but seemed unaware that it was an issue with most people and had few thoughts on the matter. His thinking was logical and linear, very structured, and very tied to the practical rather than the abstract. Language was not his strongest suit, but rules and order applied firmly there, too, as in every other aspect of his personality. His need for control was exceptionally high; he was comfortable when the content and pace were rigidly set, and subject to his influence. His need to follow process and bring matters to a close was also very high. His career profile showed jobs in fields such as engineering, construction, and manufacturing.

There were clearly two camps in the respondents to the 360-degree feedback: those who appreciated Jay's genius, his work ethic, and his efficiency, and those who were hurt and confused by him. This latter group noted that Jay had a way of ticking people off; he didn't seem to act in a hostile way, he just said things that were hurtful without seeming to know or care. One respondent said it was "almost as if the human factor was missing" in Jay.

In general, management loved Jay because he got things done and kept all the stakeholders in the loop. His meeting notes, decisions, and accomplishments were unreproachable. He also had a great way with graphics, presenting complex projects and problems in clear, understandable visuals. Yes, he had an intensity and could catch people off guard with his directness, but they appreciated him. None of them wanted to be his boss, however.

Jay was exceptionally well prepared for his job. Not only did he have an advanced project management certificate, but he invested in the very latest project management software and served on the board of a company that specialized in big data software solutions. Alice wondered what preparation he'd had for social interaction.

Weeks 4–5: Making a Deal, Making Goals

The results of self-assessments don't always come as a big surprise to coaching clients. They often know—or suspect—that they're averse to conflict or like to be in control, for example. Psychological assessments clarify and deepen their understanding, inviting them to examine new dimensions of themselves. The results of 360s, however, often come as a revelation. It's in the interactions with co-workers that blind spots are often most apparent, and most immediate.

Jay was shocked that some people described him as hurtful, abrupt, or insensitive. "I had no idea," he said. "I don't even know what I said that they're reacting to. I mean I know I'm not exactly a regular guy, but. . . ." His voice trailed off, and he looked up at the ceiling.

"I have a proposal for you," Alice offered. "How about I help you get better at your interactions and your people skills, and you teach me how to play chess. Deal?" She suggested this for two reasons. The first was to immediately establish a plan (this suited his personality and relieved his anxiety); the second was to give him an opportunity to engage, relate, and guide Alice through chess instruction, because these were skills that would improve his working relationships.

He brightened up immediately. "Deal," he said.

That week, they formulated specific goals for Jay, and for Alice. Her goal was to learn as much as she could about chess, with Jay as her instructor.

Jay's goals included:

- Assess people, and be flexible.
- Build rapport, and be engaged.
- Work on presentation and interpersonal skills.

Assess People, and Be Flexible

Jay generally got high marks for conducting meetings; he stuck to the agenda and facilitated in a way that covered all the details. However, he sometimes assigned people tasks that didn't match their competencies, and would call out people who fell short in an insensitive, humiliating manner. People rarely felt at ease in meetings with Jay.

Remedies and homework included:

- Match people to tasks based on their competencies. Not only would this produce more favorable outcomes, but it would also force Jay to learn more about people and interact with them.

- Check with people before and after a meeting about how they are doing with a project and see if they need help.

Build Rapport, and Be Engaged

Jay rarely asked about other people's lives. He was not a good listener, and tended to interrupt and change the subject. He was difficult to build a relationship with because his life consisted mainly of work and competitive chess, and he liked to discuss both at length.

Remedies and homework included:

- Learn to listen. Make eye contact, refrain from interrupting, ask clarifying questions, and restate what the person said.
- Ease into interactions and meetings during the first three minutes. Have a couple of ready-made jokes for the week, and ask people how their weekend went.

Work on Presentation and Interpersonal Skills

One-on-one meetings with Jay could be painful. His meticulous level of detail would sometimes overwhelm his boss, and Jay would get impatient if his boss didn't remember a detail from one week to the next. Jay's emails were often lengthy and complicated; he assumed that if he put it in an email, it was solved and approved. His term for that was *recorded*.

Remedies and homework included:

- Be aware of body language.
- Keep the message simple and paragraphs short. Ask if there are any questions. Remain poised and keep a pleasant tone.
- Walk calmly in the hallways.
- Practice email etiquette.

Weeks 6-9: *Star Trek*

"Which chess piece is the most powerful?"

"Um, the queen?"

"No, the knight. It goes over the top."

Alice looked at him blankly.

"You said I should practice my humor," Jay protested. "That's one of my goals . . . to tell a few jokes. And I'm using it to help teach you."

Alice was struggling to fulfill her goal of learning as much as she could about the game. Not only were there various kinds of moves for the different pieces, but there were rules that confused her.

One day, Jay gave her a book: *Great Moves by the Great Masters*. "Now that you know the basics, you can begin to really study strategy. Pretty soon, you'll be ready for the novice tournaments!"

"Aha," Alice said, "I can see that my future life is all mapped out."

He looked at her closely. "You're trying to be funny, aren't you?"

"Yes, I am. And you're catching it more often now." She grinned.

He shook his head. "Human interactions are so convoluted and random. It reminds me of a character in the *Star Trek* series. She was human, but had been part of the Borg, a culture where human interaction was not allowed; everyone in the Borg crew was connected to a central computer and acted robotically. When she escaped and came to be part of the *Star Trek* crew, she didn't know how to relate to people. She was always making mistakes, always puzzled at the nuances of human behavior."

"And you feel like her?"

"Very much. I'm constantly puzzled by the things that people say and do."

"Let me ask you, did this character learn and become more comfortable with people?"

"Yes, but it was a slow process."

"Well, the slowness may have been for dramatic effect. You're learning how to become part of the crew at this company very rapidly."

He took a deep breath and let it out. "Thank you for that feedback. It's very difficult, but you're right; I am making progress."

Why Coaching Matters

"I was surprised at how slow you are at chess. But I suppose you are smart in other ways." Jay laughed. "Say, I'm doing it again, aren't I?" This was Alice's first time playing chess and she did not do it well; but Jay now understood that there were several forms of intelligence.

After Jay and Alice had worked together for a while, Jay said, "I am a better project manager. People seem to be performing better and avoiding me less." This was Jay's way of saying that he cared about whether people liked him or not.

Alice felt especially compassionate toward Jay as he did his best to move into new ways of acting and being. She could see he was confused by interactions with people in the same way that she was confused by all there was to know about chess. Human interactions are indeed complex, but when we're accustomed to them, the subtle nuances don't appear so unusual.

She made a mental note to watch a few episodes of *Star Trek*.

Weeks 10-16: Video Practice

Video, in the context of coaching work, can serve as a powerful, real-time tool, enabling the client to experiment with different verbal and physical communication. Alice recorded some of their chess lessons for Jay to observe himself in a live exercise. It also allowed Alice to guide him in real time; if he was being too abrupt or gruff, she could point it out. Then, when they watched the videos together, she could continue to point out instances where he needed to modify his interactions. Very quickly, he took over that role, noticing when his behavior was inappropriate. And, just as quickly, he began to modify his behavior in future sessions.

Alice also recorded a couple of Jay's project updates, and they worked on those in the same way as presentation skills. They practiced different approaches for him to use in meetings, such as employing a more relaxed physical stance and allowing people to speak freely without interruption.

After a few meetings, Alice surveyed attendees to get feedback. The results showed he was progressing quickly. A fast learner and now seeing the value in the work, Jay was very motivated and engaged.

Weeks 17–18: "Who Was That Person?"

Jay had reached a new level of ease. Alice put together a short review video with a few clips of him interacting in meetings before they began to practice, and then of meetings that were held after their work together. Watching these before-and-after videos, Jay marveled at the difference between his former, detached self and his new style. The new Jay smiled, took his time, and had a relaxed, professional stance about him.

"Who *is* that person?" he asked. "Or maybe I should say, who *was* that person?"

"A human," Alice responded. "He just needed a little help connecting with the others in his crew."

"I understand where people are coming from so much better," Jay mused. "I feel more comfortable in my job here now, but I've decided to move on."

"Oh?"

"Yes—I'm ready to join the *Star Trek* crew as first officer."

They laughed, and Alice took special delight in the difference between the new Jay and the old. It's one thing to understand humor, but another to initiate it—and these days, Jay was initiating it more and more.

"Whatever planet you're on," Alice said, "I support you in your endeavors!"

Tips for the Reader

Do you recognize a coaching client in Jay? Has this client ever noticed a chill when they enter the room? Coach your client to become aware of their body language. Make sure their eyes and lips are smiling when they say hello. Remind them to nod when people are talking, to not interrupt, and to stop themselves from going too deep into detail on one topic at first. Their goal is to be pleasant and put people around them at ease.

In addition to working on nonverbal communication, coach your clients on the importance of listening—a skill sometimes neglected by those rising in the management ranks. While your client might be structured and skilled, they can be even more effective by listening to people and their concerns. Encourage your client to learn two to three things about the people they spend the most time with at work. Emphasize that they can become better at their job by helping others meet their goals. This way, your client won't need to follow such a rigid process.

If your client has a colleague like Jay, they might be having trouble handling the relationship; this kind of hyperfocus and rigidity can be surprising or off-putting for people. Counsel your client to take their colleague's rigidity and intense approach in stride. It takes all kinds, and the colleague's temperament is likely not about your client. If your client would like to connect more deeply, encourage them to find a common interest and exchange information and observations about that interest.

Jay emailed Alice a few months later with an update. "I was kind of in a parallel universe," he wrote, "unaware of how rich and exciting this world can be!" He mentioned that he had some new friends (in addition to his chess friends)—and that he'd been doing a lot of laughing.

Summary

Jay was a skilled project manager, but he had a way of offending people without meaning to. He was shocked when the 360 revealed that many of his co-workers described him as hurtful, abrupt, and insensitive. Alice and Jay practiced his interpersonal interactions for four months; by the end, he had adopted a new ease and confidence. In meetings, he now had a congenial, professional manner.

Takeaway:

- Smart, successful people often have blind spots that affect their performance and offend their co-workers. For example, Jay had a blind spot when it came to interpersonal relations. Skilled coaching can clear even big blind spots and introduce new ways of behaving.

7

THE DRAMATIC EXECUTIVE

Kyle, a creative executive for a small, up-and-coming marketing agency, was an innovative genius, and his clients adored him. Kyle cultivated and brought in interesting clients; his long-standing clients always wanted him personally on their account because of his ability to "disrupt the old model" and bring in cutting-edge ideas. However, he could be moody and adversarial with co-workers, and was noncompliant with routine administrative duties. Alice's challenge was to encourage Kyle to be more of a team player without suppressing his creative brilliance.

KYLE'S MANAGER, PARI, HAD called Alice to see if she could help him be "more in line with how we run our firm." When Alice stopped by their office, Pari explained that Kyle was a great problem to have because he cared about clients so much—maybe too much. Whatever the challenge, he would turn it upside down and inside out, brainstorming solutions that nobody else had thought of. He was also an expert in many aspects of marketing: branding, advertising, design, digital media, public relations, and more.

"He can come up with a great strategy overnight—literally," Pari continued. "He'll stay up all night and then bring the almost-final product to the team meeting the next day—website content, design, storyline, everything. And it's great. It's a great product."

"This is a problem?" Alice asked.

"It's a problem because most of his team members would need two weeks to come up with a comparable product. So this makes them feel irrelevant. But he doesn't care. His only allegiance is to his beloved clients."

"What brought this to a head was what happened at the all-staff meeting last month," Pari continued. "One of the teams had had a big win, a culmination of a couple of months' work. But right after the announcement, just as the applause was dying down, Kyle stands up, goes to the whiteboard, and draws up a better plan for the team's client. It was genius—but I think you can see the problem."

Week 1: No More Paperwork

"I just can't see the problem!"

Kyle was striding around the room. He was tall, blond, good looking, and brimming with energy. His perfect teeth sparkled as he talked.

"I mean if I was screwing up, if a client was complaining, I could see why they might call you in. But my clients adore me! One of them just called this morning to thank me again for the great program I put together."

"Believe it or not," Alice said, "I'm here to help you become even more effective."

"Aha! You're going to help me get rid of paperwork! All this preposterous stuff Pari says I have to do. Clocking in and clocking out, expense reports, online filing system, client billing . . . yech!" He waved his hands violently, as if trying to shake it all out of existence. "That's how you can help me be more effective. I keep telling Pari, and everybody, that these things murder creativity and productivity. They *murder* them!"

"I better write that down," Alice said, taking out a pen. "Let's see . . . 'Homicide in the creative department. . . .'"

He peered at her suspiciously, then grinned. "Hmm, maybe you're going to be OK."

Alice smiled back. "I think we're going to have a good time working together."

Being a good executive coach means being yourself, and it's important to have fun while you work. Humor also often brings people closer together.

Weeks 2-3: Assessment

Predictably, the 360-degree assessment came back with a lot of criticism:

"Not a team player."

"Brilliant but unstable."

"Insensitive to the feelings of others."

"Unwilling to do basic administrative work."

In the psychological assessment, Kyle scored high on creativity and competing, low on collaborating and compromising.

Kyle believed he was born this way: creative, disruptive, hardworking, questioning priorities, and questioning authority. From his personal history, Alice learned he had attended a school for creative children and was highly regarded there; he'd won local competitions in art. He'd continued his success in college and had enjoyed being a teaching assistant, and his students had loved him.

Week 4: A Ray of Light

Kyle was holding the complete assessment and shaking his head.

"You know what?" he said. "I should just go out on my own—form my own company. My clients will follow me. They're the only ones who like me, that's pretty clear."

"Yes, you could do that," Alice said. "But then you'd be responsible for *all* the paperwork, plus the hiring, firing, managing, scheduling. . . ."

"Stop, stop! You're giving me a headache. What a *ghastly* nightmare!"

"It might not seem like it, but there are real benefits to being part of this firm. They take care of most of these things. You're asked to report your information, but they take it from there. They also provide this beautiful working space." Kyle's office overlooked the main drafting room, a modern, open space with huge white drawing tables and windows that spanned from the floor to the high ceiling. There was a steady stream of music from a high-tech surround-sound system. Dogs were welcome in the office, and Kyle often brought his dog, Lucinda, in with him.

Kyle began to pace around the room. "There's got to be a way. I can feel part of me dying whenever I start doing paperwork. I know that sounds dramatic, and I know I'm a dramatic person, but it's true. Suddenly I'm this 19th-century bookkeeper, perched on a high stool doing sums by candlelight. . . ."

"Bob Cratchit—Scrooge's assistant in *A Christmas Carol*," Alice said, smiling.

"Exactly! There's got to be a better way."

She nodded thoughtfully. "Suppose we went to finance and asked them to help us? I bet they could show you some shortcuts, some easier ways of completing all their reports. And you could make a case for a shared administrative assistant."

He stopped pacing and cocked his head. "Could this be true?" he asked. "Could there be a way?"

"There are ways," she answered. "Plus, you're a creative whiz. Maybe you could find ways of re-engineering the reporting process."

"*Moi?* Financial reporting? I don't think so."

"It's possible," she said. "Creative people are often able to bring their ingenuity to other fields—sometimes unexpected fields."

He sat down and smiled at her. "Dr. Alice, Bringer of Hope. I see a ray of light through the gloom!"

Alice had seen the smile Kyle had given her on other faces. Whether her clients are in danger of losing a job, can't get along with colleagues, or simply want to move ahead, they know change is necessary. Most, however, don't know how to make the change happen, and some are doubtful that they can. But there comes a time during the coaching process when that smile appears, when they understand that they can indeed change—that in fact, it's already happening.

Weeks 5-7: Goals

Over the next few weeks, Alice and Kyle set four big goals for his coaching. They wouldn't necessarily be easy to accomplish—at first, he didn't see how they would benefit him. This was part of the problem: The strength of his passions made it difficult for him to see the long-term payoff.

The goals they set were:

- Channel client advocacy.
- Improve relationships with superiors.
- Engage peers to assist and delegate when appropriate.
- Make room for others to shine.

Channel Client Advocacy

Kyle understood clients—their needs, their pain, and their potential gain. He also was a very dedicated and conscientious worker, using his keen skills to please them. But he saw only what was in front of him, challenged people too often, disrupted meetings, sulked, and withdrew.

Remedies and homework included:
- Count to 10 before responding to others or to situations, until he's able to gain a wider perspective and think more strategically. Keep body language neutral until he's able to re-engage in a positive way.
- Think big. Strive to recognize complexities and reach for higher-level solutions that could affect many clients, not just the client at hand. (This includes designing client solutions per market or per service and using creativity to predict future needs.)
- Learn to delay gratification for larger rewards. Practice controlling emotional reactions; thinking and planning ahead can help keep composure.
- Brainstorm about which cross-functional teams at the firm could serve clients in a fuller, more seamless way (not per department). This would also help to develop employees' skills over time and build positive relationships with peers.
- Invest in outside work activities and people. Clients and a passion for work are important, but so is a passion for creativity outside work.

Improve Relationships With Superiors

Kyle and Pari had not only different styles, but also different management practices and values.

Remedies and homework included:
- Get to know his manager better, including her work, duties, values, and strengths; what she needs from her team; and what the company needs from her. This way, Kyle could understand her requests in the context of her needs and pay more attention to them. Then, over time, he could give her what she needed in exchange for what he needed.

- Pick his battles. Kyle needed to see clearly which items are non-negotiable and which are not important in the long run. This included ranking priorities by effort and time.
- Plan ahead to get maximum impact; prepare the approach and the right place and time to present it. Some conversations, for example, are better in a one-on-one meeting than in a team setting, and vice versa. Having solutions to propose enables more productive conversations.
- Set common ground, goals, and timelines together, leveraging one another's strengths, and partner with Pari in a way that minimized surprises for either party. This might even include bringing Pari to a client meeting so that she could get a better sense of the challenges Kyle and his team faced.

Engage Peers to Assist and Delegate When Appropriate

Kyle "didn't believe in paperwork" because it took time away from what he liked doing—client work. He said this often, annoying his colleagues.

Remedies and homework included:

- Reach out to finance and HR to learn more about their requests and the shortcuts in the systems. He could humanize this experience and build relationships so that he could call on them for help when needed.
- Make a business case to obtain help from a shared administrative assistant. This would ensure that the company was maxing the potential of each employee.
- Learn to engage direct reports on some of the reporting tasks and delegate parts to them when appropriate.

- Offer to help streamline some of the business processes in finance and HR. For example, Kyle believed the expense report process could be altered to improve the user's experience. He could use his creative mind to re-engineer the process in a way that made requests easier to complete for all departments. In this way, he could both help finance and HR and build better peer relationships.

Make Room for Others to Shine

Kyle had some talented people on his team, but he rarely encouraged their input or shared his knowledge with them.

Remedies and homework included:

- Coach and train two members of the team. Kyle would share his expertise with them and encourage their efforts.
- After six weeks, start coaching another two members, and so on until he's covered the whole team.

Weeks 8-9: A Very Interesting Presentation

Kyle and Alice started on his goals by practicing responses in the privacy of his office. He had recently designed a campaign for a client, and Alice was looking it over as they opened their next session.

Kyle began to explain the plan at the whiteboard as if he were leading the meeting, and Alice role-played by asking the kinds of questions team members might ask. Some of her questions were perceptive and intelligent, while others were undiscerning or downright foolish. After the foolish questions, Kyle would take a deep breath, and Alice could see him counting to 10 in his mind. Then he would answer the question as evenly as he could, all the while keeping his body language as neutral as possible. He got better at it very quickly; after a few times, he didn't even need the deep breath.

Next, Alice took the role of program designer—one of his direct reports—standing at the whiteboard. She presented the marketing plan for a new client while Kyle tried his best to avoid jumping in with better ideas. This was even more challenging for him than answering foolish questions; he was constantly taking deep breaths as Alice spoke.

When she had finished the presentation, he practiced offering some praise for the program designer; then he would work at diplomatically suggesting ways to improve the plan: "You might want to consider . . ." or "Here's a suggestion for the initial part of the program. . . ." This was the *as if* strategy: He would say the phrases *as if* he were interested; then, after a while, he would begin to sound authentic, and finally, he would begin to feel authentic.

It was important at this phase in the process for Kyle to understand that when delegating work, he had to avoid rushing to "fix" every detail he perceived to be out of place. Many executives and leaders excelled at the day-to-day work before being promoted, and it often takes coaching to help them *lead more* and *do less*.

Week 10: The Juggler

During the next session, Alice attended a meeting Kyle had with Pari.

Pari laid out the agenda: She would present her concerns as a manager, Kyle would then present his position, and, finally, they would discuss how they might work together to solve their various concerns.

Pari started out by emphasizing the difference between her job and his. Whereas Kyle dealt with his team and his clients, she had to ensure that all the employees who reported to her were working productively and harmoniously. If discord, bad feelings, and resentment cropped up, it would affect the firm's ability to produce good products. In her world, everybody was important, not just the clients.

In addition, she had to make sure that everybody was fulfilling the basic administrative work that Kyle lumped under "paperwork." She pointed out that if he didn't file his billings and expense reports, finance wouldn't be able to calculate company earnings—and this would ultimately make it impossible for them to issue paychecks.

Pari continued for about 15 minutes. When she finished, Kyle's reaction was to be uncharacteristically quiet. "Wow," he said, "I didn't realize how many balls you have in the air. You're like this master juggler."

Pari smiled. "Yes, I do feel that way a lot."

Kyle nodded. "Well, I really don't want to disrupt your act. About the reporting, Dr. Alice suggested that I might be able to make a business case for an administrative assistant to help with this. If I wrote up a request, would you consider it?"

Pari blinked. "Uh, yes, absolutely. I think that's an excellent idea."

"And about the meetings. I've been working on this with Dr. Alice. I don't want to be the one everybody hates, but I do want the clients to be the main focus. So, I came up with this idea for a new kind of meeting where the client is considered first. . . ."

The session continued this way, with Kyle and Pari each listening carefully to the other, then presenting their own views. Alice was delighted to see Kyle employ his newfound conversational skills. He was really listening to Pari—and truly processing much of it for the first time.

From the start of their work together, Alice had a hunch that Kyle had a good heart. Like many leaders, he tended to get carried away by his creative passions and was given to drama and posturing, but she sensed that at his core, he cared deeply and unreservedly about people. This insight helped her craft a long-term secret solution for him.

Later in the day, Alice got an email from Pari: "Based on past experience, I was surprised at how fruitful our meeting was today.

I'm seeing how Kyle can channel his disruptive thinking into positive efforts. I'm very hopeful. Thanks for your contribution to this."

Week 11: Ready for More

Kyle was elated by his experience in a recent meeting and by his session with Pari.

"I'm doing it, Dr. Alice! I'm actually doing it! At the meeting, I was able to hold my tongue and then respond more calmly. And guess what? People listened to me instead of just rolling their eyes. Who knew?! It feels super great to be listened to, instead of always being the bad guy."

"You've worked hard on your responses. I'm so glad it's paying off."

"And the meeting with Pari—she listened to me, too! You know, I submitted that request for an administrative assistant, and she OK-ed it."

"The wins just keep coming," Alice said.

"I'm ready for more," he enthused. "What else is on our list?"

Weeks 12-15: And on the 15th Week . . .

Now that Kyle saw their work together could bring about exciting changes, he threw himself into it completely. The things he did over the next few weeks would have left most people gasping for breath, but Kyle took it all in stride.

First, on Alice's advice, he scheduled another meeting with Pari. He was learning the concept of managing up—working with your manager for your mutual benefit. Because her coaching clients report to a chief executive, another C-suite, or a board of directors, managing up is often part of the work. They talked about how to set common ground, goals, and timelines together; leveraging each other's strengths; and partnering in a way that minimized surprises for either party.

Next, Kyle invited Pari to a client meeting so she could see more of his world and better understand the things he might ask for in his meetings with her. Characteristically, Kyle had come up with his own definition of "managing up."

"I'm teaching Pari how to manage me," he grinned.

Overnight, he designed a new way to have meetings. Instead of hourlong, operationally focused, and meandering meetings, clients were placed first on the agenda, and the meetings were only 30 minutes long, twice a day. It proved effective.

Kyle also reached out to finance and HR to learn the shortcuts in their systems. He and Alice discussed how he could humanize this experience and make it easier for their internal customers to complete their requests. This helped him build relationships with them, so that he could call on them for help when he needed it.

In addition, he offered to help streamline some of the business processes in finance—particularly to re-engineer the expense report process to improve the user's experience.

Kyle began to coach two members of his team in the finer points of marketing, and quickly realized it was rewarding to share the skills he had developed over the years. His team members were enthusiastic about the coaching; Kyle made it clear he would work with all of them in turn, six weeks at a time for each pair.

Finally, with some gentle nudging from Alice, he discovered a nonprofit that helped artists create street art for buildings. This engaged him immediately; within two weeks, he had come up with several ideas for enhancing the work of the organization. Alice's strategy in this coaching engagement stemmed from her insight of just how much Kyle cared about people. To top it all off, Kyle began to take a class in public policy.

Tips for the Reader

Do you recognize your coaching clients in Kyle? If so, urge them to think before they act. Remind them that just because they *can* disrupt a process or industry to improve it doesn't mean they need to. Encourage them to choose the time and place to create or disrupt, to maximize their impact in a way they really want for the long term. Remind them they can achieve even more when they take time to socialize their ideas and build buy-in across teams and individuals.

These issues often extend to their relationships with their managers. Perhaps you can counsel your client to get to know themselves, and their boss, to try to find common ground. Gain a full understanding of the dynamics and shift the focus onto three things that matter to both your clients and their managers, which will help both parties. This may seem kind of backward, but it works.

If your client works with people who behave like Kyle, let them know to try not to take personally the moods, being upstaged, or feeling invisible. If they must partner with such a colleague, encourage your client to do their best to demonstrate the similarities in each other's values and dedication, while also appreciating each other's strengths and areas of development.

Week 16: A Personal Guide

Kyle had become a welcome presence at meetings. Now that he had altered his way of relating, people valued his creative input. He was developing a good working relationship with Pari and was already making suggestions on how finance could improve its requests for reporting; internal customers now had an easier time completing the requests. He was even making peace with the hated paperwork.

It was time to bring the coaching to a close.

"I'll miss you, Dr. Alice."

"Didn't I tell you that we'd have a good time working together?" she asked.

"You did—though at the time, I didn't believe it. I can't believe how much I've changed. Thanks are hardly enough."

"You're the one who made the changes," Alice said. "I just helped guide you."

As a final gesture of his appreciation, Kyle presented Alice with a gift certificate to her favorite dog-friendly restaurant.

Kyle called Alice a few months later to tell her he'd gotten a promotion. He was still working with the finance manager on the client management system, and he was now on the board of directors of the street art

Why Coaching Matters

Coaching can totally turn around the working experience of your clients. And when it takes longer than expected, they'll appreciate your patience. In this case, Alice and Kyle worked on helping Kyle improve his ability to manage his reactions, which led to a promotion at work and his participation in the community. A productive executive coaching engagement often does feel like the world is topsy-turvy for a while; this is because underlying beliefs are being challenged and are often replaced, and because the process involves an element of choice that is introduced early on, like it was for Kyle.

"I'm still working with the finance manager," he told Alice. "I'm working on their client management system, and in exchange she's teaching me to make wine. It's been four months." Previously when this manager had called meetings, Kyle had preferred to skip them, so this was a great sign. He had found common ground not only at the office, but outside it as well.

"My public policy classes are great," he continued. "I never would have thought about higher-impact work and legacy in my community—it's opened up a whole new world of learning and meaning for me, and impact for the community." Sometimes, finding other avenues for high performers to channel their energy can help relieve some of the intensity in the office.

nonprofit. The people at the nonprofit must have soon realized what a whirlwind they had welcomed into their midst, but, like Kyle's marketing agency colleagues now, they were probably enjoying the breeze.

Summary

Marketing executive Kyle was a creative genius, but he could be moody and disruptive at work. The challenge was to encourage him to be more of a team player without suppressing his creative brilliance. Over four months, Kyle practiced being more pleasant and responsive in meetings and learned to collaborate with his manager. His colleagues came to welcome his presence, and his manager was pleased that she and Kyle could now work together cooperatively.

Takeaway:

- Creative brilliance is a wonderful thing, but it needs to be presented in a way that people can receive. In this case, after coaching, Kyle was able to learn to present his innovative marketing strategies in ways that his colleagues could accept. This served both him and the company.

8

THE CEO UNDER THE DESK

Sometimes executive coaching requires more than just a background in organization development. Without the proper advanced expertise in certain situations, you're better off referring the executive to a different professional. In this case, Roberto, CEO of a large manufacturing company, was struggling with erratic behavior; his executive team called Alice in because they were increasingly concerned. Roberto rarely came out of his office and was fulfilling only a few of his functions as a CEO. Alice took this on knowing it would be a tough challenge . . . but she was about to find out just how tough.

THE TOP FLOOR HAD THE usual suite of executive offices. There was a line of movable partitions shielding the office of the CEO, which struck Alice as barriers; the guard pulled one partition aside just enough for her to squeeze through into a small reception room.

"Dr. Alice Well," he announced to the woman behind the desk, then turned and left.

"Please come in," said the woman. She had graying hair and a pleasant face that was marred only by a worried frown. "And the purpose of your meeting with Mr. Rodriguez?"

Alice blinked. Secretaries were usually more knowledgeable than their bosses about the purpose of meetings.

"Oh, you're a consultant, aren't you? We've had several of those come through recently." She picked up her phone. "I'll tell Mr. Rodriguez you're here."

She spoke much longer than was needed for a simple announcement—and her frown deepened as she talked. Alice wondered if this was yet another barrier.

Finally she hung up, took a deep breath, and rose from her chair. "Mr. Rodriguez will see you now," she said, leading the way to a large door—the final barrier, Alice thought.

The office was spacious, with glass paneling and all-white furniture. Corner windows looked out over the bay, but there was no one to be seen. There was a row of Superstar sneakers lined up against a wall and a small kitchenette with neatly stacked dishes and cups. The glossy white desk was well ordered, with a sleek desktop computer—and a man underneath it.

Alice moved closer to the desk. He slid out from underneath, but remained on the floor. She realized she had been wrong about the door being the last barrier. Now there was the desk—and, of course, whatever internal forces had driven him under it.

She decided to let him check her out. She stood silently, gazing out at the bay; the sun had set, and the gathering darkness contributed to the film noir atmosphere. Several minutes passed, but he stayed put.

"How about I come back tomorrow evening?" Alice said. A few moments went by.

"Please," he answered.

Weeks 1-2: Out of Control

The following night, Alice was slightly relieved to find him sitting in his executive chair when she entered the room.

"This company is out of control," he started as she seated herself. There were no introductions, no small talk.

"People don't have any sense of ownership, no passion. I've tried putting my entire senior team on performance improvement plans, but they still don't show the kind of drive this company needs."

"This company, or you?" she asked.

He stopped, then looked at her suspiciously. "You don't understand the pressure now that this is a publicly traded company. You don't own a company like mine; you only have a small business. I knew this was a bad idea."

"We can stop at any time. Is it the fact that you have to rely on others that concerns you?"

"It was better before when it was just me. They're out of control, and they don't care."

He moved a paperweight over a few inches on his desk and straightened a file.

Week 3: The Company Without a Name

For the first two weeks, Alice felt like a lone detective with few clues. Her client, Roberto, continued to rail against his managers and resisted her attempts to expand the conversation. However, she had other ways of digging up clues—namely, her assessment tools: the profiles and the 360-degree feedback.

Those responding to the 360 made it clear they were very concerned about their CEO. When he'd first taken over the company 11 months ago, things seemed to go well. During the last few months, however, he had become increasingly unfocused and indecisive. Most people thought that he had to either make changes or resign. One respondent mentioned that Roberto "had some problems" at his previous company; she didn't know the details, but she had heard it was fairly serious.

Alice finally had something to go on. At their next meeting, she didn't waste any time in bringing this up.

"I understand you had some fairly serious problems at your previous company. What company was that?"

He slumped in his chair. "It doesn't have a name," he said quietly.

"No name?" she inquired.

He swiveled to face the window, away from her. He was silent for a few moments.

"It doesn't exist anymore."

"Can you tell me more?"

He turned back to her. "The company failed under my watch. Completely tanked. I had to lay off 6,000 employees—many without any severance pay. I had to do it on my own, with just a few consultants. My team deserted me."

"Would you like to tell me how this happened?"

"It was my fault. My team . . ."

". . . Yes?"

"No, it was *my* failing—I should have known, should have checked. . . ."

A few months ago, the headcount at Roberto's present company had just passed 6,000. But while others were celebrating this growth, Roberto was reminded of the 6,000 employees he'd had to lay off. Alice's guess was that this event had triggered his memories and set off his increasingly strange behavior.

Weeks 4–5: Coaching Goals

At their next meeting, Alice began to work with Roberto on setting his coaching goals:

- Work through stress.
- Re-enter the company.
- Create a new business environment.

Alice often worked with clients on all the goals at once, as the goals tended to feed off one another. This time, however, they needed to be sequential. Roberto would be unable to move forward until he accomplished his first goal.

Work Through Stress

Roberto had experienced a stressful event: the failure of his previous company. Before he could move on, this stress needed to be resolved.

Remedies and homework included:

- Write down a history of the perceived failure, including the names of the people involved and what happened.
- Relive, work through, let go, and neutralize the feelings associated with each part of the stress; make amends where needed (including to himself), and rewrite the story.
- Maintain an intensive coaching meeting schedule focused on the company failure and his reaction to it.

Re-Enter the Company

Roberto had retreated to the safety of his office. Once his stress had been dealt with, he needed to leave his office and start meeting with people.

Remedies and homework included:

- Rehearse one-on-one meetings with executive staff. Roberto and Alice would do this in the privacy of his office.
- Physically leave his office and walk around the building.

Create a New Business Environment

Roberto had withdrawn from many of his executive duties. He needed to reassert his leadership and work with his team to create a new blueprint for the future of the company.

Remedies and homework included:

- Create a new leadership team. Meet with existing leaders and add new team members.
- Review the existing financial projections and growth strategy.
- Draw up a new blueprint for the future.

Weeks 6-12: Extreme Stress

Alice and Roberto checked in every weekday evening for two months, winding through the series of events that had happened to Roberto over the past decade. He organized his stories in fiscal years; the most painful were those during the unwinding of his previous company. He replayed the layoffs, the announcements, the problems getting out of the lease, and these recollections were increasing his understanding about the events.

Indeed, people had failed him at his last company: The chief financial officer and the chief marketing officer had lied to him about funding and kept him in the dark until it was too late. He was forced to close the company and lay off his employees alone; the team bailed on him.

Roberto would have benefited from a brief break between jobs, but instead he moved directly from that job into this company. He had not taken the time to process the transition; he still felt guilty about the fate of the employees at his first company, and mistrustful of leaders. Now, stressed by the announcement of the 6,000th employee at his present company, he was alarmed.

There is often a company ritual when hitting a milestone employee count—a bell is rung, an announcement made. In this case, Roberto was reminded of the layoffs. Alice had encountered many leaders who had laid off employees and had themselves been laid off. Roberto's behaviors were those of stress: avoidance, negative thinking, and erratic behavior, especially when triggered by an event that brought up the past stress. The tight control he kept on the order and cleanliness of his office was related to the strong memories from his previous job.

Weeks 13–17: Leave the Office

Things moved rapidly after Roberto realized that stress had built up from his previous company, which he then brought into this company. After he gained more insight into past events, he began to see his part in the senior team's deception. He started to forgive himself, and to let go of the past. He was increasingly leaving the protective confines of his office and re-entering the company. Another sign of progress was that his office was not as organized and clean as it once was; he was starting to tolerate the messiness of humans and of his own process. And Alice noticed that the Superstar sneakers had been replaced by dress oxfords from Vegan Chic.

Tips for the Reader

Do you recognize your coaching clients in Roberto? Avoidance is a natural response to stress; they are trying to keep themselves safe from negative reactions. With support and tools, they can stop avoiding and be productive and happy at work. Building a strong executive team composed of some leaders who have experienced the ups and downs of business helps if hard decisions need to be made.

Invite your clients to list the work duties they try to avoid, and make a plan to tackle each one. No leader enjoys reductions in force, disciplining employees, or closing a business. Encourage your clients to build a support network with which they can connect. Gain a full understanding of their environment and how it is different from when they had to lay people off, fire people, or demote people. For example, certain conference rooms or the HR offices can be a reminder for many leaders and employees.

Many leaders have experienced negative events at work, and they all respond differently. Your coaching client is in a unique position to help their colleagues. Encourage them to not compare, but instead to share techniques that helped in an event such as a layoff. Perhaps your client can let their colleagues know that they are not alone—that they have had similar experiences at work (without overwhelming them with the details of their own story). Some companies have an Employee Assistance Program that could be helpful.

Stress affects those directly and indirectly exposed to the original stressful events. Read up on responses to stress—the more you know, the better equipped you will be. You can also seek the assistance of a professional mental health worker, such as a psychotherapist or a support group.

Weeks 18-30: Re-Entry and Rebuilding

For the next few weeks, with Alice's help, Roberto rehearsed for his re-entry as a hands-on CEO. It was time to look to the future. His goal was to resume his former role, but in a more defined and strategic way.

They pored over the bios and resumes of the leadership team, and Alice listened to details about his relationships with each member. When he felt he was ready, he began to hold one-on-one meetings with them.

Next, he reviewed the financial projections and growth strategy, which seemed solid. Together, they drew up an ideal organizational structure for a company of 6,000-10,000 employees, from the board of directors to the manager level. Each nameless box on the organization chart had competencies listed.

Roberto ended up rebuilding his team, adding a couple of leaders with the experience to take the company through the next phase of growth. He created a leadership compact at a couple of retreats, and changed the format and cadence of leadership meetings. He also added a few wise and experienced board members.

Week 31: A Good Sign

Alice continued to see Roberto for another few weeks, but he was getting ready to move on. At their last meeting, she'd noted that not only was his office less tidy, but his hair was even a bit tousled. That's when she knew he would be fine.

Before parting ways, they reviewed the past seven months. He noted the dramatic changes in his leadership style, and said that he now felt ready to guide this company without interference from past disappointments. He agreed to call or email if he needed.

Roberto emailed Alice six months later. He wrote that his desk was a mess, his hair needed cutting, and his new oxfords had mud on them—and he thanked Alice for creating the mess.

Why Coaching Matters

Executive coaches are not universally understood, and each are quite different. In this case, what Roberto and his company received from the coaching engagement exceeded their expectations. "We now have the right governance structure and leaders to see this company through the next 10 years," Roberto said to Alice at the end. But Roberto was also commenting on something deeper: his narrowed vision due to his previous stress. Alice felt fortunate that they had found each other, and that she could help him in a unique way thanks to her advanced clinical and organizational training.

Summary

Roberto was the CEO of a midsized tech company, and his executive team was increasingly concerned about his erratic behavior. As Alice worked with Roberto, it became clear that he had suffered severe stress when his previous company had failed. He had been deceived by two members of his executive team and forced to lay off thousands of employees. This stress had to be dealt with before he could move on. For four months they worked through his suffering, finally emerging on the other side. At this point, they began to plan his re-emergence as a CEO. Roberto reviewed financial projections and growth strategy and rebuilt his executive team. After seven months, he was again ready to function as a highly skilled CEO.

Takeaways:

- Often, people in distress need psychological counseling before they can deal with business issues. In this case, Roberto had to work through his stress before re-emerging as a CEO.
- In cases like this, it's important to engage a coach who is skilled at both counseling psychology and organization development.

9

THE DIRECTOR
WHO DID LITTLE

Bob was an expert in the field of insurance, and he knew his company like the back of his hand. He was a nice guy, and his colleagues remarked that he often had interesting stories about his weekends and knew cool facts about the city. Bob had been at the company a long time and had always met his performance goals. However, neither he nor his team grew or thrived, and Bob's manager complained that Bob didn't seem to do much. Was he just lazy? Human resources viewed this situation as a performance issue, but Bob's manager thought the company owed Bob a chance to change. Alice's job was to figure out what was going on.

Week 1: An Unusual Situation

AN UNUSUAL THING HAPPENED when Alice first met with Bob: She got bored. This surprised her, because most of her clients are anything *but* boring. They're often in difficult situations, in emotional pain, in danger of being fired, or disliked and feared, but they're almost always highly intelligent, energetic people.

Bob, on the other hand, presented in a very subdued manner. He had light green eyes with a slow blink; he mostly wore Dockers and a white shirt. He leaned on the armrest of his chair and listened while Alice told him about the coaching program's four steps: assessment, setting goals, implementation, and review.

"Do you have any thoughts about this program?" Alice asked when she had finished.

"Well, whatever," he answered, "it reminds of a retreat I went to some years ago. . . ." He related a mildly amusing story about his experience, but Alice sensed that it had been told many times before.

Weeks 2-3: Mr. Excitement

Although Bob's manner didn't change, he did apply himself to the assessment tests. Alice began the 360-degree assessment and soon learned that Bob's team called him "Mr. Excitement" behind his back; they would lay bets as to whether he would wear a short-sleeved white shirt or a long-sleeved white shirt the next day. They generally liked him, but had little respect for him, and resented him for being lazy, unresponsive, and unhelpful. One man complained that Bob didn't have the right priorities: "As a supervisor, he should be more interested in the development of our team, our skills, and our careers. Instead, it seems like he just wants to stay out of trouble and get along with everybody."

Bob had a new boss, Chivonne, who was shocked at his inertness. When Alice met with her, Chivonne wondered out loud if he shouldn't be demoted to an individual contributor—a team member instead of a supervisor. She was concerned because when she had suggested this to Bob, he didn't disagree; he simply said, "Well, whatever." This exchange had prompted her to ask Alice to work with him.

Chivonne was part of a younger generation and had higher expectations than his previous managers; those managers had grown up in the company with Bob, and many had surpassed him. In the 360, they noted Bob's level in the company, but didn't criticize him directly.

Bob's profile showed a balanced temperament, a sharp and curious mind, good creativity and imagination, an ease with language and words, and an interest and aptitude for mathematics and statistics. He was clearly in the right field. He had advanced into management simply by seniority in the company and had never had problems with HR. He attended all the required training programs, and occasionally taught a module on risk management to the junior partners. He was not totally bland; he just didn't do very much.

Alice considered several theories. Perhaps he was burned out after 10 years at the same job. Did he have "analysis paralysis"—did he overthink each decision to the extent that no decisions got made? Or was he really just lazy? She tossed these ideas around in her mind, but as she learned more about Bob, none of them seemed to be a good fit. He was bored, all right—but he seemed comfortable with his boredom. She got the sense that retirement, although still far away, was his main goal.

Week 4: History

Bob and Alice greeted each other as she made her way to a chair in his office. As she sat down, she noticed a new painting on the wall. It showed a tall, masted ship sailing between two landmasses with a gorgeous sunset in the background.

"That's a beautiful painting," she said. "Is it new?"

"I just got it at auction," he said. "It's by William Coulter, the best maritime painter in early San Francisco. The land on either side is the Golden Gate, before the bridge was built. Have you ever seen the Merchant Exchange Building on California Street? Julia Morgan, who designed the Hearst Castle, hired Coulter to do the murals."

"Sounds like you're interested in early San Francisco."

"I'm doing research for a book about historic buildings in the financial district. And I'm including all I can find about the ones that were destroyed in the earthquake and fire in 1906—the special ones."

"Tell me more about your book." Alice noticed a subtle change in Bob's tone, a note of enthusiasm that she hadn't heard before. Such moments are precious in the coaching relationship; the goal is to engage the coaching client more deeply, especially in the first few coaching meetings. Here, she was searching for Bob's areas of interest and expertise.

"Well, I've been researching it for 10 years. My friends tell me I should go ahead and begin writing, but I can't seem to get started."

After that meeting, Alice did some reassessing. Bob had shown real interest when he talked about history and his book. It occurred to her that he had simply lost his passion for the work he did and had stopped prioritizing it—he had checked out and gone on autopilot. This was understandable; he had done the same kind of work, with the same kind of people, in the same aspect of the business for at least a decade.

Weeks 5-6: Reawakening

Bob seemed unfazed by the results of his 360. Alice got the feeling that he already knew what the respondents were saying about him.

She pointed out that his manner had changed when he talked about his book, and he nodded. "Yeah, I guess I've lost interest in my work here. It's happened over time, so I just kind of got used to it. I put in my time here, then I go home to things I'm really interested in—like spending time with my partner and doing research for my book."

"That's a lot of hours to spend being bored. Suppose we could rekindle your interest in your job. I have a few ideas that we could work on together."

He started to say, "Whatever," then stopped himself. He thought for a moment, then said, "I'm open to hearing your ideas."

Over the next few weeks, Bob and Alice put together three goals:

- Develop direct reports.
- Expand subject matter expertise.
- Reinvigorate mind, body, and spirit.

Develop Direct Reports

If Bob was going to remain a supervisor, he had to prioritize his team.

Remedies and homework included:

- Build his team. Bob needed to meet with members of his staff and create individual career development plans for them.
- Hold "learning labs" in which each person on Bob's team would present a 20-minute lesson. Sometimes the content would come from the presenter's own expertise and experience, other times from a seminar they had attended or viewed or from an online video.
- Learn to delegate. List job duties and activities and rank them by most developmental and least engaging. Delegate the activities accordingly; this would help the team members in their development and eliminate the work that was the most tedious for Bob.

Expand Subject Matter Expertise

Bob had the capacity to learn. Alice thought that learning a new skill set might stimulate his passion—something she'd seen happen in other executives. She also knew he'd be exposed to another leadership style.

Remedies and homework included:

- Work two days a week in the heritage safeguard division as an assessor. His task was to assess older, unique buildings for the appropriate type and level of insurance coverage.

- Using the time saved by delegating certain tasks, Bob should complete the full cycle of assessment for the newly insured buildings and report his findings to Otsana, the leader of the heritage safeguard division. Otsana was happy to supervise and develop Bob's skills in this area.

Reinvigorate Mind, Body, and Spirit

Bob was not just physically out of shape; his mind and his spirit were also in need of exercise.

Remedies and homework included:

- Enroll in an intense program of classes on the history of the city. Although Bob was an expert on historic buildings, he agreed that he needed more comprehensive background information on the city's history. This would support him in writing his book.
- Sign up for a 14-week gym boot camp. This camp was designed specifically for people who were badly out of shape and needed to start slowly.
- Take his partner to a new bed-and-breakfast every other weekend.

Tips for the Reader

Do you recognize your coaching clients in Bob? Are they checked out or bored? Dare them to take a trip down memory lane to recall what used to energize them. What were their dreams and goals? Urge them to experiment, to try new things, or to try the same things in a new way. Encourage them to ask their friends and family about their experience lately—what seems to interest them?

This lack of enthusiasm might be leading your clients to forget about their team. Maybe they don't make or take the time to work with them, or perhaps they are not comfortable with giving feedback. Bring your clients to the realization that the more they develop their team, the more freed up their own time and attention will be in the long run. This will enable your clients to get to those other aspects of their job that they never seem to be able to access. In addition, it will be gratifying to see the team develop.

Bear in mind that development is not for the faint of heart, so encourage your coaching client to ask each direct report about their career aspirations, skills, and learning styles, and create individual development plans with them. Some will be modest, others more ambitious. Your client should remind their employees that there are other sources of development, such as training programs, buddy and mentorship programs, on-the-job learning, and stretch assignments.

A bonus of coaching is that your clients will feel empowered and able to help their colleagues and direct reports. They might identify a colleague who seems checked out. If your client is moved to help this colleague, perhaps they can try to engage and connect. Your client could ask questions about the person's interests, goals, or team, and just listen. It might be a wake-up call. If it's a direct report, you can help your client encourage them to find an area of expertise or passion that they and the manager can connect on, and try to build rapport. This rapport could differentiate the employee in the manager's eyes, and they might be able to work together more effectively. Encourage the employee to state clearly and gently what they need, and suggest a way to have fun doing it together in a creative manner. They can perhaps get a spark going.

Sometimes we simply need to know ourselves better; sometimes we lose sight of our strengths and areas of opportunity. In these cases, feedback is key. You have to ask for it, because most colleagues won't offer it. Similarly, if a colleague asks for feedback, try to be accurate but tactful. When you ask specific questions about skills, performance, and attitude, it's helpful to get feedback from more than one source. Be sure to take notes. A colleague, coach, or manager could help you sort through the feedback; this will aid you in absorbing new knowledge about yourself. They can also help you devise a plan to move forward.

Weeks 7-9: Change Can Be Challenging

The first three weeks of Bob's new program were challenging for him.

"I don't know if I can do this, Dr. Alice. I'm exhausted every night . . . but that's not even the worst of it. I told myself that if this program didn't work out, I could always go back to the way I was before. But now I see that I can never go back. It's either change or die, and right now I feel like dying is the more likely outcome."

"I've worked with a lot of people who go through these kinds of changes," Alice said. "I believe if that you continue, you'll get on top of it. How do you like your classes?"

"Well, I fell asleep in my 19th Century San Francisco class the other night. But other than that, they're good classes. I'm interested."

"Hang in there. Things will get easier."

Weeks 10-12: Progress

Bob complained a lot in general, and even expressed doubts about the coaching process, but he was continuing to engage a little more and work consistently on his goals. His work was paying off, and the results were starting to get noticed.

"I've gotten some good feedback on my meetings with team members," he said.

"You've been creating career development plans for them?" Alice asked.

"Yes, and they're very grateful. I've also been delegating some tasks to my team, and that's benefiting all of us."

"This sounds good. How's your energy level these days?"

"Well, I'm not exhausted all the time. I suppose that's progress. I've even lost a few pounds."

Weeks 13-18: Fully Alive

By week 18, Bob had come fully alive. He was accomplishing all his goals and was full of energy and enthusiasm. He had even started to come up with some creative ideas of his own.

"I have this idea for a program for new grads coming into their first year in the insurance business. I realized that I could use all I know about the field and the company, and I could work with my team members in the training program. I've run it by Chivonne and she's into it—says she'll send it on up."

Alice smiled and shrugged. "Whatever," she said lightly.

He smiled back and shook his head. "Yeah, that used to be me. I can hardly believe it."

Why Coaching Matters

While many leaders enjoy the thrill of their position, others grow accustomed and complacent. Coaching is often the most effective way to get leaders to check back in—the unbiased third party who comes in and shakes things up. In Bob's case, he was bored and missing out on life without knowing it. With a little bit of coaching, you can help your clients feel more like themselves again.

Alice got an email from Bob nine months after their work together had ended—he had just been recognized as Manager of the Year and was full of pride. He wrote about how top management liked his program for new grads coming into the company, and they especially liked how he let his team lead the effort. He also said that he had started writing his book, and had already generated some interest from a publisher.

Summary

Although Bob was an expert in the field of insurance, neither he nor his team grew or thrived. He was generally liked, but not respected; Bob's director complained that Bob just didn't seem to do much and wondered if he was just lazy. From the assessment and her conversations with Bob, Alice ascertained that he had simply lost his passion for his work and was on autopilot. Together, they formulated some ambitious goals to reinvigorate his mind, body, and spirit. Bob worked through his resistance and began to come alive. Nine months after his coaching engagement, he was named Manager of the Year.

Takeaway:

- Sometimes an individual with all the aptitude and skills necessary to be a success simply lacks the will to move ahead. When Bob rekindled his interest in his work, he became an effective and innovative manager—and renewed his enjoyment for life.

10

CONCLUSION

WE HAVE REVIEWED NINE coaching engagements with very different people and situations. But why is coaching so effective? Why is it able to achieve such dramatic results in short periods of time? How are powerful people who are set in their ways able to adopt new, more positive ways of dealing with people and situations?

I believe there are four factors that make the coaching experience a powerful force for change: the will, the what, the how, and the who.

The Will

The first factor is motivation—the will to move ahead. The client needs to have a desire for positive change, although this desire may not always be present at the start of the coaching engagement. In this book, there were two clients who were initially very dubious about the value of coaching: Jay in chapter 6 and Bob in chapter 9. It took several weeks before they began to see positive changes and became motivated to do more. Once this happened, however, they embraced the process and radically transformed their personalities and their leadership styles.

However, Madison and John, in chapter 4, weren't willing to work out their differences at the start, nor did they become any more willing as the coaching continued. This lack of motivation led to the engagement's failure.

Reluctance and doubt about the ability to change are common, but if the coaching client does their homework and practices new ways of relating, there will be change. (In other words, if they allow me to do my work, they *will* move ahead—sometimes in spite of themselves!)

The What

Once the willingness to move ahead is in place, the next question is, "What do I need to change?" The client needs to look at themselves, see what co-workers have to say, and generally become more aware of how they relate to others. There are a number of tools to aid in this process. First, there is the 360-degree assessment, in which I interview a number of co-workers at various levels about the coaching client's leadership style, personality, and competency. Then I administer business and psychological profiles, an evaluation of how the coaching client deals with conflict, and a self-assessment. I write up a full report that combines all this input—a Leader Assessment and Development Plan. The client reads through these documents and we discuss them. As the coaching proceeds, I may take videos of the client in meetings or interacting with me.

All these tools are designed to allow the client to see themselves in relation to others and to bring greater self-awareness. The client is often surprised by what they see; the 360 can be especially shocking. For example, Dr. Yelyuk, in chapter 3, and Kyle, in chapter 7, were distressed and unnerved by the critical comments from their colleagues.

The purpose, of course, is not to cause pain, but to focus awareness on areas that need attention. Once the coaching client is aware of what needs to be worked on, we can begin to formulate the coaching goals.

The How

In our quest to understand why coaching works so well, we have covered the willingness to move ahead and an awareness of the issues needing attention—the *will* and the *what*. The next step is actually working on these issues—the *how,* as in, how do we deal with these issues?

The way to start on this part of the journey is to decide where the client wants to go. With the coach's assistance, the client formulates specific goals and the means to reach these goals—the remedies and homework. For example, Tom, in chapter 1, tended to be overaggressive and insensitive in his interactions with his sales team. He and Alice set a goal of improving interpersonal skills; Tom's remedies and homework included stopping knee-jerk reactions, keeping composure while listening, and building a purposeful rapport with everyone he worked with.

In the privacy of his office, he and Alice practiced these skills. One of the most useful approaches was the *as if* strategy. Tom would say things like, "How was your weekend?" or, "Can I help you?" as if he were really interested. Over time, he began to sound more authentic, and then to feel more authentic. They also practiced active listening—that is, using language that shows you heard what the other person was saying, such as, "So what you're saying is . . ." or, "Did I get that right?"

Alice took some videos so Tom could observe himself, and they talked about what he was communicating with his body language. She also gave him the homework of seeking out and observing three other managers with more low-key and inclusive styles.

Tom and Alice worked on other goals, too, but this brief recap illustrates some of the different techniques that make up the *how* of coaching. It may also demonstrate the effort that goes into a successful coaching engagement. It takes a great deal of work on the part of both the client and the coach to effect positive change.

The Who

Executive coaching takes skill. When entering into the change process, the coaching client is in unfamiliar territory, and it's the coach's job to guide them. I have guided more than a thousand clients through this process, most of whom were very enthusiastic about the results. The correspondence months after the engagements illustrates this enthusiasm.

A critical component of successful coaching is a skilled coach. You need someone with the right skills and experience; anything less could be ineffective at best, and counterproductive at worst.

Final Words

I hope the stories in this book have inspired you. You have watched as individuals dramatically refined their personal styles and leadership capabilities. You've seen them overcome their resistance, illuminate their blind spots, and adopt more effective ways of relating and managing. And you've seen how these personal changes can affect entire departments and even whole organizations.

By now, you should have a pretty good idea of the how, what, and why of executive coaching: how it works, what it entails, and why it's so successful in effecting positive change. The wish to change and better oneself is a powerful human drive; a skilled coach helps their client channel this drive and guides them through the necessary shifts to realize their ambitions.

I also hope these stories have entertained you. I realized a long time ago that learning happens best in an atmosphere of relaxed enjoyment. In fact, a sense of humor is an excellent quality for a coach and a coaching client; a good laugh can relieve the tension around making difficult changes.

In the end, I applaud the courage and perseverance of my clients. Their stories celebrate their fortitude, their dedication to positive change, and their good humor under fire. It is a privilege to work with them.

REFERENCES

Anderson, M.C. 2001. "Executive Briefing: Case Study on the Return on Investment of Executive Coaching." MetrixGlobal. http://researchportal.coachfederation.org/MediaStream /PartialView?documentId=681.

International Coach Federation (ICF), Association Resource Centre, and PricewaterhouseCoopers. 2009. *ICF Global Coaching Client Study*. Lexington, KY: International Coach Federation.

McGovern, J., M. Lindemann, M. Vergara, S. Murphy, L. Barker, and R. Warrenfeltz. 2001. "Maximizing the Impact of Coaching: Behavioral Change, Organizational Outcomes, and Return on Investment." *The Manchester Review* 6(1). www.performanceconsultants.com/wp-content/uploads /maximizing-the-impact-of-executive-coaching.pdf.

Olivero, B., K.D. Bane, and R.E. Kopelman. 1997. "Executive Coaching as a Transfer of Training Tool: Effects on Productivity in a Public Agency." *Public Personnel Management* 26(4): 461-469.

ABOUT THE AUTHOR

 Nadine Greiner, PhD, is an executive coach with a dual doctorate in organization development and clinical psychology. She has helped more than a thousand people become more effective and fulfilled at work, which has positively rippled out to 10,000 of their colleagues. Recognized for her immense success rate, Nadine has more than 30 years of experience in the field of coaching. In addition to her advanced academic preparation, she has held several high-level positions in privately held and publicly traded companies, and served as CEO at the age of 38. This trifecta of psychology, business, and executive leadership makes her a unique and effective coach who produces excellent results for her clients. Nadine speaks and lectures in postgraduate programs globally.

On a personal note, Nadine is dedicated to animal welfare, and has fostered, rehabilitated, and trained thousands of cats and dogs. Twenty percent of all her profits go to animals. Nadine stays fit by running after them, and by joining the dance party with her friends at Zumba.